*Gunnie Rose:*

BOOK 2

# A LONGER FALL

## CHARLAINE HARRIS

PIATKUS

PIATKUS

First published in the US in 2020 by Saga Press, an imprint of Simon & Schuster, Inc.
First published in Great Britain in 2020 by Piatkus
This paperback edition first published in 2020 by Piatkus

1 3 5 7 9 10 8 6 4 2

A CIP catalogue record for this book
is available from the British Library.

ISBN 978-0-349-41806-3

Printed and bound in Great Britain by Clays Ltd, Elcograf S.p.A.

Papers used by Piatkus are from well-managed forests
and other responsible sources.

MIX
Paper from
responsible sources
FSC® C104740
www.fsc.org

Piatkus
An imprint of
Little, Brown Book Group
Carmelite House
50 Victoria Embankment
London EC4Y 0DZ

An Hachette UK Company
www.hachette.co.uk

www.littlebrown.co.uk

**Charlaine Harris** is a *New York Times* bestselling author who has been writing for over thirty-five years. Born and raised in the Mississippi Delta, she is the author of the Aurora Teagarden mysteries, basis for the Hallmark Movies & Mysteries Aurora Teagarden original movies; the Midnight, Texas series, now airing on NBC; the Sookie Stackhouse urban fantasy series, basis for the HBO show *True Blood*; the Lily Bard mysteries; the Harper Connelly mysteries; and the co-author of the graphic novel trilogy *Cemetery Girl*. Harris now lives in Texas with her husband and two rescue dogs.

Visit Charlaine Harris online at charlaineharris.com and on Facebook as CharlaineHarris.

# BY CHARLAINE HARRIS

**Gunnie Rose Series**

*An Easy Death*
*A Longer Fall*

**Aurora Teagarden Mystery Series**

*Real Murders*
*A Bone to Pick*
*Three Bedrooms, One Corpse*
*The Julius House*
*Dead Over Heels*
*A Fool and His Honey*
*Last Scene Alive*
*Poppy Done to Death*
*All the Little Liars*
*Sleep Like a Baby*

**Midnight Texas Series**

*Midnight Crossroad*
*Day Shift*
*Night Shift*

**Sookie Stackhouse Series**

*Dead Until Dark*
*Living Dead in Dallas*
*Club Dead*
*Dead to the World*
*Dead as a Doornail*
*Definitely Dead*
*All Together Dead*
*From Dead to Worse*
*Dead and Gone*
*Dead in the Family*
*Dead Reckoning*
*Deadlocked*
*Dead Ever After*

*The Complete Sookie Stackhouse Stories*
*The Sookie Stackhouse Companion*

**Lily Bard Mystery Series**

*Shakespeare's Landlord*
*Shakespeare's Champion*
*Shakespeare's Christmas*
*Shakespeare's Trollop*
*Shakespeare's Counselor*

**The Cemetery Girl Trilogy**
(with Christopher Golden)

*Cemetery Girl: Book One:
The Pretenders*
*Cemetery Girl: Book Two:
Inheritance*
*Cemetery Girl: Book Three:
Haunted*

**Harper Connelly Mysteries**

*Grave Sight*
*Grave Surprise*
*An Ice Cold Grave*
*Grave Secret*

**Graphic Novels**
(with illustrations by William
Harms)

*Grave Sight Parts 1–3*

**Standalone Novels**

*Sweet and Deadly*
*A Secret Rage*

*To all the people who have handsold my books through these years: bless you for believing in me and my stories.*

# ACKNOWLEDGMENTS

Thanks to Paula, my friend and assistant, for her help and encouragement and tenacious research. Thanks also to Dana and Toni, who are friends, allies, and sounding boards; to Sarah Byrne, who volunteered her name; to my editor, Joe Monti, whose faith in me never seems to waver.

Saint Moses the Black (also known as Abba Moses the Robber and Moses the Ethiopian) was a real man who lived from 330 AD to 405 AD. He was one of the first Africans to achieve sainthood. Though he lived his early life as a criminal, he became a patron saint of nonviolence.

Canada

Holy Russian Empire

New America

★San Diego

Mexico

Traditional Lands Restored

Independent Hawaiian Nation

PACIFIC

N
W · E
S

# A
# LONGER
# FALL

# CHAPTER ONE

It had been a long time since I was on a train, and I found I hadn't missed it a bit. The rocking made me a little uneasy in the stomach, and also sleepy, a real bad combination. Our crew sat at the west end of a car on a train going roughly west to east, from Texoma to Dixie. It would be a long ride. We'd have to switch trains in Dallas.

"Was that your boyfriend who brought you to Sweetwater?" the woman sitting across from me asked. Her name was Maddy Smith. She was wearing guns, like me.

"Nah," I said. "I've known Dan Brick since we were yay-high." I held my hand out. Maybe I'd been four years old.

"Good-looking man."

"Really?" I'd never thought about Dan's looks. "He's a good friend."

Maddy looked at me, smiling. "If you say so. He don't feel that way."

"Huh." As far as I was concerned, talking about Dan was at an end. I looked out the window again.

The land outside was open to view till there was a ridge of low hills. The sun was beginning to cast long shadows for the small trees, the few farms. The towns were far apart in this stretch of Texoma.

We'd gone through miles that were entirely empty. The population of Texoma wasn't what it had been before the fields dried up and the farms got repossessed and the influenza took people from every family. When it had still been Texas.

Our car was half-empty. Not too many passengers wanted to share space with gunnies.

My new crew, the Lucky Crew, was all in the same half-drugged condition I was. Across the aisle, gray-whiskered Charlie Chop was out and out snoring. Rogelio was staring out the window looking angry and handsome, which seemed to be his resting face. Jake, the crew leader who'd hired me, was looking ahead resolutely, making sure he was alert. He and I had run out of things to talk about thirty minutes before. Jake and I were turned toward Maddy, who was about my age, as she sat on the crate. That crate was our cargo.

Even if I was going to Dixie, it felt good to be working. My last job had almost killed me, but the long recovery had ended in me feeling as antsy as I'd ever felt in my life.

So I'd needed a new crew. Jake had needed another shooter. Here I was. This was not the job I'd have picked for my first one back, but it was better than none.

"That your grandfather's rifle, you said?" Jake remembered what I'd told him about the Winchester.

"Yep. He left it to me."

"He a shooter?"

"Not by profession, but he shot just about everything we put in the pot."

"So it's a family trait."

"If so, it passed my mom completely and came to me doubled."

Jake laughed. "Your mom teaches school in Segundo Mexia, doesn't she?"

I nodded.

"She married?"

"To Jackson Skidder." Who had spotted my shooting talent early and encouraged me to learn. Didn't matter to him that I was a girl. A skill was a skill.

"He's a well-to-do man," Jake said.

I nodded. Jackson worked hard, was clever about people, and took chances when he had to. He also took good care of my mother, Candle.

Jake glanced at his watch. "Time to shift," he said.

We all stood and stretched.

Maddy looked grateful to get onto some padding, as she took her new seat by me. Jake took the crate. Rogelio and Charlie took the seat Jake and I had vacated. Some of the other passengers turned to look at us, though they should have been used to the drill by now.

A couple of them were from Texoma, like we were. Then there were some older and more prosperous people returning to Dixie from wherever they'd been. Lots of trains terminated in Dallas. Not too many went from Dallas to Dixie.

There were two passengers I was keeping my eye on. They didn't fit in. The closest was a blond woman, about ten years older than me and Maddy (both of us were around nineteen). She was dressed in a straight skirt and short-sleeved kind of tailored blouse, with a little hat and low heels. She was no Dixie woman, for sure, and no Texoman, neither. Either. I guessed Brittania.

The other passenger to watch was bareheaded, short, and black-haired. He wasn't nearly as impressive. But he hummed with power. When he stood for a moment and I saw his vest, I knew for sure he was a grigori, a Russian wizard. When I looked hard, I could see the ends of a tattoo above his collar. Another sign.

Jake was crate-sitting, facing the west end of the car with a line of sight over my shoulders. I heard that door open. Jake's hand went to his gun. The newcomer was a fancy man, dressed sharp like the blond woman, and also wearing a hat. He took a seat by her and they exchanged a few words. Jake turned to watch them.

From the other end, two new men entered, and we all tensed.

"Dressed too nice," Maddy muttered.

"Dressed too new," I said. The two were young, early twenties, one blond, one brown-headed. Everything they had on was brand-spanking new. Levi's, shirts, gun belts. Down to their cowboy boots. They'd gotten a payout of some kind.

I stood with my rifle pointed at the blond man, a step or two ahead of his friend. "Turn around, man, and go back where you came from," I said. "We don't want any trouble with civilians around." Unless the two were prepared to kill everyone in the car, there would be witnesses. I registered that the grigori had stood and turned to watch.

The two newcomers didn't seem to know there was a wizard at their back. Unless they were the wizard's employees, they were fools. I knew there was other movement in the train car, but I kept my eyes on Blond and Brown, and past them on the wizard. Everyone else had to shift for themselves.

The wizard's hands went down. He was not protecting the two. So they were idiots.

Then a lot of things happened in a flash.

The blond one pulled his shiny new gun, and I killed him. The brown-headed one had drawn his weapon, too, when Jake took him down.

I kept the Winchester aimed at them, just in case. My eyes flicked around, trying to see what was going on around me. There was an old couple crouching low on the floor in front of their seat, like the seat would protect them from a bullet. The fancy couple, both with guns in hand, looked down at the two dead men in the aisle right by them. The wizard had resumed sitting with his back to us like nothing had happened. A couple of other people were yelling, the usual "Oh my God!" and "What happened?"

Didn't take too long for the train staff to get there, and Jake took over the task of explaining. All the rest of us lowered our weapons and sat down, so we wouldn't look like we were going to shoot someone else.

Maddy and I ended up carrying the bodies to a freight car. Guess Rogelio didn't want to get his hands dirty, and Jake was still talking. Charlie was sitting on the crate. After we'd gotten Brown deposited by Blond, we took the opportunity of going through their pockets. They were both twenty, both lived in Shreveport, and they had a lot of cash, which Maddy and I appropriated since they didn't need it anymore. This was not something I usually did, but it was either we got it or the railway people.

Maddy saw the picture in my wallet as I put the money away. "Who's the baby?" she said. "Yours?"

"No. A friend's." Not strictly true, but I didn't want to tell Maddy the whole story of my friend Galilee, how she'd run away from Dixie pregnant by her employer's son, how the baby had turned out to be a boy she'd named Freedom. Galilee Clelland had been my best friend, and when she'd died in the middle of a road, I'd gotten a hole in my heart. "I may see the grandparents on this trip, and I brought a picture to show them," I said, despite myself.

Maddy looked at me curiously, but she could tell I didn't mean to say any more.

The car was quiet again when we got back, at least until Jake began to talk.

He told us a bunch of stuff. We would be getting into Dallas soon, and getting off with the cargo. The Dallas law would come to our hotel to talk to us. When he was through, we all leaned in.

"What did you find on the bodies?" he asked.

I said, "They come from Shreveport. They lived on the same street. Stewart Cole and Burton Cole."

"No letters or telegrams or receipts?" Jake looked disappointed. His mustache seemed to droop.

Maddy shook her head, her braid whispering across her back. "Not a damn thing," she said.

"Take off their boots?" Charlie pointed to his own in case we didn't speak English.

I nodded. "Only this." It was a scrap off an envelope. It had *3rd car from rear* written on it. Our car.

We had targets painted on our backs.

Or maybe the bull's-eye was on our cargo.

At the Dallas station, we were met by the law. They were pretty anxious to know why we'd shot the two men. We watched the Coles' bodies being unloaded from the freight car as the detective questioned everyone who'd witnessed their attack. To my surprise, everyone agreed that both men had drawn before Jake and I had shot them. Didn't often happen that everyone agreed, and it sure made life easier for us.

The well-dressed couple acted like they were in charge of everything. The blond woman introduced herself to the police as Harriet Ritter, and she showed them something she carried in her purse, some badge or identification. They acted real respectful after that, to her and her companion, whose name was Travis Seeley.

I'd hoped to pick up more information, but they moved too far away for me to hear any more.

Next morning we walked to the station, Jake and Rogelio carrying the cargo. It wasn't awful heavy, but the crate was bulky. Maddy and I took front guard. Charlie brought up the rear. People gave us quick glances as we went through the street on the way to the station, and then did their best to avoid us. Which was good. I hardly knew my new crew, but they were working well together.

Maddy was a poor girl from a farm in the middle of nowhere, Jake had been Lavender Bowen's former second, Charlie had made a name for himself throwing his hand ax in the border skirmishes. As far as I could tell, Rogelio handsomed people to death. He hadn't shown me another skill, but Jake vouched for him. Which is to say, we didn't look well dressed or equipped with fancy stuff, but we all had experience.

We loaded up into our car, eyes and guns at the ready. No one kept us company today but the fancy couple. The grigori had reached the end of his journey, or he'd chosen another car. The Dallas police didn't show up, so we were good to leave.

It was the most boring day of my life.

Jake gave me ten minutes to stretch my legs, so I wandered through the train, giving Harriet Ritter and Travis Seeley a good look as I passed them. They smiled at me. They looked glossy and well rested.

Two cars away, I happened upon another gunnie, who grinned at me when she saw my Colts. I asked if I could sit for a moment.

"Have a seat, and welcome. I'm Sarah Byrne." Sarah was in her thirties. From her clothes and her possessions, she was down on her luck.

"Lizbeth Rose," I said, shaking her hand. "You working?"

"No such luck. I've been getting over an injury." She had a scabby cut on her cheek, must have been bad when it was fresh. "You?"

"Yeah, I'm with a crew new to me."

"You all need any help? I'm free." She looked eager.

"I'll tell our crew leader."

"Maybe I know him?"

"Jake Tutwiler."

"No." She looked kind of relieved for just a second. Not a good sign.

"You're heading away from home," I said.

"My sister married a man in Jackson. I'm going to visit. I have to switch trains twice more."

Two seats ahead of us, a man who'd been fighting with his wife, not too quietly, hauled off and belted her one.

Next thing I knew, I was right beside him and I was putting my gun in his face. "Not here," I said. "Don't you do that." The wife was just as shocked as he was, and she looked down, wouldn't meet my eyes. He blustered and blew, but he shut up. A Colt is a powerful argument.

When I was sure he wasn't in a hitting mood, I said good-bye to Sarah.

"I got to get back to my crew," I said. "Nice talking to you. Always good to meet someone else in the business."

"If your crew leader needs an extra hand, I'd sure like to get work before I go to my sister."

"I'll tell Jake," I said.

I did tell Jake about Sarah Byrne. He just grunted, but after a minute he said, "Good to know." This trip had already produced some surprises. It might produce more. Maybe an extra gun and pair of eyes would be a good precaution.

We spent another night in a cheap motel in a little town, don't even remember the name of it. After being jiggled around all day in the train, we slept like logs. Charlie snored so loud, Maddy and I could hear him from our room right beside the men's.

I was getting used to Maddy. I liked her. She wasn't an exciting person, but she was agreeable, and she was determined to do her job. She'd decided our cargo held the crown jewels the Russian royal family had smuggled out with them when they'd been rescued. I tried to figure out why anyone would hire us to guard them, and why they'd send the jewels to Dixie, of all places. But Maddy had her fantasy. She pointed out that Tsar Alexei's first wife had been from Dixie. So it all made sense, to Maddy.

Jake, our leader, talked a lot about his boyfriend. Charlie talked about anything and everything. Rogelio was a silent brooder.

Third day, we crossed into the country of Dixie. We were approaching Sally, our goal, a little town in Louisiana. I wanted to get off that train so bad I was itching, and the others were the same. We had fallen out of our best readiness because we were too warm and no one approached us and we were sick of guarding the crate, which didn't tick or ring or do anything but sit there.

Everything was boring until the train blew up.

# CHAPTER TWO

The sound seemed to come out of nothing: the shriek of metal twisting, a deep rumble, the squeal of brakes, the yells of passengers. It was like death became able to scream.

Charlie was standing up when the train left the tracks, so he died first. He leaped up when the screeching began, somehow feeling it before the rest of us, so he had nothing to hold on to.

Lunch baskets and suitcases and books, every kind of thing, hung in the air along with Charlie as the north windows became the floor. Charlie flew through the air higgledy-piggledy, falling across a row of seats to crash into a window. I'm sure he died as soon as he hit the window, which shattered and cut into Charlie's neck . . . though that neck had most likely broken first.

I saw it clear and separate, each little thing.

And then the hundreds of things happening came together in a blur of noise and sight when our car hit the ground beside the tracks and skidded on its side, along with the car before and the car after.

Maddy and I, we'd been sitting on the same seat. We ended up in a heap on what was now the lowest point, the north side of the train. The crate came with us. I grabbed hold of it when we began to tumble. I landed on top of Maddy, so I got the better of the deal. I heard her cursing. Not only was she alive, she was mad as hell.

Jake and Rogelio were almost hidden in the pile of items that had landed every which where—purses, suitcases, maps, a box of candy. The two men lay still. I feared the worst. Then I saw Jake's arm move, the fingers flex.

After a long minute of trying to understand what had just happened, Maddy and I scrambled to get untangled. When I was sure the train wasn't going to move any more, I rose to my feet. I wasn't sure what or who I was standing on. "Up you go, Maddy," I said, my voice a far-off buzz to my own ears. I didn't know if she could hear me or not.

I had put my rifle under my seat, and I scrabbled for it and slung it around my neck. My Colts were still secure in my gun belt.

I wondered briefly about Ritter or Seeley, but they weren't my crew.

"Someone's gonna come to take our cargo," I yelled, to make sure Maddy heard me over the screams and groans. Maddy and I pulled our guns and stood flanking the crate. It was splintered bad on one corner. I saw dark wood inside, but couldn't make out anything else.

"You sure?" Maddy yelled back.

I thought my head would fly off. It seemed real logical to me. We'd been waiting and waiting for someone to try to take the cargo from us, and this train wreck gave 'em the opportunity. And I realized, all of a sudden, *This is why we got blown up.*

"I am sure," I yelled. I felt blood running down my right cheek. Maddy was bleeding too. "You able to shoot?" I yelled, and she patted the air to get me to quiet down.

"I can hear you," Maddy said. "I can shoot. Should we help?"

People all around us were asking for help.

I had a confused trail of thoughts. We should help 'em, but we weren't doctors, and the cargo was our responsibility, and the men were going to show up shooting, and we had to shoot better or the people in the car would get shot anyway.

"We got to defend," I said, and Maddy seemed content with that.

After a long pause, she said, "Charlie's dead."

"Saw him," I said. I found I was shaking all over from the wreck, and with the waiting. I could not help myself. I heard gunfire. Yes, this was it.

"Jake," Maddy called, real loud. "Jake, Rogelio."

"I'm alive," Jake called back. He didn't sound too sure. "You see anyone coming?"

"Not yet." I had to raise my own voice to be heard over the screams. "But you hear the shooting?" It wasn't constant, but the sound was getting closer.

"I hear it."

"Jake, you and Rogelio out of the running?" Maddy sounded scared but determined.

"I'm trying to figure that out." Jake sounded dazed and slow.

I spared a glance to my right. Jake was struggling to untangle himself from Rogelio and from another passenger who'd fallen across his legs, one of the old men, who wasn't going to get any older now.

"You saw Charlie's dead," Maddy called to Jake. She was worried, trying not to sound it. "We can sure use you."

Jake said a few things. I couldn't understand him.

Maddy muttered, "God lay Charlie's soul to rest."

We had to shift around to get good footing, the crate tight between our feet. Maddy faced east, I covered west. There was more light coming from the east. I risked a glance behind me. Now that the choking dust was settling, I could see the east end of the car had been split by the force of the impact, just where the roof met the doorframe. The gap was tall as a man, but narrow.

Facing west, the car was darker. There was no new opening. Half the windows faced dirt. The door—now sideways—was intact, though splintered.

Maddy yelled, "I see someone coming." She didn't mean a rescue crew.

Jake crawled over to us, slowly and painfully. "All right, I'm here," he said. "Where's the fire?"

There was blood flowing quick and bright from a gash in Jake's scalp. "You're addled," I told him. "Don't try to stand."

"I think I won't." Jake's voice was groggy. But he was aware enough to prop his back against the crate and draw his pistol.

"Here they are!" I don't think Maddy knew she was shouting. She was pretty excited, and in truth there was still a lot of noise coming from the people badly hurt or badly shaken. At the moment no one could get in our car from my direction, so I turned to look.

Two men with guns were squeezing through the crack, one at a time. That made it easy. Maddy shot one the instant he appeared. As he dropped, I shot the next one, who had just started to flinch back. There were screams of protest from the other passengers. Like "No!" and "What are you doing?"

Might be we *had* just killed two men coming to the aid of the injured. But Good Samaritans wouldn't have had their guns drawn.

With those two disposed of and none more in sight at that opening, I turned back to guarding my end of the car. For a couple of minutes, the screams of pain and appeals to God for rescue battered at my ears. But the voices began to die down—for real, *die* down. And the live passengers realized no help was arriving anytime soon.

"They won't come as fast this time," Maddy said, her voice at a reasonable level.

"No," I agreed. "But they'll come. They went to all this trouble; shooting a couple of 'em isn't going to stop 'em."

After a few minutes I heard a big noise, like a giant can was being opened with a knife.

Turns out, that was pretty much what was going on.

Outside the east end of the car, someone was prying at the narrow opening. At the same time, I could hear sounds coming from the door on the west end. Might be rescue, but I didn't think so. We weren't that lucky. Jake had sure picked a bad name for this crew.

"What if they're helpers?" Maddy said, stepping right on my thoughts.

"They ain't. Shoot 'em." Jake's voice was slurred, but he sounded sure. He was holding his gun, but it wasn't pointed at anything. A quick sideways glance told me Rogelio was stirring. I was relieved he wasn't dead, but I wished he'd rally faster.

After the screeching metal sound of the cutting tool quit, a big pry tool took over. More and more light poured into the car, and the people—the ones who had not fallen silent forever—were once again convinced help had arrived. They got excited. As if a group of men had known the train would derail and had gathered their tools and waited to assist stricken passengers.

Of course it wasn't rescue. Someone fired in at us. The screaming resumed. Shit.

Maddy fired back. And Jake, too, so he was at least capable of that. I don't know how close he came to his target. I had other problems. The glass window on the door at my end of the carriage smashed. I saw a crowbar inserted through the hole to pry open the door.

Hard to understand why they were doing that, since they'd have to crouch down to crawl through. It would be like shooting ducks at a fair arcade. I'd kill 'em as soon as I saw 'em.

But I couldn't. See 'em. I only spied a hand in the opening, tossing in something. This was real bad. I fired at the spot where the hand was, hoping to wound someone, and a yell told me I'd done that.

The cabin started to get hazy. The "something" was a smoke bomb.

I'd heard of them but I'd never seen one. Kids sometimes built them to use for pranks. The people I'd talked to—people who knew arms and weapons—told me smoke bombs were dangerous because the chemicals could ignite.

I don't know diddly-squat about chemicals. But everyone who'd spoken against the smoke bombs were right. The damn thing did ignite. There was a pop and flame in the middle of all that smoke.

And then there was *more* screaming and moaning. And the smoke grew thicker.

Maddy began coughing. "I can't breathe," she said between hacks. Something about this smoke was getting to her lungs particularly bad. I wasn't coughing as hard, though my eyes were streaming. I forced myself to keep looking in the direction of the door, though I wanted to squeeze my eyes shut.

A face came out of the smoke, and I shot it.

"Can you see enough to shoot, Maddy?" I said.

"Just barely." I could just hear her breath sawing in and out.

"It's going away," I said. Some wind was coming through now that the east end of the carriage was open. Most of the windows had been down when the wreck occurred. Thank God. I could see better. Maddy would be able to breathe.

But under cover of the smoke, other gunnies slipped into the car.

We began shooting in earnest. I killed a woman with bristly hair, then wounded a white-haired man. The white hair almost made me hold back, but he had a gun. I got him in the right shoulder.

It was great that we could make out who was coming in . . . but they could see us just as well, and we couldn't move because of the damn crate.

I could feel Maddy trembling against my back. Maybe she could feel me, too. This was long, for a gunfight. They're over quick as a rule.

Rogelio had risen to his knees, and one of the incoming gunnies tripped over him. Rogelio had a knife in hand and he cut the guy, who collapsed right beside him. But then Rogelio passed out again, before one of the others could shoot him in retaliation. I didn't know if our crewmate was really out or if he was faking it, but either way, he'd finally done some good.

One came from either end, and they were both shooting as they entered. I felt Maddy get hit. I heard the noise she made. She was down. I was alone.

Rifle wasn't good in these close quarters, but soon it would be the weapon I had to use. I was out of bullets in one Colt, had six left in the other. I am good with my left hand, almost as good as I am with my right. I got creased, between my shoulder and elbow. It burned. Pain leaped up my arm. I could feel the blood soaking my shirt. A big man loomed up out of the wisps of smoke, and he aimed to hit me with the stock of his rifle, but I shot him instead. Got a bit of blood spatter.

It got real hard to stay upright.

You can tell yourself your wound is just a graze and you won't die. But getting shot hurts. Don't let anyone tell you there's an easy gunshot wound. My arm was on fire. I spared a glance for Maddy. She was now stretched full length over a couple of other bodies, gunnies or just passengers, I didn't know. Jake was barely upright in his seat on the floor. He fired at the next attacker, missed, tried again and got him. But he had gotten hit in the exchange.

I was gonna die here, I figured, and I was so focused on the next person wriggling through the sideways door that I didn't see anyone coming up behind me, across Maddy, until I felt a blow to the back of my head.

I knew I was done, but I twisted to fall across the crate.

I'd tried my hardest. I couldn't do any more. I was out.

# CHAPTER THREE

I was lying on the ground and Harriet Ritter was sitting on a tree stump a few inches away. She was talking to Sarah Byrne, the gunnie with the scabby wound on her cheek.

". . . so it seems," Ritter was saying, "that there's an opening on the Lucky Crew, which should maybe be called the not-so-lucky crew." If she was smiling, I was going to kill her. I opened my eyes a little wider. Ritter was not smiling.

"You can live," I tried to tell her, but it came out more like a croak.

"Thanks. Glad you woke up." Ritter had blood on her clothes and she smelled like engines and metal. So did Sarah Byrne. I expected I did, too.

"Who is dead?" I sounded clearer this time.

"For starters, most of the gunnies who came after you. We got out quick through the hole. We shot two of 'em from outside. The old man on your team, the one who carried the ax, is the only one dead from your crew. Jake Tutwiler has a head wound from the wreck and a bullet wound in the arm, not likely to kill him. The big girl was shot in the thigh. That good-looking Mexican who doesn't smile has a broken nose, a sprained shoulder, and a broken rib or two."

That didn't seem like many wounds, for someone who'd been slumped on the floor last I'd seen him. "The other gunnies get the crate? The ones shooting at us?"

"No. Travis and I stopped them. Just in time."

"Thanks for rushing to help us," I said. Maybe sounded a little bitter.

Ritter's lips tightened. "We got to it as fast as we could. We climbed out of the car before anyone else got moving. I twisted my knee, and Travis dislocated his shoulder. He's got a cut on his chest that will need stitches. We kept about six of 'em off. You heard the shots, I guess. Couldn't help it that some got in."

Maybe I should have apologized. I just didn't have the energy. I looked at my arm, to see I'd been bandaged. Felt like the wound had been slathered with something. "What's on it?" I looked up at Ritter for an answer.

"A new medicine, supposed to prevent infection," she said. Her face had relaxed. "It's hard to find."

"And yet you had some," Sarah Byrne said. Sarah didn't sound like she cared much for Harriet Ritter.

"Yes, I had some." Ritter sounded real calm.

"What's happened?" I asked. I had no idea how much time had passed.

"The dead are over there," Sarah said, pointing.

I lifted my head, trying to get the lay of the land. I was on the ground close to the wreck. The train had been running just about west to east, and I was on the north side in a fallow field. About a quarter of a mile away was a road running parallel to the tracks. On the north side of the road there was a low hill. I could just see a row of bodies lying side by side on the slope. I counted twenty.

"And that many again, or more, likely to die," Harriet said. "No telling how many were hurt. They've put up a tent for the wounded, and got nurses over there. They're bandaging them up and taking them to the little hospital in Sally, a nurse said."

How much time had passed? More than I'd figured when I'd first come to. "Who did it?" I said. "How'd the train leave the tracks?"

Sarah Byrne answered me. "Something blew up. I don't know who set it off. There's been some unrest hereabouts recently. Maybe it was because of that. Maybe whoever was after your cargo just seized the chance to make a grab."

"Pigs may fly." It stood to reason—at least to my reason—the tracks had been blown up to make an opportunity to get the crate. It had happened between towns, when the tracks ran through fields, where there wouldn't be many witnesses. Maybe the plan had been made up on the spur of the moment, but that was what its goal had been.

"The derailment might have been an accident. Or an equipment failure. Or something on the tracks," Ritter said, like she'd made a promise to be fair.

"Something on the tracks like dynamite." Sarah started pacing, her hands jittery around her guns. Her traveling bag was on the ground.

Was mine somewhere close? I had to look for it. Where was my rifle? Though I was worried, I couldn't seem to get up just now. I would. Real shortly.

"Travis has gone to get his shoulder popped back in place and to gather information," Ritter told us, though we hadn't asked.

"You want a drink of water?" Sarah knelt beside me.

More than anything. "Yes."

She slid an arm under to lift me a little and put a canteen to my lips. The first gulp, though warm and metallic, was just what my throat needed.

"Thanks. You look in good shape," I said after she'd put my head back down.

"I landed on the asshole we had the talk with—man who hit his wife? Broke his fucking neck, which saved me."

"Justice," I said. "Listen, can you look for my bag? Do I have my rifle and my Colts?" Suddenly, I decided to sleep a little.

I woke up, alone, in the same spot. I felt a little bit better. There were more bodies laid in the line on the slope, which seemed very far away. Women wearing white nurse uniforms were going around from one bandaged person to another. Some men had almost completed setting up a tent to shelter them.

I could not spot Sarah Byrne or Harriet Ritter. I could not see anyone I knew over by the tent. By the sun, it was afternoon. I turned my head to the left and discovered Maddy, who had a bandage around her left thigh. It was stained with blood. Her eyes were open.

"Where's the crate?" I said.

"Under Jake's arm. He's propped up against that tree yonder." She pointed.

I followed her finger to see Jake maybe twenty feet away, kind of behind me and to my left. He was under a big tree, which was smart, since the sun was beating down. There was a bandage around his head. The crate was by his side.

"My guns," I said.

"You're still wearing 'em. That gal with the scab put the rest of your stuff over by Jake. He's got my bag, too. He was scared someone would steal our things while we were out of it. That Harriet Ritter helped me get over to you, keep an eye out."

"Think we could go over there?" It felt wrong, being away from the cargo and my Winchester. Would be nice to have my extra clothes, too, considering I was spotted in blood.

"We ought to," Maddy said. "But I'm scared about walking on this leg. It stopped bleeding. Don't want it to start again."

She was white as a sheet and sweating. She looked bad. "They should have taken you to the wounded tent."

"Couple of men said they'd come get me, but I guess they forgot. Lots of hurt people here."

I rolled to my hands and knees and slowly pushed up to my feet. Didn't feel too bad. I held out my good arm to help Maddy pull up.

Maddy was heavier than me, but between us we got her upright. "Don't put weight on that leg," I said. We hobbled and hopped over to the tree. I helped her to sit by Jake. It was a big tree, so she got a share of it to lean against.

"Might as well change from the Lucky Crew to the Cripple Crew," he said by way of hello.

"I guess we're lucky we ain't all with Charlie over there on the slope," Maddy told him.

"True enough." Jake made a weak try at a smile. He looked like death warmed over.

"Is the crate okay?" I said.

"Have a look." Jake eased away so I could see.

A few slats were broken. What was in the crate was an old chest. I was only able to make out a little, but the dark wood looked heavily carved and had some gold glinting on it.

We'd been guarding a box that held another box.

"It weighs the same," Jake told us. "I was out for a bit, but it sat exactly where it had been when I came to."

"Last I knew, I was on top of it," I said.

"I was by the side of it. After you got clipped on the head, some farmworkers came in who'd seen the wreck. They were helping people out. Right away, the two men who'd been about to take the crate pretended they were there to help people too. They were going to lift you off first, so they could get a chance to grab it, but a doctor came in just then with that Ritter woman and Seeley, who had their guns out. The doctor got the farmhands to take other people out first. The gunnies lost their chance. By the time the farmhands carried you and Maddy out, I was myself enough to wrap my arm around it. The men who carried me out carried out the crate too. Then Ritter and Seeley got that Sarah Byrne to sit with me. But she said she had to walk to town after you came to, and that's what she did. Ain't seen the other two since then. So here we are."

"Then we're okay. We've done good." Maddy gave a firm nod.

I wasn't too sure about that. "We killed some people," I pointed out. "You think we'll get called out on that?"

That wasn't necessarily something the law would get us for at home. We'd been doing our jobs. But the law in Dixie could be different.

"I don't think any of the other people in our car are in any shape to call the sheriff on us," Jake said. "Most of 'em are up there on the hill."

"Where's Rogelio?" Maddy glanced around.

"See that tent over there?" Jake said, pointing. It was all fixed up now. "That's the wounded. You should be over there. They're doing good for a little town, one not expecting this to happen. I wished they'd come get you, Maddy."

"What about you, Jake?" I said. "You need some doctoring, seems to me."

"After we get Maddy some help, we'll figure out a way to get me and the crate to town together."

They'd left the side flaps up on the tent. Lots of movement inside it. A big wagon was pulling up to it now, and I figured they were going to load up the ones who needed to go to the hospital. I could just hear a distant siren. There must be an ambulance, and it had already gone. Maybe it had made several trips. Didn't know how long a time I'd lost.

"We're close to Sally?" I looked at the landscape as if that would tell me, but the plain was broad and featureless except for a few low, rolling hills.

"We almost made it to town. This is the second time the wagon's come back to fetch wounded to take 'em there."

"I will go see what's happening with Rogelio," I said, pushing myself to my feet. I had to do something. I reloaded my guns, put 'em back in their holsters. I started to sling my rifle over my shoulder, but I hesitated. I was doing good to take one step after another, much less carry any more weight than I had to.

"Jake, I'm gonna leave the rifle and the bag with you," I said. "I'll be back for 'em."

"Not too many armed women in Dixie," Jake reminded me. "Specially not ones in pants."

"Maybe they'll think I'm a boy," I said.

Finally, I'd said something Jake thought was funny. He laughed long and hard.

Walking to the tent was an adventure. The ground was hummocky, and it didn't stay put, thanks to my head. Each step had to be careful and slow. But I got there.

I stepped into the tent without anyone looking interested, though I had drying blood everywhere on my shirt and my head. I felt invisible. I'd been that for a while on my last job. It was weird.

The shade of the canvas was welcome. There was a lot of movement inside, nurses in their uniforms and conscripted men (all black—these must be the farmworkers who'd taken people out of the cars) helping with the wounded as needed. The lucky ones were on canvas-and-wood cots.

I went from bed to bed, looking at the faces. Finally, I spotted Rogelio. I wasn't at all surprised to see a nurse in a starched white uniform, complete with a white apron, squatting by him. How did she keep the apron and her white stockings clean?

Rogelio looked past her and saw me coming. To my amazement he smiled. He could see me. That was good.

The nurse looked over her shoulder to see what Rogelio was grinning at, and she could not hide her surprise that it was me.

Since Rogelio was going to so much trouble, I smiled back. The bump on the back of my head throbbed.

"Hey, Rogelio," I said, when I came up to him. His broken nose was all swollen up. Maybe he was smiling because his looks were no longer perfect and he felt obliged to make an extra effort.

I nodded to the nurse, being polite. I thought about kneeling to talk to Rogelio closer—felt like I was shouting down at him—but wasn't sure I'd be able to stand.

"Lizbeth." Rogelio reached out to pat my calf, which was all he could reach.

"How you doing?"

"I think some of my ribs are cracked, and my arm is banged up. Only thing broke is my nose. This lady has been taking good care of me."

Thus acknowledged, the nurse turned red.

"Thank you, ma'am," I said. No one minds having respect, I figured, though she wasn't much older than me. She had a fuller body and strong shoulders. She was wearing a name tag on her uniform. It read FINCH.

"Do you want me to see if I can find your luggage?" Nurse Finch said to me. "So you can change?" The nurse seemed sure that that was something I needed urgently.

I couldn't understand what she meant. Then I realized she thought I was a scandal, had maybe had to wear someone else's pants while my dress was being mended by a maidservant, or something. Ha!

"Don't worry about it," I assured her. "I got a friend guarding my bag. These are my clothes, and I intend to keep wearing them until I get to a hotel. In my line of work, dresses are not practical."

Nurse Finch stared at me like she'd stare at a snake crawling from under a rock. "Oh, my Lord, honey, what do you do?"

Probably the guns should have been a big clue. "I'm a shooter," I said. "A gunnie."

Nurse Finch shrunk away from me like I'd told her I had the plague. Rogelio smiled wider. "Lizbeth is a famous shooter," he said. "She's the best."

"Why, thank you, kind gentleman," I said, fluttering my eyelashes.

He laughed again. Probably a record. "You had some drugs, Rogelio?" I had figured out where the cheer was coming from.

"Maybe they gave me something for the pain," he admitted.

"I suspected that was the case. You gonna ride to Sally in the wagon?"

"If Maddy can come in the wagon too. She don't need to be on that leg for long until she's had some days to heal. It's worse than she thinks."

Not only had Rogelio smiled, he was thinking of another person. Had the real Rogelio vanished in the wreckage, and another one been substituted? I wished he were on pain medicine all the time.

"Would that be okay?" I asked Nurse Finch, since she was still standing there with her mouth open.

"Okay to . . . ?"

"Bring our crew member, Maddy, over here to get on this wagon to ride into town," I said, holding on to my patience with both hands. "Better if a stretcher team went and got her. Her wound is pretty bad." I was trying to be patient. *I* hadn't had any pain medicine, and my arm was throbbing with my heartbeat, felt like.

Might have shown on my face, because Nurse Finch said, "You got hurt in the wreck." Her eyes went from the dried blood on my face to the bloody bandage around my right arm.

"I got hit on the head." I felt around for the wound on my scalp. Wasn't but a lump.

That was too much for Nurse Finch. She mumbled something about telling someone and hurried off.

"Sorry to scare your friend away," I said to Rogelio, only half-joking. "You need something?"

I could see him open his mouth to make a joke out of that, and I could see him change his mind. Which was good.

"Can you get Maddy over to the wagon?" he asked instead. "I don't see any men who aren't already busy, and if you can help her, she'd be able to leave for the hospital now." Sure enough, I could see two big men raising up a stretcher from the ground, which was a hard task, and loading it onto the wagon.

"I'll try." I trudged back to the tree and told Maddy that Rogelio's deepest wish was to have her by his side when he rode into Sally.

She laughed, but she flushed, too, and I could tell I'd embarrassed her. "Sorry," I said. "He is sure different when he's full of drugs."

"Good," Jake said. "Because he's been a pain in the ass on this trip."

"He's not always like a sore bear?"

"No, and I thank God for it. Maybe getting hurt knocked something off his shoulders."

I shrugged. "Okay, Maddy, let's do it again," I said, trying not to sound as tired as I felt. Once again, I pulled her to her feet. I left my rifle and bag with Jake, because I figured I'd come back to get him and the crate.

I hesitated for a long moment. Maybe I should get Jake to the wagon first. Jake's color was bad. But I'd already gotten Maddy up, and I couldn't see repeating the process.

After ten halting steps with Maddy's arm around my shoulders, I knew I needed help.

But there was none. I had to keep my eyes fixed on the ground to avoid any rocks or ruts that would upset our wavering progress. The sweat was running down my back. My arm throbbed worse and worse. I glanced up to see the tent was not as close as I had hoped.

I forced myself to lurch ahead, Maddy hanging on to me silently as she struggled.

"Do you need help?" an accented voice asked.

I stopped dead in my tracks. I looked to my left, real slowly, not breathing, which didn't help a bit. There stood someone I'd been sure I'd never see again.

# CHAPTER FOUR

I felt like someone had struck me in the chest. I sucked in air from deep in my middle.

Maddy said, "Is this guy okay?" She began to reach for her gun with a trembling hand.

"He's a friend," I said, my eyes fixed on his. "Maddy, this is Eli Savarov. I worked with him a few months ago."

Eli looked down at me steadily. I could not read his face.

I had so many questions and I could not squeeze out a one of them. They'd kind of gotten stuck in my throat from all trying to get through at once.

Eli bent a little to put his arm around Maddy. It touched mine. I said, "Now." We began moving again. Eli was a lot taller than me, but he bent and I stretched, and we got her there much faster than if I alone had been supporting her.

Maddy surely had a lot of questions, but the pain sapped her curiosity. I was glad of that.

We delivered Maddy to the wagon as it was about to leave. There was just enough room for her next to Rogelio, who had already been loaded up. He looked pleased when Maddy was deposited beside him, to the point of grinning at her. Even with the broken nose, it was not a bad effort.

"I'll see you in town," I told them, and Rogelio blew me a kiss. The wagon lurched into motion.

"Those are friends of yours, I take it," Eli said in a funny way. He was standing about a foot from me, too close, but it would be prissy to tell him to take a step away.

"New crew," I said. "What are you doing here?"

"You first," Eli said with a polite smile.

Huh. Okay. "I'm on a job with my new crew," I said. "Hardly likely I'd come to Dixie for sightseeing." I glanced up. Eli's eyes were narrow and green, just like I remembered.

"That's for damn sure," Eli said, and it sounded funny, with his slight Russian accent.

"How's my sister?" I couldn't think of anything else to say.

Eli took my hand. "Felicia's well. You got her letter?"

"I think I've gotten three now. I hope she keeps writing." I took a deep breath. "Why are you here?"

He did not let go of my hand. "I'm on a . . . business trip."

Since Eli was a grigori, a wizard of the Holy Russian Empire, which used to be California and Oregon (my mom had taught me), that might mean almost anything.

"Got a partner with you?" His previous partner, Paulina, was dead. She'd died twice. That I knew of.

"No. I had hoped to hire you."

"I didn't see you in Segundo Mexia knocking on my door," I said, my voice level. I had to stay hard.

"You were already gone when I got there," Eli said. "I missed you by a few hours."

I didn't know what to do with that news. "I've got to get back to Jake," I said. Eli let go of my hand and we began walking to the tree. My crew leader was where I'd left him. But now he was sitting funny.

A few seconds ago I would have told you I couldn't run, but I did. When I was close enough to see clearly, I stopped dead and covered my face with my hands for just a moment. Then I made myself look again.

Jake still had his back against the tree, but now he slumped to his left. His shirt was soaked dark with blood from where he'd been stabbed in the throat. His eyes were open. He was dead. The crate that was tucked under his arm had been pulled away and ripped apart. The chest inside it was gone.

"I left him alone for ten minutes," I said through clenched teeth. I felt Eli behind me, but I wasn't exactly talking to him. I just had to say it out loud. "*Ten damn minutes*. And he couldn't even stay alive that long." *Dammit.* I was yelling when I finished.

After a moment of letting the world settle into a new pattern, I was able to understand that my Winchester and Jake's guns were still on the ground by his side. In fact, one of his guns was in his right hand. Whoever had killed him had wanted to get away with the chest so bad they hadn't stolen the guns along with it.

Nothing was more sellable than guns. And my leather bag was lying right there too.

I was so angry I was shaking.

Eli said, "This was your new crew leader?"

I jerked my head in a nod.

"And two of your crewmates are hurt badly enough to be going to the hospital in Sally?"

"Yes. One's already dead, in the crash."

Then there was a lot of silence from Eli.

I wheeled around to face him. "You didn't . . . ?"

"I did not make your train derail," Eli said.

Because I knew he could. I had seen grigoris do things that made even *me* feel queasy.

"All right." I believed him. "But someone did."

"I know. What were you here to guard? People? A thing?" When I didn't answer—I was still too stunned about Jake—Eli said, "What will you do now?"

That was an important question. I fumbled through my thoughts. It felt like I had fog in my brain. I fixed my gaze on my feet, noticed my boots were bloodstained, and shoved that thought away while I pondered.

There weren't going to be any trains leaving out of Sally for a while. How long would it take to clear and repair these tracks? How would I pay my fare?

I could go into Sally and consult with Rogelio and Maddy. Or maybe Harriet Ritter would help me find the chest. For the life of me, I couldn't figure out what part Ritter and her henchman had to play in this, whether she was a friend or foe. I thought about joining up with Sarah Byrne for about a second, but I was obliged to find whatever had been in the crate. I was the last crew member standing.

The third thing I might do was find the Sally sheriff to tell him my boss had been murdered.

Sure, I ought to do that.

The sheriff would be glad to hear some more bad news on top of what must be one of the worst days Sally ever had. It had probably escaped his notice that the train had been derailed on purpose.

And the stab wound in Jake's neck would look an awful lot like the sharp glass wound that had pierced Charlie's neck and killed him. Were doctors going to examine every single body real thoroughly after a massive loss of life? I didn't think so. And whoever our employer was, surely that employer would want to know what had happened . . . that we'd failed.

What with the bop on the head, the arm wound, and the tossing around I'd gotten in the wreck, it took me a bit to think through all this. Eli's feet shifted restlessly, but I did not look up.

Eli said, "Come with me, Lizbeth. Please."

"Where to?" I had too many problems. I couldn't organize them enough to make a plan to solve them. I gathered up my rifle and my bag.

"Come with me to Sally."

"What are *you* going to do there?" I asked. I made myself look up at Eli. Who was also Prince Ilya Savarov. And so many other things.

Not like me. I was one thing.

Eli's long, light hair was braided clumsily. He had beard stubble. He wasn't spanky clean. When we'd been on the road a few months ago, he'd shaved every day. This made me worry even more.

"I have to find a man who hired some people to bring a chest to him." Eli looked like he'd rather be anywhere on earth than standing in front of me telling me this.

"Did you know?" I said, suddenly angry.

"Did I know . . . ?"

"That it was me? Did you know *we* were bringing it? That was our cargo." Because what had been in the crate had looked exactly like a very old and carved chest with something important in it.

"No," Eli said. "I swear, Lizbeth. Your neighbor told me you'd left on a job, but she didn't know where you were going. I had no idea you were here until I spotted you across the field."

We looked at each other for what seemed a long time.

"So . . . where is it?" Eli glanced around.

I pointed to the broken wood around Jake's body.

"We got it this far. After the wreck, there was a gunfight. Jake got wounded. We all got wounded. I was least hurt, but I was unconscious for a time." I should have known Eli was in the vicinity, just from that. I'd never spent so much time unconscious as I had while I was working with Eli. "When Rogelio asked me to bring Maddy to get on the wagon to the hospital, I left Jake guarding it," I said.

"And this was Jake." Eli glanced down at the body. Luckily we were far enough from the other survivors that no one had noticed Jake had been killed. Yet.

"Yeah. This was Jake."

"Let us get away from here, Lizbeth. Unless you feel you have to tell someone, officially, that Jake is dead? Murdered?"

"I think that's pretty clear without me pointing it out." Though I'd been wondering the same thing myself, I sounded tart to my own ears. Like I resented his thinking for me.

"Lots of people saw you together?" Eli started walking in the direction of the tent, slowly, clearly hoping I would trail along behind him. For lack of a better idea, I did.

"Lots," I agreed. "But most of them are injured or dead, or too . . . too shook up to think about what happened to us and the crate when the train left the track."

"And why did the train leave the track, do you think?"

I almost said, *To get to the other side.* "The tracks were blown up.

Wait, you weren't on the train?" I was having a hard time getting this picture together.

"I was in an automobile. Trying to beat the train into town." Eli was so patient with his answer, I knew he must have told me this before.

"You didn't see the tracks blow up?"

"No. I was ahead of the train, closer to Sally. But I heard the noise. It was terrible. I turned back after I heard it."

"Hear the gunshots?"

"No. So the tracks were blown up, the train began to derail, and your car went sideways?"

I nodded. Though Eli's words didn't seem adequate to sum up the awfulness.

"You were hurt in the wreck?" Eli said, nodding at my arm.

"No, I was *shot*," I said, for what seemed the tenth time. "There were people, lots of 'em, trying to take the cargo after the wreck. They were coming in from both ends of the car. Maddy and I were the only ones standing. Charlie was already dead by then—that *was* the wreck—and Rogelio and Jake were banged up, but they helped, especially Jake. We stood over the cargo until we went down. I got shot in the arm. Maddy got shot in the leg. And someone snuck up behind me and hit me on the head." I felt my scalp again. The minute I touched the bump, it let me know it was ready to hurt. To make it all better, Eli's fingers went over it too. Thanks.

"Why didn't they take the cargo then? I was down." I tried to figure it out, but my thinking felt as clumsy as my wounded arm. Then I remembered. "Oh, the man and the woman."

"What man? What woman?" Eli wanted to move and he wanted to talk, and he couldn't seem to make up his mind which was more urgent.

"That Seeley and Ritter," I said. "I saw her after the wreck, her and Sarah Byrne."

"Now someone else!" Eli flung up his hands. "Let's get in my car and go."

"Okay," I said. I couldn't think of a better plan. Eli and I in a car in a strange country. Felt like old times. When I'd seen a man's blood leave his body, and a dead woman walk into a house. A man being hung. A woman shriveling into a mummy.

*When I'm with Eli I see awful things*, I thought, clear as a bell.

And that was the thought I should have stuck with.

# CHAPTER FIVE

C ome this way." Eli glanced back to see if I was still trailing him. I was. I couldn't see that I had a lot of other choices, but I was doubtful I could walk much farther.

"Just a little now," Eli said coaxingly, like I was a blindfolded baby. He took a hold of my arm, the unshot one. Eli's car was on the other side of the road from the tent, at the base of the low hill where the bodies lay. They were now being loaded into the back of a truck. It had a mortuary name printed on the door.

"Charlie is in there," I said, nodding toward the truck. "I guess when they find Jake, he will be too." I felt a little distant.

Eli looked at me, his eyes all narrow. "You don't sound like yourself."

Maybe I wasn't. It had been a long day already. And I'd thought I'd never see Eli again, to top off everything else. But here he was.

I climbed into the car. It was not the fancy Celebrity Tourer he'd had in Texoma. It was an ordinary Carrier, which was—if cars could be averaged out, the Carrier would be on that line.

"The refrigerator's working great," I said, as he pulled onto the road. Always grateful for the refrigerator, Eli's gift.

"Good." Eli gave me another narrow look. Worried.

I hadn't seen him since right after I'd killed his father. I had a history of killing fathers, I realized all of a sudden.

"Water under the bridge," I said out loud.

"What?" Eli kept his eyes on the road. It was paved, but that was just a notion the work crew had had. The potholes were more like tiny caverns. "Lizbeth, you're not making sense."

"How is the tsar?" I asked, to change the subject.

"He's well. Thanks to the young man we found, and your sister to back him up." Talking about the tsar made Eli feel that I was just fine, because that was a right and proper topic.

"Have you used Felicia's blood yet?" The tsar had a bleeding disease. Grigori Rasputin's blood had kept him alive long enough to take the throne when his dad, Nicholas, had passed away. But when Rasputin had died, grigoris had combed the continent looking for his by-blows, since all of his legitimate kids were dead. My half sister was Rasputin's granddaughter.

So was I. But Eli had kept my secret.

"Once, Felicia gave him blood. When the older boy was ill."

"How did she do?"

"She was very brave, I am told."

Felicia would not have wanted them to see her cry. "She's young for that," I said, not happy. And there was something wrong with the way Eli had said "I am told." Why hadn't he been there? He'd been in the inner grigori circle taking care of the tsar before.

"I warned you it might happen," Eli said, all touchy. "That we'd need to try Felicia's blood. The time came sooner rather than later. One of Rasputin's other children . . . died."

"I understand." In return for her blood, my little half sister, Felicia, who was maybe ten (she wasn't sure), got room and board and an education, things she would never have had in Mexico, where we'd found her. What I didn't like was Eli's pause. How had "one of Rasputin's other children" died? But I felt too tired to ask. "So her blood helped," I said.

Eli gave a quick nod.

There'd been some question as to whether Felicia and I had had the same father, Oleg Karkarov, a bastard son of Rasputin. If her blood had worked, she was *definitely* my half sister. I hadn't been lying when I'd told the grigoris that so they'd give her a home and an education. That should cheer me up, when I got over being shocked and shot and so on. I knew there was an important fact beckoning from somewhere right beyond my grasp, but I could not quite reach it. I put it aside to think of later after I'd had some sleep. I was so tired.

And then I was asleep.

I was lying down flat in the back seat when I woke up. There were trees all around us, which took some getting used to. All the car doors were open, a breeze was blowing through, the sun was shining, and I felt pretty well.

Still filthy. But my arm didn't hurt, and my head only ached a little.

"Thanks," I said. I knew Eli had cast a healing spell.

"Glad to help."

I got out of the car very slowly and carefully, testing my muscles. Sore. Bruised. But three days ahead of where I should have been. One of the good things about having a grigori around—at least, one who meant well.

"Plus," Eli said, "I wasn't going to get any good out of you until you'd recovered some."

That was more like it.

Eli was sitting up against a tree, just like Jake earlier. His hair was moving in the breeze. He looked older. Older than the few months it had been since I'd last seen him.

"I only have a little magical talent in me," I said. "But it would be handy if you could teach me a healing spell. Couldn't hurt."

"I'll be glad to try. Since you can withstand magic to a startling degree, maybe you will be good at performing some spells." Eli tried to look like he believed that.

"You had better tell me what's happened to you and your family," I said. "You're here by yourself, in a banged-up Carrier, no partner. You were the golden guy last time I saw you, despite your father the traitor."

Eli shook his head. "You're always so quick."

Didn't take a genius to figure it out.

But Eli didn't leap at starting the conversation. This was going to be like pulling nails out of a board. Okay, I'd start with his family. "How's your little brother?" Peter was not so much younger than me in age. Experience . . . way younger.

"Peter is back in school. One more year and he'll be out, maybe helping me. It would be nice to spend time with him."

Peter had gone into the grigori business, like Eli. Since it was okay for Prince Ilya Savarov to be a grigori, it was okay for Peter, too. Lucky they hadn't wanted to be carpenters. "And your mom? Your sisters?"

"They live a retired life."

That didn't sound like any fun. Maybe they were in mourning for Eli's dad?

"Your stepfather and your mother?" Eli asked politely.

"Fine. If we're down to talking about the health of our families, we better get a move on." Being closed in by the trees and the high growth was making me feel blind. Eli obviously wasn't ready to talk about whatever was wrong.

"You haven't asked where we're going."

"I assume you need to go to Sally. You were on your way there."

"Yes, I was."

"So, let's go." I wanted out of this green. I wanted to see the sky.

"All right." We shut the two back doors and climbed into the car.

"I want to tell you some things about Sally, about Dixie," Eli said. He was backing out of the cage of green, very carefully. We'd pulled into a sort of rutted excuse for a road that ran into the woods off the main road to Sally, apparently. It was lucky he'd done some healing on me. Otherwise, the ruts and bumps might have knocked me senseless again. "Since we'll be there for a few days, I think."

"So talk."

"I met a friend of yours when I went by your house looking for you," Eli said, with an edge to his voice.

This was not talking about Sally. Eli already knew Chrissie. "Who?"

"A young man named Dan." Dan hadn't impressed Eli, or they hadn't struck it off, or something.

"What was he doing at my house? He lives west of town." I was even more confused.

"According to Dan, he is your boyfriend and keeping an eye on your house in case some stranger like me happens by, perhaps intending to rob you." Eli's voice was dry as a salt pan.

"My boyfriend?" I was some kind of amazed. "I wonder when that happened? Somehow he forgot to tell me."

Eli laughed and relaxed. "Tell me all about the trip you had to get here," he said. "How heavy was the crate?"

"I helped carry it once," I said. "I don't think it weighed more than forty pounds. I could have done it by myself."

"Do you know what was in it?"

"'Course not. We weren't paid to open the crate. Just to get it here. And we almost made it." Almost was no good.

"When did you sign on with Jake? What's his whole name?"

"Jake Tutwiler. Less than a week ago."

"You'd known him for a long time?"

"No. Just met him. But he had a good reputation."

"What about the others?"

"I had known Charlie Chop for a while."

"Your other crew members?"

"The man in the tent, the one with the broken nose, that was Rogelio Socorro. The woman I was helping to the wagon was Maddy Smith, another gunnie. I knew Maddy by sight, hadn't met Rogelio."

"So how did Jake hire you? I mean, how did he know about you?"

"I have a reputation," I said, somewhat stiffly.

"I remember," Eli said, but he was thinking about something else.

"So when I was free and well and ready to work again, Jake sent Charlie to let me know Jake was making up a new crew. I needed a job."

"Maddy was Jake's partner?"

"What? No. Jake has a guy back home." These were odd questions.

Eli kept his eyes on the road, which was good, because it was a rotten road and there were slow farm machines on it, and all kinds of trucks and cars going out to the wreck site. This must be the biggest thing that had ever happened in Sally.

"So what do you plan to do next?" I thought I'd better find out. I'd had enough surprises for the day. "You were coming to get me to hire me to help you, you said."

"I plan to find the man to whom the chest would have been delivered and talk to him. I want to know if he has ideas about who stole it and where it is now. And I expect after you have had a rest, you'll want to go see your friends in the hospital. Maybe they know more about the crate than you think. After we determine all these things, we'll know what to do next."

I couldn't think of any response to this.

"Will you take some advice?" Eli said. This was what he'd wanted to say all along, I could tell.

"Maybe." Depended on the advice. He'd sure gone the long way around the bush to get there.

"You need a dress and other . . . other lady things to pass, here. To move around."

"To pass as what?" I'd pulled on a skirt in Mexico so I wouldn't be odd. Did no one like women in trousers? Surely up in Canada, where it was so cold, women wore practical clothes?

"To be spoken to, to be treated decently, to be accepted as a woman worthy of respect. I've been here often enough to know that."

I had known I was going to stick out in Dixie, but I guess I hadn't realized how much till I saw the women on the train. Also I hadn't known I'd be walking around without my crew. I was sure Eli wouldn't be saying that because my appearance embarrassed him. And when you considered all my mixed feelings about him, it was strange I was sure.

"I don't have money for clothes." I didn't think Dixie was like Mexico, where you could buy used garments from street stalls for pennies.

"I want to hire you to help me. I just didn't think I'd have to come here to do it. The clothing is part of the job."

"I accept, as long as it doesn't conflict with my original hire."

"All right. First, we get you togged out. Then we start to work."

Sally seemed like a pretty little town, lots of white houses and green lawns and so on. Paved streets. At the moment those streets were clogged with traffic, with wagons and cars all heading toward the hospital or out to see the wreck.

There was plenty of time to look from side to side.

"There!" said Eli. On a side street to the left there was a store labeled FANCY.

I had been thinking of a dry goods store. Eli thought higher than me, which didn't surprise me.

"I don't know if they'll let me in," I said, and I was being honest. Being healed hadn't changed the dirt and blood and sweat.

Nothing was going to stop Eli now. His head was up and his stride was manly. I was going to get some damn clothes. I sighed and trailed after him, wishing I could go in armed. He'd asked me to leave my guns in the car.

Nothing more exciting had happened in that shop, ever. Eli commanded some respect, since he acted like he was used to having money; and he was, well, pretty good-looking in his own way—kind of gawky and exotic, with his cheekbones and his accent and his hair. The Fancy ladies fluttered when he came in the door.

Then they saw me. It was like they'd seen a rat running across the floor. And I didn't really blame them.

The next forty minutes ranged from painfully embarrassing to just painful. I asked where their washroom was and cleaned up as best I could short of stripping and bathing in the sink. I didn't want to get grime on these ladies' dresses.

Lady One (stout, brown-haired, heels) looked relieved when I came out, so I'd done some good.

In the interest of getting me out of the store as soon as possible, Lady Two (blond, thin, red lipstick) had put several things in a dressing room already. I had never seen a dressing room, but it wasn't hard to figure out. I'd heard Eli explaining I'd been in the wreck, trying to drum up some sympathy for me to make this easier. Hadn't worked very well.

After ten minutes I was thinking, *Fuck these women*. I didn't often even think that word, but it made me feel better while they yanked at me and turned me around. I tried to tell myself this was like picking out a new gun, but that didn't work too well. I love guns.

I left Fancy with a dress, two blouses, two skirts, two pairs of shoes, underwear, and a nightgown. And a hat. And a purse. I had no idea what I was going to carry in the purse, unless it was extra bullets.

Eli had added the nightgown to the pile, which had made the ladies look at me out of the corners of their eyes.

"So, to the hotel," Eli said as he was putting the bags in the back seat. I was silent, trying to get my sense of me back.

The bustle on the streets had not abated. A lot of the people were wearing uniforms of one kind or another: police, firefighters (who would be volunteers), railroad employees. I saw clusters of weeping women and stricken men. They'd come here to meet someone on the train, and now they were wondering if that someone had lived.

"They'll never forget today, here in Sally," I said. I never would either.

When we reached the Pleasant Stay Hotel, located right off the main street, I saw it was a pretty big place: white painted brick, with a screened-in front porch twice the width of a regular one, set with round tables and chairs arranged a decent distance apart.

There was a crowd sitting on the porch, a real subdued one. And a steady stream of people coming and going out the big front door. Eli found a place to park, which was kind of a miracle.

"Take me around back," I said, just as Eli was about to turn in.

"What's wrong?" Eli frowned at me.

"Your reservation might get lost when they see you have someone with you who's not proper." Now that I knew I looked like a dumb rough shooter, "unwomanly" according to Dixie standards, I felt like a sore thumb. I knew I was being stupid, but those women had done a job on me.

(Not that Eli himself was so proper, with his long pale-brown hair and his grigori vest with all its little pockets, and his tattoos. But still, since he was a man, and had money, he'd get the benefit of the doubt.)

"You heard 'em," I said. "The ladies in the store."

"Those women? What do you care what they say?"

A good question. "I didn't understand it," I said stiffly. "Why would they say, 'raised by wolves'?"

Eli looked angry, impatient, embarrassed, and like he didn't want to have this conversation.

Neither did I, but we were finishing it.

"If I promise to explain later, can we go inside?"

I nodded. "But you know what, Eli? I don't think you need to explain." They didn't know my mother, how hard it had been for her to raise me on her own after my grandparents died. They didn't know how smart and pretty she was. I had never felt like I did her no credit, though. Until now.

# CHAPTER SIX

With his mouth set in a grim line, Eli drove around to the rear and parked. We had a lot to carry. Our real bags and the extra stuff. I locked my rifle in Eli's trunk.

There was a door up a short set of steps, neatly labeled GUEST ENTRANCE. It led into the big hall that ran the south length of the building ending in the porch. Eli walked forward to the front desk, just inside the wide front door. I kind of lurked in the back of the hall with all our stuff.

I stood in the darkest corner I could, but still passersby gave me the narrow-eyed look that meant they thought I was real out of place. One of the black workers did too. She was wearing the uniform all the black people did at this hotel: a dark green dress with a white collar for the women, dark green pants and a lighter green shirt for the men. I sighed, and reminded myself that according to my mother, patience was a virtue.

Eli strode toward me, and he'd gone from frowning to scowling.

I figured the hotel proprietor had said something about me. Come to find out he had, but he'd also said something to Eli about Eli. "Told me to be sure and keep my magic to myself inside the walls of the hotel," he muttered. "Told me people in the town of Sally didn't tolerate godless magic spells and the people who cast them."

"Did he tell you he didn't suffer a witch to live?" I said.

"Yes, as a matter of fact. I'd like to see how he could stop me living before I stopped him."

"I'd put my money on you." For the first time in many hours, I smiled.

The black man carrying our bags up the stairs had been a perfect blank, but his mouth twitched too. I could swear he came close to smiling along with me. Eli tipped the man generously, and the man actually did smile as he said, "Thank you, sir."

I looked around the room, which was plenty large, with the usual bed with night tables, and an easy chair with a little table beside it. I spotted another door and opened it with hope. Yes! The Pleasant Stay Hotel was fancy enough to have a bathroom attached to each room! I would put up with a few nasty remarks for the lovely convenience of having a bath whenever I wanted one, and not having to wait in line for a turn at a common bathroom in the hall.

There was soap, too, and it smelled really nice. "I have to bathe," I said. I really felt nasty to the last degree.

"Your arm," Eli reminded me. "Let's have a look."

He unwrapped the bandage real gingerly. We wanted to save it, since bandages were going to be in short supply in Sally.

The furrow in my arm was red and crusty, but it looked good for a bullet wound only a few hours old. Eli's healing and the salve Harriet Ritter had smeared on the wound had done a great job. I asked Eli if he knew the name of the germ-killing salve.

"I'll try to find some more, and another bandage," Eli said. "Though it hardly needs a bandage now." He looked pleased.

"I owe you more and more." I couldn't sound happy or even content about that.

"I have a strong feeling the scales will balance," Eli said, and gave me a crooked smile before he left. I locked the door behind him.

I stripped off my clothes in record time. The bathtub was nice and deep, and I started the water running. It got hot pretty fast, and I put in the stopper. There was a bottle of stuff on the stool beside the tub, and it was labeled FOR THE LADIES. Maybe it would turn me into one. The water foamed up and the smell of lavender filled the room. I smiled again. Things were looking up.

There were lots of towels and they were all thick, not a thread-bare one among 'em. Even the washrag was thick. I climbed in, feeling better than I'd felt in days.

I was humming when I took out the stopper. I stepped out onto the fuzzy mat and glanced in the mirror. I felt more like myself, more in balance. "After all," I said, "I can always go back and shoot those ladies." That cheered me up. I hummed as I washed the bandage in the sink.

Eli, too, was in a better mood when he returned with a couple of small shopping bags. "I had to walk several blocks," he said. "Every pharmacy in the area is selling out of first-aid stuff. But I have fresh bandages and some of that ointment." He'd enjoyed stretching his legs and tracking down what I needed, I could tell.

I sat on the bed wrapped in a towel while Eli emptied out the drugstore bag. Didn't take Eli long to re-dress my arm. He read the directions on the ointment and dabbed it on the wound, circled my arm with gauze twice, pinned it in place.

"That antiseptic stuff seems to work great," I said. "Thanks for getting more." I wasn't sure I would need it after today, but I was glad to have it on hand.

"It's going to change everything," Eli told me. "That's what the pharmacist said." Then his smile faded, and he had that look. He was going to tell me something he knew I wouldn't like.

"Spit it out," I said.

"When I was going out, Mr. Mercer at the front desk stopped me. The man who's not going to suffer me to live." Eli grimaced. "Mr. Mercer told me he had not realized I was taking a woman up to my room, a woman to whom I was not married."

I stared at Eli. "He really said that?"

"He really did."

"I bought dresses. I got underwear. I have a purse. Now this man I've never met wants me to be married, too. Who made these people God?"

"Themselves, apparently." But Eli did smile just a little. "Mercer's more than a desk clerk. He owns the hotel."

"So Mr. Mercer can have us thrown out, and then we wouldn't have anywhere to stay. I bet every hotel in Sally is full by now." Plus, I was in love with the bathtub. "Does he want me horsewhipped or stoned?"

"Mercer just wants some whitewash, apparently." Eli sat beside me on the bed. "So I told him we were married."

"Okay." It didn't make any difference to me. I knew who I was.

Eli looked like he was relaxed all over. "Then we're all right," he said. "I got you this, to look the part." He opened the second bag, the smaller one, and withdrew a tiny box.

"This" turned out to be a plain, thin gold band. Eli took my left hand and slid the ring on.

Something about the ring, about Eli putting it on my finger instead of handing it to me . . . that made the air in the room suddenly feel fraught.

Eli had bought himself a wedding band too.

"I hadn't thought I'd marry so young," I said, making myself smile, willing the tension to go away.

"Good God," Eli said. His eyes flew wide. "Lizbeth! How old are you? I've forgotten, if I knew."

"I'm still nineteen," I said. "Same as when you asked me in Mexico."

"Lots of people are married by the time they're nineteen." But Eli looked uneasy.

"I don't think anyone's going to ask to see my birth certificate," I said, wondering if I even had one. "In Texoma, I've been counted grown up since I left school when I was sixteen. And that was kind of late to still be in school."

"I thought you might get mad about all this," Eli said.

"I got other things to worry about, things a lot more important."

Maybe I could have put that nicer. But Eli only raised his eyebrows, to tell me to go on.

"I have to find out what happened to our cargo. I have to check on Maddy and Rogelio. Harriet Ritter and Travis Seeley can connect me to Jake. If anyone looks close, they'll see he was murdered. I may get accused of killing him."

Eli smiled. It was like the sun coming out. "We do have a lot of things to do. Can you wait to check on your friends? So we can try to get a lead on your cargo? Are you feeling well enough?"

I noticed he had said "we." And I felt the biggest sense of relief. Doing everything by myself had seemed like a huge, steep mountain. I knew no one in Sally. I knew nothing about who'd employed the Lucky Crew. I had almost no money. But I tried not to let it show. I didn't want Eli to feel I was a burden on his shoulders.

"I wouldn't call them my friends," I said, just to break my silence, which had lasted too long. "I like Maddy, though she's not real bright. But she's steady. Rogelio is an ass. Good-looking ass, but an ass." I shrugged. "But they're my crew for now, they got hurt while they were working, and I should make sure they're getting good treatment."

"I noticed that," Eli said out of the blue. "That Rogelio was what you'd call a handsome man."

"What?"

Eli had focused on the least important part of what I'd told him. But when he looked off into space, obviously wanting me to forget he'd made that remark about Rogelio, I was confused. And I was slow enough to say something about it. "I didn't think you looked at men that way." I cocked my head. Something was going on that I didn't understand. With my wizard buddy, that seemed to happen often.

Eli flushed red. "It's not a hard-to-see thing. His looks."

"Okay. I guess." But I didn't understand. "That Harriet Ritter is a good-looking woman," I said, just to give him some company.

"This is the third time you've mentioned this Harriet Ritter." Eli's voice was sharp. "Can you describe her?"

Eli seemed to be listening to a different conversation than the one I thought we were having. I said, "Blonde, in her thirties, built trim. Sharp clothes. Made up. She and Travis Seeley were on the train, same car as us. They were armed. We could tell they knew how to use their guns. And they stuck to us for a couple of days. I figured . . . well, I figured someone had sent them to make sure we were doing our jobs. As backup."

Eli had his thinking face on. I gathered my new clothes and went in the bathroom to dress. I was tired of sitting around in a towel.

I put on the garter belt and the brassiere, then the hose, then the panties, then the slip. Though I'd seen garter belts and hose before, I'd never put 'em on. I felt I was already wearing a lot of items, and I hadn't even finished yet.

Next I put on the blouse. The saleswoman had called the color "rose pink." I guess some roses were that color.

As "accents"—that was what she'd called 'em—the blouse had a white collar, white trimmed pockets, and white cuffs on the puffy sleeves, which came halfway to my elbow, covering the bandage. The skirt was full and to my knees, and it was covered in flowers, some of them the same pink as the blouse. At least the material was cotton and the shoes were tolerable, though not real practical.

I hated to think what Eli had spent on all this gear. For a mean moment, I hoped it was a lot. If I had to wear this, he should pay for it.

I wanted to strap on my gun belt, but I knew it would look ridiculous on top of the skirt. Also, going armed openly would spoil the whole point of the . . . costume. I was wearing all this to blend in, which Eli had assured me was absolutely necessary in Dixie.

I told myself that several times.

I stood in front of the mirror while I combed my hair as much as I could. My curls were spring-loaded. I could only see myself down to the waist, but that was enough. I made a sour face. I looked like I was going to a fancy-dress party.

I made myself leave the bathroom. Eli glanced up, looked down, then looked up again with the funniest expression on his face. "You look very nice," he said.

"I know you're trying not to laugh," I said, sounding just as snippy as I felt.

"Far from it."

Then I correctly interpreted the look he was giving me. "No, sir," I said. "It took me a long time to put on all this rig, and I'm not getting out of it anytime soon." Our past history had not always been what my mother called "platonic."

"There's always later," Eli said, sounding hopeful.

"Later is not now." I didn't want to promise anything. I didn't know how this new Eli was going to act compared to the old Eli. If I had changed a bit, he must have also.

"So where to, Eli?" We needed to get out of this room, away from the bed.

"Just remember," Eli said as he stood, "we're married now." He gave me a sly smile.

I could not forbear laughing. "Let's get to work on that list of jobs."

"If you insist." His accent was right at the front. "First we will find out what we can about the chest."

I had no idea how we were going to do that, but he sounded as though he had a plan in mind. We went down the stairs together and toward the front door. I had the gratification of seeing Mr. Mercer, who had a narrow face and receding dark hair, actually drop his jaw. I gave him a cool look to let him know I had registered his presence. I was tempted to raise my ring finger and waggle it at him.

We swept out the front door.

"That was fun," I murmured.

"Yes," he said, smiling broadly. "It was. Of course, we now have to walk all the way around the building to get the car."

"It was worth a walk."

Eli drove west out of town. We were returning to the site of the derailment.

I thought of it as a battlefield.

When we got out of the car, Eli insisted I put my hand in the crook of his arm, as if I needed support to walk on the grass. It went contrary to common sense, but I managed to match my pace to his.

"You looked like you were going to bite someone," he whispered.

"Sorry," I muttered. I made my face relax and go vacant.

"Much better. Now you look lack-witted." We were approaching a short, stout man with a badge pinned to his coat. His face was full of a large, white mustache. The sheriff was giving instructions to a small group of men. He ended by saying, "And the sooner we get all this cleared up, the sooner the railroad crew can repair the tracks, and the sooner trains can come in and out."

After a few comments, all the men dispersed.

"Yes, sir?" The sheriff turned to us, looking us up and down. Eli earned his deep suspicion because of the grigori vest. The sheriff looked at me with more favor, so the clothes were paying off. I introduced us, and the sheriff waited to hear what we wanted.

"My wife was going to be receiving a chest, arriving on this train," Eli said. "It contained a wedding gift from my family. And two of our family friends are in the hospital in your town. We would like to check on their baggage. Is there a place where it's all gathered?"

The sheriff looked real tired. He didn't care that we were newly-weds, that we had injured family.

"Luggage and gifts aren't important, considering the people who've died," I said. "We're doing what we can, Sheriff. Anything is better than hanging around the hospital."

That struck the right note. The white-mustached man straightened his back, and after a glance around at the debris and the empty slope where the line of dead had lain, he said, "I'm Clyde Lathrop, sheriff of this county, Mr. and Mrs. Savarov. Do you know which car the chest was in?"

"It was in a car with a group of guards," Eli said. "My brother told me the guards were in a passenger car, not a freight car."

"Oh. Oh, my goodness." The sheriff looked unhappy. "Well, the account we got, there was such a gun crew in one of the derailed cars, and most of the people in the crew are dead or in the hospital. In fact, just an hour ago, we found one of them in the field over there, with a very suspicious injury. There was a smashed crate beside him."

"I'm sorry," I said. "I don't understand. An injury not caused by the . . . derailment?"

"No, ma'am."

I can't tell you how strange it felt to be a "ma'am."

Sheriff Lathrop continued, "I'm pretty sure he was murdered. I'm real sorry to tell you this, but maybe that crate was a temptation to someone who took advantage of the chaos."

"Oh, no," I said. I leaned heavily against Eli. That was easy, because I was just as tired as the sheriff. I tried to make tears come to my eyes as I looked up at Eli, but I could not make that happen. "We have to find out what happened to the poor man, and to the crate. I'm afraid your brother will take it personal, if we can't retrieve . . ."

"It was a family piece," Eli told Clyde Lathrop. "We're very anxious to track it, if that's possible. And of course, we want to claim the poor man's body for burial."

"Mr. Savarov, everything we've gathered together from the wreck is in that tent yonder, now that the injured have all been moved," Sheriff Lathrop said. "The crates and boxes and so on are on one side, the personal luggage on the other. You are welcome to

look. I don't believe there's anything that would shock your missus."
The sheriff cut his eyes toward me significantly.

I had to bite the inside of my mouth to keep my face still.

"Thank you, sir," Eli said.

"If you don't find what you're looking for, you may feel free to
look among the wreckage. But Mrs. Savarov should remain here if you
do so. And the dead have all been taken to the funeral homes in town."

"Again, thank you for your advice, Sheriff." Eli nodded gravely
and we started over to the tent that had formerly housed the
wounded. Now it was the salvaged goods depot.

If I had truly been a gently bred lady, there were still some things
that would have distressed me . . . maybe. There was blood on some
of the items that had been retrieved, and of course blood had dripped
on the ground from the injured. Now it had dried on the trampled
grass. No way to get rid of that until the tent came down and there
was rain.

I bravely pretended I didn't see it. I didn't want to come all over
faint. I held a hand to my forehead, palm out, to mask the awful
sight.

"Would you stop it," Eli hissed. "I can see you're trying not to
laugh."

"Yes, my manly protector," I said. I didn't dare look up.

I wasn't laughing after ten minutes' hard searching. No chest.
I hadn't believed it would be here. No one would murder Jake and
then leave the booty to be carried to the lost-and-found. But we had
to look.

Jake would have used his gun if he hadn't believed the person
approaching him was a friend. That idea popped into my head, crys-
tal clear.

"He did the best any crew leader could do," I said.

"Don't you think I should go look over the wreckage?" Eli said. I could hear that encouraging note in his voice that said he really wanted to do that. And I could also tell he knew the fact that I couldn't go with him would be real irritating to me.

"That might be a good thing to do," I said. "Sweetheart." I tacked that on since we were newlyweds. Eli squeezed my arm a little too hard.

"Then consider it done," Eli said gallantly. *"Solnyshko."*

And he led me to an intact wooden crate in the shade in the middle of the tent, so I could sit while he hared off and saw what there was to see. I puredee hated that.

A Negro trustee—at least that was what I thought his black-and-white-striped uniform signified—came over to me, eyes lowered, and asked if I would care for a glass of water. The sheriff thought I might be feeling a little overcome. I thanked him nicely, and accepted.

When he came back, eyes still lowered, I said, "You know a family around here, Reva and Hosea Clelland?"

I'd kept my voice low, but he still flinched. "Yes'm."

"I don't want to make trouble for them, but I knew their daughter Galilee. If they can come to the Pleasant Stay Hotel, or let me know where to meet 'em, I'd like to talk to them."

"Yes'm," he said, and scuttled away as fast as he could. I'd kept our exchange too quiet and quick for anyone to take notice, on purpose. If I behaved wrong, this man would pay. Not only had Galilee told me stories, but I could tell from the way the Negro people acted that they'd rather do anything than draw attention to any conversation they had with white people, especially white women.

Bored and restless, I began to pick through the personal bags and luggage we hadn't yet checked. I found one I was sure was Maddy's. Her initials were scratched on the outside. There were so many that were similar I had no way of knowing which were Jake's and Rogelio's, but I found Charlie's. I could send its contents back to his family.

After that, all I could do was drink water, sit on the damn crate, think about how lucky I was to be in the shade, and wonder what "*Solnyshko*" meant.

# CHAPTER SEVEN

B y the time Eli came to fetch me, I was almost stunned with boredom. It wasn't really that hot, but the air was a lot wetter than I was used to. I didn't know how anyone could live here. Or why they'd want to. It was supposed to be fall.

"Ready to go back to the car?" Eli said. He looked grim and sweaty.

"I have been ready since you left me here," I said.

"Look sweet," Eli reminded me.

"I don't have any idea how to do that," I snarled.

He raised my hand to his mouth and kissed my knuckles.

It tickled, and I smiled.

"There now, not so hard," Eli said, clearly pleased with himself.

"Let's go to the hospital now," I said. "Oh, here are two bags from my crew. Since you're such a big, strong man, you can carry them."

"Of course," Eli said smoothly. "Anything for you, my frail flower."

I snorted.

The hospital was only two blocks away from the hotel, so Eli parked the car behind the Pleasant Stay and we walked. Turned out that had been a good idea. We couldn't have found a parking spot anywhere closer to the hospital. I was so tired I was staggering, though. Despite my nap in the green forest, I was exhausted. And I wasn't looking forward to going inside the hospital.

I'd only been in one once. In Segundo Mexia, most people believed you went to the hospital to die, and the only hospital was quite a distance anyway. We did have a real doctor, who lived a few miles outside of Segundo Mexia. He was a drinker. You had to get there in the morning.

Ballard Memorial Hospital was a long one-story building shaped like a T. Its outside was red brick. It was built up off the ground like most structures here. After we went up the steps and through the big double doors at the front, we were blocked by a large desk. You could walk around it if you went right, but clearly that would be a terrible thing to do.

Behind the desk sat a nurse in a starched uniform with a ledger in front of her. *Like she's waiting to admit people to heaven*, I thought. She had a name tag that read MISS MAYHEW.

"How can I hep yawl?" Miss Mayhew said. Her accent was so thick it was like molasses.

Eli and I looked at each other, at a loss.

Miss Mayhew gave us a sharp look. Then she repeated, "How can I hep yawl?" in a louder voice, in case we were hard of hearing.

It *was* noisy; the floor was wood, and heels made big sounds on it. Since the hospital was full of people, there were lots of voices crossing each other. Somewhere in the building behind a closed door, a man was screaming.

Miss Mayhew wasn't listening to the screaming at all. It might as well not have been happening.

My brain burped up a translation. Miss Mayhew wanted to know how she could help us.

"We're here to see Maddy Smith," I said. I tacked on a "please, ma'am" after Miss Mayhew's gaze got even sharper.

Miss Mayhew deigned to look down at her ledger. "Maddy Smith," she said. "One of the injured from the train?"

"Yes'm." I'd learned my lesson.

Miss Mayhew pointed to a set of doors behind her, in the left wall. "She's in the open ward with all the other women just brought in. The ward's completely full. First time I can remember. Please limit your visit to ten minutes. We have an *awful lot* of people coming in and out today. Sign in here, please."

She reversed the ledger and Eli bent to sign it for us. I'm not sure what I would have written.

"Thank you, Nurse Mayhew," said Eli, with his best smile.

But Miss Mayhew was immune. Blank stare. I loved it.

We walked past the desk into the wide hall. There was a sign sticking out on the left: WOMEN'S WARD. The men's ward was across the hall. A door at the far end said EMERGENCY—OPERATING THEATER—PRIVATE ROOMS. The screaming came from there.

The double swinging doors to the women's ward were closed, I guess to cut down on the noise or for modesty. Eli pushed one open and we went in. It smelled, of course, though maybe it would have been clean and clear if the train wreck survivors hadn't been there. The engine smell was strong. Fear, sweat, blood, dirt, and all other body fluids added to the bouquet.

The women's ward was a long, open room containing twenty beds. As Miss Mayhew had said, they were all occupied. There were also a few cots set up running in a line down the middle of the room. They were occupied, too.

I could tell most of these women had been on the train; they had broken limbs, head injuries, and fresh bandages. Though there were three nurses, and they were all working diligently, some of the patients had not been cleaned yet. Their faces were smudged with dirt or blood, and they were still in their train clothes, just as soiled.

I saw Maddy halfway down on the left side. She was in a hospital gown. Due to the heat, she was on top of the sheets rather than under them. Her leg was heavily bandaged. She didn't look good.

Maddy looked at me as I stood by her bed. For a moment, she didn't know me. It was almost funny, the expression she wore when she figured out who I was. I'd put the new outfit from my mind. I put a finger across my lips to let her know not to make a big to-do about my transformation.

"Lizbeth?" Maddy said cautiously, kind of feeling her way through the situation. I nodded. She looked past me at Eli. "I remember you from the wreck. Thanks for helping me."

"We came to see how you are feeling," I said.

"My leg isn't as good as I had hoped," Maddy said. She was unhappy and worried and in pain. "They did some cutting and stitching on it, got the bullet out. I just woke up. I thought after they'd bandaged me I'd get back to the station to see if I could get a train going the other way. But the doctor says I can't walk on it for a week, at least, and then I got to use crutches. If I don't take care of it now, I'll be a gimp the rest of my life, he said. If it opens up again, I might bleed to death." Maddy looked gloomy, as well she ought. "But I have to get home and get work. And I got to pay the hospital bill. Maybe you can send Jake in here? He should be willing to front me the money for the return trip, plus my wages."

I could tell she'd been sitting there thinking and fuming and worrying. Who wouldn't? I hated to bring more bad news down on her. "Maddy, I have to tell you something. After I helped you onto the wagon, we went back to Jake, to fetch him and take him to town, along with the crate. But when we got there, he was dead. Someone had cut his throat. And they stole our cargo."

Maddy looked at me. After a long moment she gasped real deep and rough, like she was taking the first breath after a blow to the chest.

"We left him to get killed," she said, her voice ragged. "We left him."

I had already thought that twenty times. It made me sick. "Yeah, we did. I did," I said, so she'd know I wasn't sparing myself. "No way around that. But Jake was alert and armed. I went directly back to him after we'd talked to you and Rogelio. Couldn't have been more than ten minutes."

Maddy looked down at her clasped hands, her lips pressed together. "I've been with Jake for three years," she said, presently. "I've been to dinner at his house. I introduced him to his boyfriend."

I kept silence until she got herself under control. After a bit, she took a deep breath.

"So, who's this friend of yours?" Maddy asked. She jerked her head at Eli. "Where'd you find him?"

She didn't remember we'd talked about this at the train wreck, and that was not surprising. "I knew Eli from my last job," I said. "I had no expectations of seeing him here. His job has crossed mine, again." I didn't want Maddy to think I'd arranged some kind of rendezvous.

"He a wizard? Holy Russian?" She leaned a little to look past me, her face telling me clearly that Maddy didn't trust Eli as far as she could throw him.

"You can talk to Eli directly." I was having my own struggle, to sound neutral. "I'm not his mouthpiece."

"He why you're all rigged up?"

"No." Yes. "I'm all rigged up because women here have to be, or they get . . . mistreated. I have to track the cargo."

"What can I do?" It was clear Maddy was not pleased with me, or trustful of my ally, but she knew we had to finish our job.

"Get well," I said. "Jake would be the last person in the world to want you to get crippled, trying to find out who killed him. And Rogelio is here, he'll help, unless he's more busted up than I figured."

Maddy looked angry, and frustrated, and then . . . resigned. "It is true that I can't do any good while I'm bleeding from the leg," she said grudgingly. "I have to be able to walk, or no more jobs for me. And the pain is more than I'd counted on." She was white around the mouth.

I nodded, being no stranger to pain. "Do you know a name or address where I can get in touch with our employer? To see about what to do now, how to get paid? At least they owe us for the trip here."

Maddy shook her head. "Maybe Rogelio does. Jake treated Rogelio like he was second-in-command. I guess you checked Jake's pockets?"

I *hadn't* checked Jake's pockets. I clenched my fingers into fists to keep from smacking myself in the head. "We'll do that," I said. "You know where Rogelio is?"

Maddy said, "I haven't laid eyes on him since the wagon brought us here. I guess he's over in the men's ward."

"I'll come back when we find out something. I don't know how long that'll be." I patted Maddy's hand. "And look, I found your bag."

"Mr. Eli, if you'd draw back a minute, I need to talk to Lizbeth," Maddy said. Her voice was steady and determined.

Eli nodded politely and wished Maddy a swift recovery. I watched him stride out of the ward, his long braid swinging across his back.

Maddy barely waited until Eli was out of earshot.

"Thanks for looking for my bag, but Jesus, Lizbeth! What are you doing with him? You know he's a grigori! Where's your sense, girl?"

"Me and him worked together," I said again. I had a hard time getting the words out between my teeth. I was running out of sympathy. "I trust Eli, Maddy. He's all I got to work with. I have no money, no contacts here, no names to track."

"Okay," Maddy said slowly, thinking it over. "You don't know this place. People here are different, seems like." She stared at my face some more. "I wish I'd never come here," she said, suddenly, in a burst of anger.

"You and me both. I'm going to find you money to go home," I said, promising her and myself. "I'll be here again to see you. Please do what the doctor says, so you can get well. I'd like to work with you again."

Maddy smiled, a little shy now. "I feel the same way. You're good to have on a crew, Lizbeth. You're a fine shot and a reliable woman."

"You know it's going to be days before anything moves in or out of here," I reminded her. "They got to clear away the wreck. They got to repair the track. I'll figure out a way to get us home. We're owed."

"Watch out for that grigori," Maddy said, just as I was turning away. "Trust him or not, you know he bears watching. And that woman, that Harriet Ritter, and her sidekick. Those two are wrong."

"I'll keep my eyes open," I said. I was glad she hadn't noticed the wedding ring. I gave her a final wave before I followed Eli out to the main hall.

Maddy was right to think the man and woman we'd met on the train had a lot they should tell me . . . if they would. But tracking down Harriet Ritter and Travis Seeley wasn't at the top of my list.

First we needed to visit Rogelio, and then we had to track down Jake's body, since I'd been so stupid I hadn't gone through his pockets.

Eli was waiting for me in the hall. It took me a minute to spot him because there was so much traffic. Doctors, nurses, visitors, patients who could walk . . . on their own, or with crutches. Orderlies who were mopping or sweeping or pushing rolling bins of laundry.

"After we finish here, we're getting some sleep," Eli said, putting his big hand on my shoulder. He looked as tired as I felt.

"You're right," I said. "But first . . ." We went back to the desk at the entrance, and I asked where Rogelio was.

"Who?" Miss Mayhew shook her head. Her white starched cap was anchored so firm to her scalp that it didn't wobble. "We haven't admitted anyone by that name. I'd remember. We don't get many Mexicans." She was matter-of-fact about that. To give the woman credit, she checked the list of patients despite her doubt. But after, she looked up at us and shook her head again.

I was stunned.

Eli didn't seem so surprised. "He must have been well enough to walk away on his own," Eli said. "Miss Mayhew, we need to find the body of another friend. Where would we be able to view the dead?"

"I'm sorry for your loss," Nurse Mayhew said automatically. "The unclaimed deceased have been taken to Hutchison Funeral

Home or Debenham's Funeral Home. Here are the addresses." She handed us two business cards. I didn't know if it was funny or outrageous that the funeral homes had cards at the hospital desk, but at least it was convenient.

"Can you tell me if the bodies will be autopsied?" Eli said delicately. Miss Mayhew, a nurse but also a Dixie woman, might find this unseemly.

"I doubt it," Miss Mayhew snapped, kind of angry, kind of shucking him off. "Sally has four doctors total. There are lots of the living to take care of before they can start looking at the dead."

"Thanks so much for your help," I said. I let Eli take my arm and lead me out of the hospital. We went down the steps and past the benches and bushes and flowerbeds. Everything was decorated here.

We turned right and began walking.

Eli said, "We need to talk. And how long has it been since you ate or drank anything?"

"I'm real thirsty." I was trembling, which is one of the things that happens to me when I'm parched. It had been the longest day of my life and it wasn't over yet.

"There," Eli said, pointing to a sign that read BEVERLY'S RESTAURANT. The dim coolness of the place was welcome. It was quiet after the clamor of the hospital. A gray-haired woman in a flowered dress seated us and said, "Your waitress will be right here." It was too late for lunch and too early for dinner, and there were only two other customers having a quiet, sad talk. We could speak without being overheard.

"You're thinking . . . what are you thinking?" I said, after the ancient waitress had brought our sodas and glasses full of ice. Eli called her back and asked her if they had pie. They did, banana cream or buttermilk. We got one piece of each. "You reckon Rogelio died? I didn't think he was hurt bad enough."

"He's the kind of man who stands out," Eli said. "Maybe he had treatment at the hospital but didn't need a bed, since the place is so full right now."

"Maybe he had bleeding in his brain? Or he was kidnapped right off the wagon? We could question the nurses in the men's ward." I was eating the banana cream pie. I couldn't put myself into the right frame of mind to enjoy it a lot. But it was much better than going back to the hospital.

Eli made the buttermilk pie vanish. He yawned widely. "I need sleep," he said, and he sounded utterly tired.

Once Eli had mentioned the word "sleep," it was all I could think of. I had to make myself sit up in my chair and down my drink. It had chipped ice in it. It felt like heaven going down.

"We have to check the bodies," Eli said, with great regret.

"Yeah." We couldn't wait on that.

We finished our drinks and set out for the funeral homes.

# CHAPTER EIGHT

The closest one, Debenham's, was swamped with the dead. The men who worked there were completely overwhelmed. One employee, a man about my age, was sitting on the front steps, his head in his hands. When we told him why we were there, he simply pointed to a gravel path leading around the building to the backyard. "They're in the shed," he said. "The refrigerator's full of locals." He closed his eyes so he wouldn't have to think about us anymore, or anything else.

The Debenham's people had tried to be respectful—but when you place twenty bodies in an area meant for four, it's not possible to mind your manners. They'd piled the women to the left and the men to the right, which was . . . well-intentioned, best I could come up with.

There were fewer women. I recognized the old woman who'd been in our carriage when Maddy and I had shot the two young men. Wondered if her husband had survived. I also spotted the woman whose husband had been beating her. She wouldn't get to enjoy being free of him.

Eli and I began looking through the men.

This was not the most unpleasant half hour I had ever spent, but I was glad I had a strong stomach.

I regretted my nice clothes more than ever. I had to take care not to get anything on my skirt. Eli couldn't identify Jake, so I had to stay close while he moved the corpses around so I could see each one.

Neither Jake nor Rogelio had been brought to Debenham's.

We left without talking to any of the staff. Aside from the one young man, I don't believe anyone noted our presence or departure. There was an old pump in the backyard of the funeral home, and Eli held his hands under the water while I pulled the handle.

Hutchison Funeral Home was larger and fancier-looking than Debenham's. The yard and the business itself teemed with people, a lot of them weeping. Parking in front had lost all order. Apparently most of the local victims' bodies had landed here, families had already identified their own, and funeral arrangements had begun.

Hutchison had all hands on deck. Four men and two women in dark suits were moving from group to group being quiet and smooth. I liked that. I hoped the place was so busy our request to see the bodies would be automatically granted. But the man who glided over to us—he introduced himself as Donald Barton—was only persuaded to let me see the bodies after I told him I was the only one who could identify my brother, and my parents were desperate to learn his fate.

Donald Barton did not like my proposal, not one little bit. I thought we were going to have to knock him senseless in a quiet corner. Finally, the oldest woman employee, a white-headed stout lady dressed all in black, stopped by while he was arguing with me. She said, "Donald, if this lady wants to look for her brother, you must let her."

"Thank you, ma'am," I said, with a lot of gratitude. "I appreciate it."

Donald Barton wasn't going to let us go by ourselves, though. First we toured the large ground-floor room normally used for the preparation of bodies. That room was full to capacity, held no one I recognized.

Like the first funeral home, Hutchison had parked the overflow in a detached building—their garage. Hearses had been pulled out, the bodies moved in.

Still grudgingly, Barton held open one of the wide doors. "If you don't find your loved one here, we don't have him," he said with some satisfaction.

Eli thanked him. I couldn't open my mouth.

These bodies were laid out in a less jumbled way, which was good. But each body had been covered with a sheet, which was going to make this take even longer. I was sagging on my feet.

I'd been just about praying Barton would leave us alone. Surely he had better things to do? But no. The man had decided it was his duty to draw away the cloth from each face in turn. It made me so aggravated I could hardly stop myself from smacking him. Maybe he hated Eli's grigori vest. Maybe he thought I deserved to faint right by the bodies.

I could not oblige. I am not that good at pretending.

Rogelio was not among the dead (a relief and a puzzle), but we found Jake, finally. He was still clothed. "Mr. Barton, this is my brother Jake," I said, and I didn't have to act being sad. "I need to take the contents of his pockets to my parents." I looked at him expectantly.

Barton was trying to think of a reason not to help me. But he couldn't come up with one. He carefully checked every single garment, handing each item he found to Eli.

Jake had much more money than I'd expected. It was a miracle no one had looted him. There were some receipts, too, looked like.

I said, "Mr. Barton, please check Jake's boots. He had the habit of stowing things there."

Barton looked disgusted, but he couldn't think of a reason to deny us the boots. Those were not bloody at all.

"You were right," Eli said to me after Barton silently handed him two items. There'd been an envelope in Jake's right boot and a knife in Jake's left.

Even if the envelope held a love letter from Jake's boyfriend, we were to the good. Never hurts to have an extra knife.

Eli slid the money into one of his pockets, all the scraps of paper (including the envelope) in another. We would wait to read those. I hoped I'd get the answers to some questions.

"Mr. Barton, thanks so much," I said. "I'll let my family know, and they'll be in touch about what to do with the body. This body is Jake Tutwiler's."

"Ma'am, they'd better call or wire soon," Donald Barton advised me as he wrote Jake's name in a little notebook. He tore out the page and tucked it in Jake's shirt pocket, protruding a little. "You can tell this place has to be emptied out quick."

"I understand." I let Eli lead me away. I even leaned against him.

"I need to telegraph his boyfriend," I said, once we were out of earshot. "Maddy said she introduced them, so she'll be able to tell me how to do that. Why didn't I get his name while we were at the hospital? I have to find out what happened to Rogelio. And I need to find that Ritter and Seeley."

"We'll do all of that, but not right now," Eli said. "We need to eat a real meal, and we have to sleep."

"I haven't got much of an appetite."

"Me either, but we need to eat, anyway."

The dining room of our hotel was not yet ready for dinner, but they were able to bring us some soup and bread. Soup was not what I would have picked, considering the weather, but when it came I was glad of it. I needed the chicken and the vegetables, and the biscuits that came with it were real good. And the cold sweet tea. With ice. That was best of all.

In twenty minutes we were going slowly up the stairs, and then we were in our room. I was really, really glad to be away from the crowd. The whole day had bruised me, body and spirit.

I began unbuttoning my blouse, and then paused. Was it all right to undress in front of Eli? Was it right to assume we were comfortable with each other? Would he assume we were back on *that* footing?

At this moment I decided I just didn't care. Without casting a glance his way, I took off my new clothes, hanging them and shaking them out, giving the underwear a quick rinse in the bathroom sink when I went in to wash my face and put on my nightgown. I had not had a nightgown since I was a child, and this one was real pretty, but I wasn't in a mood to be pleased about it.

Though it was still light outside, Eli had drawn the curtains to dim the room. I pulled a string to make the fan turn. It whirred in a pleasant way, making just enough noise to blur the voices on the stairs and out the window. The minute I lay down, it all sounded far away. I felt the mattress move as Eli crawled in beside me.

"Go to sleep. We're safe," he said.

I took him at his word.

## CHAPTER NINE

When I woke, early light was coming in around the curtains. I could just make out the outlines of the furniture. It was as cool as it was going to get. I slid out of bed and padded quietly into the bathroom, easing the door shut behind me. I bathed, and as I toweled off I thought, *I should get dressed now.*

I just couldn't face all those underpinnings and a frock on top of it all. I pulled the nightgown over my head again. It was very thin and light. I climbed back into bed, trying to be stealthy, hoping I could sleep some more.

The sheet was pulled up to Eli's waist. His broad shoulders were bare, and I could see all his tattoos. He'd added one since our trip. His braid had come undone, so his light hair was spread across his pillow. I had forgotten how lovely he was without his clothes. You thought he was gawky until he was naked. Then you could see how well he was put together.

I couldn't help but remember another hotel room in Mexico. I pulled the sheet up a little and settled my head on my pillow. I told myself, real strictly, to sleep.

But it turned out Eli was awake too, and he had other ideas. He slid my way a couple of inches and put his arm around me. Then he left it up to me.

He was good about that.

It wasn't much of a decision. The minute I'd seen Eli at the train wreck, I'd felt restless.

(I'd told myself not to assume Eli would feel the same way. I'd told myself that in Mexico, we'd been on the edge of dying every minute, which makes you ready to enjoy something, anything.)

After thinking all this, which took one shake of a lamb's tail, I turned on my side to face Eli. That was all the encouragement he needed. He began working the nightgown up, his hands reacquainting themselves with me, and we kissed about a hundred times. To my astonishment, he said, "I missed you, Lizbeth," so intently I couldn't doubt he meant it.

It started out sleepy and tender, like a gentle reunion. But it turned into . . . forceful and exciting. I forgot how sore and bruised I was. Eli was *really glad* to be inside me, even with a condom on. He said "Lizbeth" in a hoarse, deep voice, like it was torn from inside him. He had strength and stamina. "*Now*," he said, in the same voice. And that excited me so much I took off into my big moment, right before his. My body jerked, like it had a mind of its own, and I had to clamp my teeth over a moan. It seemed to last a long time, pleasure after pleasure.

I was panting like I'd finished a race as he slid out of me. We lay together in silence for a few peaceful moments.

"Lizbeth," Eli said, his voice real quiet. "You good?"

"I think you could tell I was 'good,'" I said, not able to hold back a big smile. "You sure were." It was hard to say something so personal, especially something about sex, but I wanted to give credit where it was due.

Eli looked a little embarrassed, and a lot pleased.

I wondered if Eli would say something more about missing

me, because that had really surprised the hell out of me. But if he thought about it, he decided against it. Which was probably for the best, because we had a job to do.

"Lizbeth," he said ten minutes later, in an entirely different tone. He had showered and he was toweling off. I was brushing my teeth. I turned, raising my brows, since my mouth was busy.

Eli was looking at me silently. He couldn't seem to go on with his sentence.

As the silence grew in the little room, I even thought of saying, *Someday maybe we'll see each other when we're not working.* But the differences between me and Eli made such a wide chasm, you couldn't begin to reach across it. It was real silly, real stupid, to even let such a thought in my head.

Eli bent down to me and kissed my forehead, something my mother hadn't even done when I'd been little. "What do you want to do first today?" he said. If he'd been going to say something different, he'd made up his mind not to.

There were things we had to do, he was right. And they were things I knew how to do.

I said, "First, we need to get Jake's boyfriend's name and address from Maddy. We got to send him a telegram about the body. Charlie's family, too. Also, we need to go around the hotels to see if we spot the gunnie I met on the train, Sarah Byrne. Maybe she saw something while she sat by me on the grass. I got to talk to Harriet Ritter and Travis Seeley. And maybe spot Rogelio." I had no other ideas. I was counting on some cropping up. "What about you, you got a list?"

Eli looked kind of shifty, which he did when he wasn't supposed to tell me everything. It was a timely reminder that Eli had an allegiance that trumped any other.

"First, we need to eat and we need some coffee," Eli said.

So we ate breakfast at a table on the big screened-in porch: sliced peaches in cream, bacon, and pancakes. It was one of the best breakfasts I've ever had.

"Would you like some more coffee, Mrs. Savarov?" our waiter said. For a minute, I didn't realize he was talking to me.

"Thanks, please pour me some," I said after an awkward pause.

"And you, Mr. Savarov?"

Eli nodded. "Please."

The waiter, a short man with gray hair cut close to his scalp, eyed Eli real closely. While the man poured our coffee, Eli put his hand over mine on the table.

I started to pull back, startled, but I remembered we were supposed to be married.

We had sure done some of the things married people do.

I didn't know what to do with that idea—whether to laugh, or feel wicked.

I didn't have to pick, though, really. I would always laugh. I didn't have much respect for a God who would watch you in the bedroom and judge on that. If you weren't hurting each other, and if neither of you was married to someone else, you were okay having sex. It was a free pleasure, in a world that didn't have that many.

I managed to smile a little at Eli. He smiled right back, keeping his hand over mine. Mr. Mercer strolled through the tables, talking to guests. He noticed our hand-holding. So he had to see the rings. But we were not among the favored.

I was fine with that.

A young woman was trailing in Mercer's wake, dark-haired and narrow-faced like him. A daughter, for sure. She was learning how to greet guests herself. We didn't make her personal greeting list either, but she sure had some eyes for Eli. It was hard to tell from her staring if she liked what she saw or if she thought he'd sprout horns. I saw her speak to our waiter before she strolled back into the reception area.

When the waiter came with our bill, Eli signed it and asked that the charge be put on his room account.

"I'm sorry, sir," the waiter said. He was trying not to look embarrassed. "The management asks that you settle each charge as it comes up."

Eli got out his billfold with more calm than I could have shown and gave the waiter cash. In fact, he told the man to keep the extra as a tip.

"That is petty harassment," Eli said, just loud enough to hear, as we passed Miss Mercer at the desk on our way to the stairs.

We still had an hour before visiting time at the hospital. We'd spread Jake's papers out to dry the night before, anchoring down the corners with ashtrays and Bibles so the fan wouldn't blow them around.

The most bloodstained paper was the one that had been in Jake's chest pocket. I puzzled it out slowly, reading each word out loud to Eli. "*Dear Jake, I already miss you and you are just leaving. I bless the day I met you. You are a handsome man inside and out. You have honor and integrity and a beautiful cock.*" I decided to read the rest to myself. "More of the same," I told Eli, trying to sound matter-of-fact. "It's signed 'Burke.'"

Eli said, "Burke was in love."

"That makes me sad." Burke would want to know, as soon as I could get his full name and hometown from Maddy.

There were receipts, too, but I knew where we'd been so they weren't that interesting. Eli unfolded the other note with his long fingers, the one that had been in Jake's boot. Eli read it out loud in a voice just above a whisper. "*Mr. Tutwiler: When you get to Sally, a representative of mine will meet you and assume responsibility for the cargo. Once you have handed it over, you can return to Texoma. My representative will say 'Let my people go.' If you're approached by someone who doesn't say that, he's a thief. Act accordingly.*"

It wasn't signed. This was so aggravating.

"How'd Jake know this letter was actually from your employer?" Eli said.

"Maybe something was enclosed. Or maybe there was something on the envelope. Or maybe he knew the person who handed it to him." I was ready to learn something solid. You needed to know who your enemies were. That was even more important than knowing your friends. "I don't like maybes."

"I knew that about you," Eli said. He was smiling, just a bit. "I don't either."

Mr. Mercer's shadow of the morning was at the desk as we walked by on our way out. As I'd guessed, her name tag read MISS MERCER.

"Mr. Savarov," she said, kind of cooing. "A moment, please."

We went to stand in front of the desk. She looked almost pretty and round in a light green dress with a dark green scarf at the neck.

"Will you be staying with us longer, Mr. Savarov?" she asked, not even bothering to look at me.

"I made my reservation for three more nights," Eli said. "Was that unclear?"

"No, sir." Miss Mercer couldn't think of a lie quick enough.

Eli looked puzzled. "Then there's no problem," he said carefully, trying to figure out what was going on.

The girl flushed. She didn't know where to look while she talked to someone as outlandish as Eli; her big brown eyes went from his long braid to his neck (his collar was askew and one of his tattoos was just visible) to his grigori vest. And back again.

"I hope you have a lovely morning, Miss Mercer," I said, and started toward the front door.

When we were safely out the door, I said, "Eli, never be alone with that girl."

Again, he looked puzzled. "I don't plan on it," he said.

"I think she does," I told him. Eli flushed and we walked the rest of the way to the hospital in silence. I watched my feet in their strange shoes move across the sidewalk. Today I wore my pale-blue skirt with little white flowers, and the white blouse. I felt like an idiot.

Maddy was awake, but right away I saw she had a fever. Her face was flushed, her eyes were dull, and she was listless. "Good to see you," she said. "I was glad to have my bag. But one of the nurses locked it up with my guns in it. She said we couldn't have those lying around."

"Are you okay with that?" I didn't know what I'd do about it if she wasn't, but I'd try to do something.

"Yeah, I guess. I ain't going to be doing any shooting for a day or two, I reckon." Maddy managed a smile. "And I don't need my clothes." She plucked at the white hospital gown.

"What does the doctor say about your fever?"

"You can tell, huh? He gave me a shot to kill the germs, he said. I should start getting better today." Maddy tried to smile.

"Can I trouble you for Jake's boyfriend's name and how I can send him a telegram? I figured he'd want to claim the body."

"Burke Printer. He prints the newspaper in Sweetwater. His office is at . . . let me think . . . it's on Armstrong . . . sixty-two." I checked on Charlie's information while we were at it.

Eli wrote everything down on one of the scraps of paper he seemed to always have in one of his pockets. "I hope you get better," he said. "If you need us, ask the nurse to call us at the Pleasant Stay Hotel."

Maddy looked a little surprised at the offer. "Thanks, I will."

I spent a little more time with Maddy. We talked about the food, which she said was fine, and her leg, which looked okay. I wondered where the fever was coming from. Was the wound infected? Or one of her cuts? But I could tell Maddy was nervous about the fever and didn't want to discuss it.

I asked Miss Mayhew, on duty at the entrance desk again, where the telegraph office was. I'd figured it would be somewhere around the train station, and it was, from her directions.

Eli and I decided to go there first, then work our way from the station out through the town looking for Ritter and Seeley, or Rogelio, or Sarah Byrne. Anyone familiar. "We can cover ground faster if we split up," I said, which was common sense.

"I think we need to be together," Eli said, sounding real firm.

"Yeah? Why?"

"For one thing, we're married. For another, women on their own here can . . ." Eli stopped, at a loss for words.

"Do you think I can't take care of trouble?" I could hardly believe what I was hearing.

"You can't wear your guns," he said, taking care to speak really quietly. "You don't want to draw attention to yourself. I know you can take on a small army by yourself when you're armed. But Dixie is different, and believe me, we want to get in and out of here with as little notice as possible."

"Why don't I want to draw attention to myself?"

"Lizbeth, can't you take my word for it?"

That was a good question. I looked up at him and thought. Eli's face showed worry rather than anger. Eli was seriously troubled about my well-being in Dixie . . . yet he'd seen me fight. I had to take him seriously.

"All right," I said slowly.

He bent to give me a kiss on the cheek. "Thanks," he said. "This is a terrible place, sometimes."

"You've been here before."

"Yes, I came last year."

"With Paulina?" She'd been his partner. She'd died twice.

"Yes. It was a nightmare. You knew Paulina. How could she comply with the rules here?" Eli looked away. And then he said in a completely different voice, "Could this be your gunnie from the train?"

"Yes! Sarah Byrne."

Sarah was still wearing pants, but she was not toting her guns. She spotted me the next minute, and made haste to join us. "I'm glad you're feeling better," she said. Her eyes went up and down me. "Wow, you look different! Did all your clothes get burned up in the crash?"

"Sarah, this is my friend Eli." Sarah looked up at him, and a little line appeared between her eyebrows.

"Grigori, huh? I never talked to one before."

"I am a grigori, yes," Eli said, springing all his charm on her. He had quite a bit, when he chose. "It's a pleasure to meet you."

"Uh-huh," Sarah said, looking back at me. "Well, if you say so. Lizbeth, your arm feeling better? Any muscle damage?"

"No, just sore," I said. "Harriet's salve and Eli's healing helped a lot." I paused; this was going to be awkward. "Jake died, though."

"Sorry to hear it. He didn't seem that badly hurt." She shifted her feet. "Well, if you need me . . . I'm at the Darby Hotel, one block over. It's real cheap."

"I'll remember. Hey, have you seen Harriet Ritter and Travis Seeley since yesterday?"

"No, but I ain't like to. Why?"

"You do see 'em, tell 'em I'm at the Pleasant Stay, and we need to speak. Or Rogelio, too. He kind of vanished."

"Lots of people trying to find other people in this town. Hope they're not down at the funeral homes."

"They're not," I said.

Sarah was surprised that I'd checked. "Oh, what happened to your cargo?"

"Stolen from Jake. He was murdered."

Losing your cargo was a disgrace. Sarah made an effort to look like it wasn't such a big thing. "Well," she said abruptly. "You know where I am if you need me. If I've left there, I've found some means to go on to my sister's place."

"Good luck with that," I said, and Eli told her good-bye. Sarah gave him another doubtful look and was on her way. I had no idea where she was going, but she walked with purpose.

I didn't feel easy about the whole conversation. I didn't know for sure why. Eli, too, seemed uneasy. He asked me exactly how I'd met Sarah, where she was from, where her sister lived. I didn't know all the answers.

We passed a drugstore on our way to the next hotel. The gold lettering on the window read BALLARD PHARMACY, SODAS AND SHAKES. When I glanced in the window I saw familiar faces.

"Speak of the devil," I said to Eli, gripping his arm to make him stop. "Those two, Eli, are Harriet Ritter and Travis Seeley." I was as proud as though I had planned this. "We been looking for 'em and we found 'em."

They were seated in a large booth with another man whose back was to the window. Looked like the three were having a serious conversation, all hunched over and their heads together.

The fans in the store were going, and I thought it might be fifteen degrees cooler than out in the sun.

As if Travis Seeley felt me looking at him, he stopped talking and raised his head, looking directly at me. His mouth fell open. I'd almost forgotten how different I looked in the white blouse and blue skirt, with its tiny white flowers.

I gave him a cheery smile and wave. Seeley nudged Harriet Ritter and jerked his head in my direction. Ritter, too, gave me a startled look. If I hadn't been so uncomfortable in the new clothes, it would have made me feel kind of smug.

The third person at the table, the one with his back to me, twisted around to see what his friends were looking at. Rogelio Socorro. The suspicion I'd had after he'd vanished from the hospital? Justified.

"Well, well, well," I said, when we were standing at the booth. "We all meet again."

Eli said, "Please introduce me."

"Eli, you met Rogelio yesterday, when he was on his way to the hospital. Because he was so badly hurt." I thumped Rogelio on what I hoped was his sore shoulder.

We made it clear we were sliding into the horseshoe-curved booth with them, and Rogelio scooted toward the middle. Slowly. I got in next to him. He'd know I had a knife.

Rogelio's face was a study. The two others from the train were not abashed in the least.

"I have seen your friend, Lizbeth, but we haven't officially met," Harriet Ritter said, smooth as glass. She tilted her blond head as she gave Eli a little smile. And a devil bit me in the butt.

"Harriet Ritter, Travis Seeley, this is my husband, Eli Savarov," I said. "Prince Ilya Savarov."

Some moments are just *perfect*.

Eli gave the three a gentle smile all around before leaning in to speak to Rogelio. "Mr. Socorro, we've been very worried about you. We talked to Maddy Smith, who is in some difficulty. Then we went to check on you, but you weren't listed as a patient. Your injuries weren't as serious as they seemed?"

By that time, Rogelio had gotten his feet back under him. "I didn't want to take up a bed at the hospital when I could walk out of there," he said. "I was sure there was someone who needed it worse than me."

"That's noble of you," I said. "And to think you met up with our other two companions on our journey! Miss Ritter and Mr. Seeley!"

"Please, call us Travis and Harriet. All of us who were lucky enough to survive the crash are wandering around Sally," Travis said mildly. "We were bound to bump into each other. As witness our meeting with you now. And your . . . husband." He didn't try to keep the doubt out of his voice.

We were all doing a lot of disbelieving.

A young waitress arrived just then to ask us if we wanted to order. Eli ordered a glass of ice water and ice cream for us both. I had only had ice cream a handful of times, and I sure wanted to try it again. Especially since Eli ordered chocolate flavor. The waitress brought our water immediately and bustled off to get the ice cream. I took a long and welcome swallow.

"We found Jake's body at one of the funeral homes yesterday," I said.

"But I thought he wasn't hurt too bad. And he had the crate to guard," Rogelio said, very slowly. I was convinced he was having a hard time believing me.

"While we came over to the tent to talk to you, Jake got murdered," I said. "Stabbed in the throat." I let that sit there for a minute. Rogelio was silent, his mouth slightly open. He was staring straight ahead of him. I would swear he was shocked.

"The crate was there, broken open, its contents missing," Eli said.

"We figured you and Jake were holed up somewhere with your cargo," Harriet said, looking at me. "We were going to track you down today, Lizbeth. Make a plan for delivery."

"And how are you involved, Miss Ritter?" Eli asked. He was still smiling.

"How are *you* involved, Mr. Savarov? When did you get to be part of this mission?"

"My superiors sent me," Eli said. "To find out what was happening."

"And who are your superiors?" Travis was doing his best to sound just mildly curious.

"Ultimately, I answer to the tsar."

Travis's eyes widened, Harriet's lips mashed together in a straight line, and even Rogelio seemed startled.

At this interesting moment, we got our ice cream, and the waitress took the opportunity to clear the empty plates in front of the others. I took a bite of the ice cream. It was . . . so cold and so chocolate. It was all I could do not to close my eyes and go "Mmmmmmm." I began to eat it steadily. After all, it was lunchtime.

Eli gave me my own little smile. Then he became all business. "Who is your employer, Harriet?"

Finally.

"Iron Hand Security," Harriet said, after a glance at her partner.

I had heard of Iron Hand, a company that had offices in every country in North America, even in Canada. Iron Hand had a very tough reputation. Very tough was what you wanted in a security company, which was the glorified version of a gun crew, in my estimation. I had dreamed of hiring up with a security company someday.

"Did you send the first two shooters into the car to test our mettle?" I said, leaning forward to look that Harriet Ritter right in the eyes.

"I wouldn't send two men to their deaths to test how good your crew was."

I wasn't sure that exactly answered my question. "Why were you there in the car to watch us? Were you hired as backups?"

Harriet Ritter deliberated. Then she lied. "We were there on another matter entirely," she said.

"Sure," I said, not bothering to sound like I believed her.

"I'm sorry you don't think I'm telling you the truth," Harriet said, not sounding sorry at all. "But we weren't there to watch your crew. And we tried to help you out after the train wreck."

"And yet here you are with Rogelio," Eli said. "Who didn't tell the truth about his painful injury."

"Yet here we are," Travis said, with a smile and a sweep of his hand. "Survivors of the same disaster, coming together to share our experiences." He made it sound like they'd been having a fellowship hour, and we'd arrived to add to the fun.

Eli made a little noise expressing scorn. A snort sounded funny coming from his high-bridged Russian nose.

"If you won't be truthful, we're wasting our time," I said, though I had no idea what else we were going to do. I had finished my ice cream and so had Eli. He left some money on the table for payment, and we slid out of the booth. I looked up at him. "Let's go do some work."

What work did you have in mind?" Eli said, once we were out on the sidewalk.

"First, I got to send a telegram to Jake's boyfriend."

I found the Western Union shop easily thanks to Nurse Mayhew. I had enough money (from Jake's pockets) to tell Burke Printer the bad news, but I had to be economical. I finally wrote, *So sorry Jake and Charlie killed train wreck at Sally. Bodies Hutchison Funeral. Who is employer?* I signed it, though I wasn't sure Printer would recognize my name. I put our hotel on the form so any reply could be delivered there.

The telegraph office was busy, but I stayed until the operator sent the message. I hoped Jake's boyfriend would notify Charlie's family.

"I think we better have a talk," I told Eli when I was back on the sidewalk.

"I figured," Eli said, gloomy all over. Men never look happy when you say that.

It was hard to find a place in the crowded town where we could have some privacy and shade. We went back to our hotel, though I had misgivings about being in a room with a bed and Eli when we needed to say things rather than do things.

But those things had to be said, no matter how much I enjoyed his company—which I did, especially when we were naked. I didn't want us to be at the same cross-purposes we'd been at the last time we'd worked together.

Maybe we were already there.

As we went up the stairs to our room, I glanced over the bannister to see the waiter we'd had that morning and the night before. He was looking up at me curiously, and when he saw me looking back, he shot out of sight like a bullet. I wondered what was on his mind, but not for long. I had other fish to fry.

When the door was locked behind us, Eli pulled off his grigori vest and his hat, and I shed the shoes and stockings I'd hated all morning. I sat cross-legged on the bed while Eli took the easy chair. "Tell me how you came to be here," I said. "You know why I'm here. And I swear you know everything I know."

Eli took a deep breath, and he let his unhappiness show. "I am not in favor at the court anymore," he said, as if he were confessing to torturing cats. "My father was a traitor. So no matter how faithful I have been, I've been regarded with doubt ever since the plot against the tsar was uncovered."

"But the grand duke begged off, the guy your dad was backing as the next tsar, right? If the grand duke got pardoned, why didn't his followers? And their families?" If you forgave the head of the snake, you had to forgive the body, too, seemed to me.

"The grand duke said he was ignorant of this plot to do away with Alexei. He wept with grief that he could be considered guilty, when he loved his nephew so much. My father could not have said that believably; there was too much proof against him. It was a relief to the tsar when Father didn't have to go to trial, though his death was a great puzzle to everyone."

Eli's father had died in a little hotel in Segundo Mexia. Yep, that had been mysterious to everyone but me, Eli, and Eli's younger brother Peter.

"Even though your father is dead, and he was the plotter, you and your family are in the doghouse?"

Eli looked confused.

"Your whole family is tainted?"

Eli nodded grimly. "Even after my service to my tsar. Even after I have had the privilege of tending to him personally when he was ill."

"Your older brothers?" His half brothers. They'd had another mother.

"My oldest brother denounced my father, swore his loyalty to the rightful tsar, and gave the tsar an ancient icon, one we brought with us when we escaped, as earnest of his devotion."

I wasn't sure what that meant, but I got the gist.

"Alexei has a son now, and he wants to protect that son's path to the throne more than anything else. Nothing else is as important as that."

I could see that other things were more important to Eli. I had a lot of other questions about his family and how they would manage, but it wasn't the time. "I can tell your family's in big trouble. And I'm sorry. Maybe everything depends on how you do here, huh? And what you have to do here is find the chest stolen from my crew and make sure it gets to the right people." I paused. He nodded. "So what was in the chest?"

Eli hesitated. Finally, he said, "That is a long story. I want to tell you, and I will, but not at this moment. Too many lives are hanging on it. Let me think."

I took a minute to recite the alphabet in my head. When I was able to speak without cursing, I said, "Take all the time you need. Who do you believe stole it?"

"First thought? Someone who had no idea what was inside. Someone who happened upon Jake, saw through the splintered crate to the carved chest, decided it was valuable . . . and saw Jake could not defend it."

Eli had said that not like it was a thought, but like it was a hope. Whatever was in the chest was powerful. Eli very much hoped it was not in the hands of the enemy, whoever that enemy was.

"Jake would have been waiting for that to happen," I said. "And he had his gun."

Eli took a deep breath. "My next guess is that someone was searching through the wreck for the chest and spotted Jake with a likely looking crate. Approached him, maybe to ask if he needed help. That person killed him and took your cargo."

"Do you know of anyone who would fit that bill?" I asked.

"There are many, many people here in Sally who would do that."

"Eli, this is like Mexico all over again. You've hired me to help you and then not given me the information I need to do a good job. You better rethink this soon. Is there a third thought?"

Eli's jaw was set hard. He stared at me as if he was trying to send his ideas into my head, because he didn't want to say them out loud. "Yes," he said. "My third thought is that the people for whom it was intended stole it, hoping they wouldn't have to honor the agreement that . . ."

A knock at the door interrupted Eli. We'd both been concentrating on the conversation, keeping our voices low. I jumped. I'd been too intent.

I had a gun in my hand in a flash, and I nodded to Eli.

"Who is there?" Eli used a calm voice, though I saw his hands were spread and open. He was ready to use magic.

"I brought your drinks, Mr. Savarov." The voice was a little familiar.

We hadn't ordered any drinks.

"Leave them outside the door, please," Eli said pleasantly.

"Sorry, can't leave glasses on the floor," said the voice. "Please, sir."

If he hadn't added the last two words, we would have told him to take the drinks back. But there was a desperate note when he'd said "please" that made me believe this man was afraid. I met Eli's eyes and nodded. I got up from the bed and went silently to the door, stood to the left of it against the wall. Eli went to the door and opened it, stepping back quickly as he did.

The man outside was the waiter I'd noticed earlier. He'd served us at breakfast. He stepped into the room, his eyes going from side to side to find me, and when he did he had a gun at his head.

"God almighty, don't kill me," he said.

Eli shut the door behind him and took the tray with the two glasses from the man's hands. He placed it carefully on the little table by the easy chair. "Now, why are you here with drinks we didn't order?" he said.

"Tell her to put her gun down, please, sir," the man said.

"My name is Eli Savarov, and this is Lizbeth Rose," Eli told him. "What's your name?"

"James Edward Johnson, sir." The waiter took a deep breath, seemed a bit more composed now that he saw we weren't going to kill him straightaway.

"You don't have to call me 'sir' every time you speak to me," Eli said. "What do you need to tell me?"

"I had to talk to you in private, and this was the only way I could think of to do it." His eyes cut toward me. "Please, lady, put down the gun."

I lowered it. But I kept it in my hand. "Talk," I said.

"Where is he?" James Edward asked Eli.

## CHAPTER ELEVEN

A lot happened in the train derailment," Eli said. "The chest is missing. Someone took it."

James Edward looked as though he was going to keel over. "Oh, no," he breathed. I pointed to the chair, but the waiter shook his head.

Eli said, "It's just temporary. We'll keep our promises to you."

"Maybe the train wreck was God telling us to back down." James Edward sounded kind of hopeful, and also kind of angry.

"The train was derailed on purpose," Eli said. "By humans, maybe the Ballard thugs. Not by God."

I had no idea what any of this meant, but at the moment, that was not my job. My job was to keep this man from harming Eli, or making any outcry drawing attention to us.

But for sure, later, I would understand, if I had to beat it out of Eli.

James Edward didn't look homicidal. He looked scared. "We're dead," he muttered. "They know. I might as well get back to work." He half-turned.

"But we haven't even started yet," Eli said, putting some push into his voice. "There's so much to do."

James Edward's shoulders were slumped. "Like what? Sir?"

"Like finding out where he is," Eli said. "And getting him back."

"How we gonna do that?" James Edward Johnson looked at Eli like Eli was a fool. I bet he'd never looked at a white man like that before, not with the white man looking back.

"I'm sure someone you know saw something, noticed someone, at the train wreck. Your people were everywhere that day, carrying the wounded, lining up the dead, picking up the debris. White people don't pay them any attention."

I heard someone coming up the stairs. I held up my finger to tell Eli and James Edward to shut up. Sure enough, after a moment there was another knock at the door.

James Edward, his face full of alarm, pointed from me to the bathroom door with a lot of you-better in his gesture. I looked at Eli, who nodded. I hurried into the bathroom, glad I was barefoot. I left the door open just a crack so I could hear.

"James Edward, where've you been? Excuse me, Mr. Savarov, I wondered if James Edward was keeping you and the missus from your drinks. Every now and then, he does tend to go on." The voice was hearty, cheerful, and as false as a hair-bow on a pig.

"Not at all, Mr. Mercer," Eli said. "I asked James Edward for the latest news on when the train tracks would be repaired."

"All right then, James Edward, duty is done. We need you downstairs."

"Yessir, right away."

I could hear him leaving, his step heavy and regular. But Mercer didn't leave.

"Mr. Savarov, I hope your stay here is going well?"

"Just fine, thank you."

"My daughter says you are staying on?"

"We are, for the other three days I'd reserved. I certainly hope after that we will be ready to leave. We've tracked down a relative of my wife's who perished in the accident, and there are other friends we're searching for."

"I'm so sorry for your loss. I've puzzled at your arriving here on your business. But then her relatives being on the train? What a coincidence."

"Not really," Eli said pleasantly.

"Of course, of course. Well, have a good stay and be sure and let us know if there is anything we can do to make your time here more comfortable."

"You can let us charge things to our room," Eli said, as if he'd just thought of it. "We've never been told before we couldn't do that. Surely that's the normal procedure?"

"But of course you . . ." Then Mr. Mercer seemed to catch himself. "That should have been done automatically. That James Edward! I'll have a word with him. Sometimes you just have to give them a good talking to."

"I believe Miss Mercer told him not to let us make charges to our room. But if you're going to correct that mistake, all's well."

After a tense moment of silence, Mr. Mercer said, "Good we had this little talk. I'll let you have your privacy, then." And I heard more steps and the door closing.

"You can come out now. Unless you want to take another bath?" Eli said. He was trying to sound like everything was fine.

I opened the door and gave my temporary husband a good, hard look.

I didn't like what I saw.

Eli looked as unhappy as I was. "You're waiting for me to explain my conversation with James Edward. And I want to. But I swore to a priest I would not tell anyone what I'm doing here. I swore."

"Swearing is a serious thing, no matter who you're swearing to. But it's hard for me to help you—in fact I can't—unless I know what you're aiming to do. I have my own goal. I'm obliged to find our cargo so we can make good on our job. Now you want me to help you out. Can those two things go together? Or had we better split up?"

Eli had objected strongly to our separating this morning. Now he hesitated. "I didn't know it would be so hard," he said, as if he was talking to himself. He looked at me directly. "I need you, Lizbeth. Our goals march together, for the most part. If I don't accomplish this, my family . . ." He stopped.

I wanted to pound him in the head. "What about them?" I said, trying to *make* him speak.

I could practically see the words inside his mouth, begging to come out, but it wasn't going to be at this moment.

I looked down at the floor and breathed deeply while I thought. I didn't have a lot of choices. If I grabbed my stuff and walked out, I had nowhere to go. If I could find a hotel with a vacant room, which didn't seem likely, I didn't have enough money to pay for it. And since Eli had paid for the clothes on my back, I'd be pretty damn ungrateful to leave him to fend for himself.

Also, if I became that awful thing in Dixie, a woman on her own, it seemed pretty certain I'd end up killing a person or two.

Shooting someone sounded pretty good right now.

It was lucky the white edge of a note appeared under our door just at that moment. It was even luckier the note was for me. I read it hastily.

Eli waited for me to hand it to him, assuming it was for him, too, but I tucked it in my pocket. (I was lucky the skirt had something so useful sewn in.)

"I'll be back in a while," I said, sitting on the bed to put my shoes back on. I decided to skip the stockings. I got a couple of things out of my traveling bag and put them in my new purse, which only held the money from Jake's pockets. I put on the little straw hat, which did no good at all to keep the sun off my face.

Leaping up, I rooted in my bag until I pulled out a boot. In the bathroom I banged the bootheel hard, sideways, against the edge of the toilet. The heel obligingly went a little crooked.

I nodded to myself and left with the boot under my arm. I didn't tell Eli good-bye. I tried to go down the stairs very quietly. I succeeded, even in the stupid shoes. The lobby and hall were mostly empty. Only one couple was standing at the desk, checking in. They both looked hot and weary and not interested in anyone else at all. I turned left instead of right at the foot of the stairs, because I'd gotten a hand-drawn map to follow.

I looked just like anyone else as I went out the back door of the hotel, or at least I hoped I did. I was carrying my stupid handbag, wearing the stupid hat, the boot tucked under my left arm. At least I had a knife in the handbag and one strapped to my leg. It was a relief now. The top of the stocking wasn't interfering with it.

It was midafternoon, and though there was still some activity in the streets—mostly a couple of blocks east, around the hospital—Sally had sunk into a heat-hazed drowse. I figured this was more typical than the bustle of yesterday. I made myself walk slower. I tried to stick to shadows as I made my way through the parking area, then through a little alley, which was as clean as the main street.

I came from the shade of the alley into the glare of the sun beating down on the south side of the next parallel street, Singer. Though I didn't need to, I found myself pulling the note from my pocket to make sure I had the directions right. I glanced to my left and then to my right. Bingo. I headed for the dark green awning over Kempton's Shoe Repair, trying to keep my pace down to a seemly saunter.

A bell on the door tinkled as I pushed it open. The shop interior seemed very dark after the dazzling day. The floors were bare wood, and the wall opposite the door was filled with cubbyholes holding shoes and leather and all kinds of items I couldn't figure out in the dimness.

"Yes'm?" The ancient black man behind the counter was hard to see until he stood. As my eyes adjusted, I could see his hair was almost white. So was his mustache. His hands were massive, thick with muscle and scarred all over.

"I'm Lizbeth Rose. Lizbeth Savarov," I added, just in case. "My bootheel is loose. I'd appreciate it if you could take care of it." I handed him my boot, and he looked over the heel.

"Yes'm, I can do that," he said without looking up. "You care to rest in the back room? You can get yourself a drink of water. Mr. Kempton won't be back for another half hour. I can take care of your repair right now, if that suits you."

"Thanks so much." By now I had noticed the door to the left of the counter. I pushed it open and stepped into the back room. It had one window, which was curtained. There were two people sitting on an ancient sofa covered with dark velvet, worn in places.

"I'm Lizbeth," I said, tired of wrestling with my two last names. "Are you Hosea and Reva Clelland?"

"Yes'm," the man said. He was not as old as the shoe repairman, but he was getting a sprinkling of gray in his hair, and his face was heavily lined. She was bent over almost double, and her hair was drawn back in a bun. It was secured with metal pins and a little hairnet.

"You knew our girl?" the woman asked. Her skin was like a pecan shell in color, and her eyes were dark brown. The whites were yellowish. She was thin and looked to be somewhere in her late fifties. Her husband looked healthier, and he'd always been taller and straighter.

"Galilee was a friend of mine," I said. "My best friend. We lived together for a while, after her son left home to make his own way."

They regarded me with . . . it was almost disbelief.

"Really?" said Hosea. He shook his head as if he'd never heard of such a thing.

"We were on the same gun crew."

"She shot people for a living?" This from Reva. She didn't seem to know whether to be horrified or proud.

"Galilee guarded things for a living," I said as gently as I could. I guess I am not very gentle. "Sometimes when you guard things, other people try to take them, and you have to shoot."

They glanced at each other, a look I couldn't read. "How did she die?" asked Hosea.

"You knew. You did get Freedom's letter." At least I didn't have to break the news. That was a relief.

"We got it, but we were scared to answer it. They look at the mail here, you know. See who you're writing to."

I had to believe them, but this seemed incredible to me. "Galilee died while we were on a job," I said. I explained that Galilee and I had been in the back of the truck with the cargo, in this case two farm families, who were trying to escape their commandeered farm in Mexico to get to New America. Such people made good human chattel, and bandits had attacked us. They'd killed our driver, and in the resultant crash, Galilee had been thrown out of the back of the truck and killed instantly. I would have said that anyway, but it happened to be the truth.

"So she was left lying in the road?" Reva's voice quavered, and her eyes had that shimmer eyes get when they are holding on to tears.

"I had to keep on with the job and get the stolen people back," I said. "But her man's brother came along right after and buried them."

"She had a man friend," Hosea said. "They married?"

"No, sir, but they were headed that way," I said. It might have happened.

"He didn't bury her hisself?"

"He died too. That night."

"You the only one left?" Reva said very softly.

"I was the only one left."

"You must be one tough woman."

"I am."

I opened the handbag and handed Reva the picture Freedom had given me.

"Your grandson wanted to be sure you had a picture of your great-granddaughter," I told them. The two old people bent over it.

"She is light, like Freedom is, the letter said," Reva murmured. "But most of the Ballard is bred out of her. She'll be okay."

"Ballard" again. The hospital was named after the Ballards. They seemed to be the local high panjandrums to the white community, and the boogeymen to the black citizens of the town. It seemed to me that I'd heard the name before; it felt somehow familiar.

There was a sharp rap at the door I'd come through. Reva and Hosea stood immediately and started for the back door. "Get out there quick and sit on the bench like you waiting for him to get through with your shoe," Hosea said over his shoulder.

A few seconds later I was sitting on the bench with my legs crossed, studying a map of Sally from a rack on the counter. The owner of the shop came in, mopping his face with a handkerchief. Mr. Kempton was short and white-haired and red with the heat, dressed in white shirtsleeves and black trousers. He'd loosened his necktie.

"Good afternoon, young lady. Has Phineas taken care of you?" he said, real loud. I thought Mr. Kempton was at least a little hard of hearing. He wouldn't hear the back door closing on Hosea and Reva.

"Yes, sir, thank you," I said. "My boot is just about finished, I imagine."

"Boot? You ride? Sorry, I'm Brent Kempton." A glance at the boot Phineas held in his hand told Mr. Kempton that this was no shiny riding boot, but a strictly everyday item.

"I live in some rough country," I said. I didn't introduce myself. Instead I took my boot from Phineas, pretending to examine the heel. "Good as new," I said. "How much do I owe you?"

"A quarter," Mr. Kempton said. "Just took a nail or two to fix that."

Phineas never raised his eyes to mine or reacted to my presence in any way while Mr. Kempton was there. But then, Phineas didn't show emotion. He seemed deadened, somehow.

I walked out of Kempton's Shoe Repair with my boot again tucked under my arm and a debt discharged. It galled me that I'd had to meet with them in secret. In fact, it made me angry.

I realized I was walking pretty fast. I had to remind myself to slow down. One, no one else was hurrying. Two, did I really want to be back in that hotel room, mad and confused?

But what else could I do? I passed the hotel, too restless to check in with Eli.

I went to the telegraph office to see if I'd had a reply to the message I'd sent Jake's lover.

"We were just about to deliver this to the hotel," the middle-aged man at the counter said. "You didn't need to come walking over here, Mrs. Savarov."

Just now, being called Mrs. Savarov was awful irritating. But that wasn't this man's fault. "Thank you," I said, accepting the message.

*In touch with funeral home shipping body home have talked to Charlies wife do not know employer. Burke Printer*

Brief and to the point. I hadn't really thought he'd know who our employer was, but it would have been handy.

I couldn't face another trip to the hospital just now, with the big echoing rooms and the pain and Nurse Mayhew. I went back to the hotel. Not exactly to my surprise, Eli was waiting for me on the porch.

"Let's go to the park," he said, and off we set. He was wearing a white linen shirt and tan slacks, but no grigori vest. (His shirt pockets did look real bulgy.) He'd rebraided his hair with care. He looked nice, and he blended in as much as he ever would. (Not at all.)

I hadn't seen the park. It was right across the street from the courthouse. It was green and neat, full of big old trees, a Confederate cannon, two water fountains (one for white people and one for black people, the signs said), and quite a few wooden benches in good repair. Eli picked one on the shadowed side of the big war memorial, and we sat down under a tree. It was a pleasant afternoon when the breeze sprung up. The sun was shining but we were in the shade. The town was a few steps closer to normal after the train wreck, looked like.

There weren't many other people around: a woman pushing a baby carriage, two men talking seriously as they walked, and a groundskeeper picking up trash with a spike on the other side of the park.

We were side by side in body, but not in mind. I spoke first. "We got to be honest with each other. Since you hired me, am I not an . . ." I couldn't think how to end the sentence.

"An extension of me?" Eli looked thoughtful. "That is a good way to think of it. How can you help, if you don't know what I want to do? I can tell you a few things." He looked around us for anyone close. This was the land of listening-in, all its people seemed to think. The groundskeeper was wandering out of the park, maybe to pick up trash somewhere else.

Eli said very quietly, "I got assigned this job, one no one else wanted, because of my father's treachery. I have to hand the crate's contents over to certain people here in Sally. If I'm successful, I'll change the course of events here in Dixie forever. If I'm not, I'll probably be killed. My brother Peter will be expelled from his school, half-trained. My two sisters will not be able to marry."

I let all that settle in my head. "Can't your sisters do anything for themselves?" I asked.

"Young women in Russian aristocratic families are not taught how to do anything but run a household," Eli said. "And usually that means directing the servants."

I thought if you watched a servant work you could learn to do the servant's job, if you had a little grit. I kept that to myself. "Can your sisters shoot?"

"They've never held a gun."

He expected me to be shocked, but I wasn't. My neighbor Chrissie had never carried a gun, because it would be crazy to give her one. "Your sisters, they don't want to be grigoris like you and Peter?"

"They don't have the slightest affinity that I can discern," Eli said. "Which is a real pity. It's an honorable profession."

I thought of Paulina and her ability to kill people in exotic ways. I remembered the terrifying Klementina. That little old woman had bowed to no man, and she hadn't suffered fools gladly. She had died like a hero. I could feel the corner of my mouth lift in a smile, remembering. Full of pepper and vinegar, she'd been.

"Your older brothers won't take care of 'em?"

Eli's two older brothers were also sons of the now-deceased Prince Vladimir Savarov, who had backed the wrong horse (Grand Prince something) when he believed Tsar Alexei would die of his bleeding disease without leaving an heir—or if he had a boy child and died, that child should not inherit the throne because Alexei's wife (his second) was very unpopular.

"They have said they'll be responsible for finding the girls suitable matches." It was easy to see Eli didn't trust his older brothers, at least not entirely. "Though how that's to be done, since the girls are the daughters of a traitor, and I doubt my brothers would give them much money . . ." His voice trailed off.

"So their only hope is for you to be back in favor? That's the way you see it?"

Eli nodded.

"What about Peter?" Peter had made an attempt to kill his father. Unfortunately, it had taken place at the exact same time *I* was trying to kill his father much more efficiently. I would not have gotten shot if Peter hadn't stuck his oar in.

"My little brother is more in favor since he tracked my father to Texoma. Some say Peter killed him." Eli rolled his eyes toward me and smiled. "He's back in school, and has determined he has an affinity for air." There was a list of elements or talents. Each grigori was better at spells involving one of them, Paulina had told me. "Peter is also in love," Eli said, and looked at me like I should know what he was talking about.

"With who?" I felt like I was walking into a trap, but I had no idea where he was going.

"With a beautiful young black-haired woman who saved his life in a hotel in Segundo Mexia."

I tried to remember such a person being present that day. Then I winced. "You can't be serious," I said.

"Peter has asked a hundred questions about the girl who got shot for him," Eli said.

"He sure did his best to screw everything up."

"He's smitten," Eli said. "When everything else in the family was going so wrong, I didn't have the heart to tell him."

"Tell him what?" I was blundering through this conversation.

"That you are spoken for."

This was making me very nervous. "Eli, for God's sake!" I threw up my hands, and a woman on the sidewalk glanced at us curiously.

Eli could tell I was all out of plumb. "After all," he said teasingly, "we are married."

Teasing, I could handle. "Yes, thanks for the fancy ring," I said, making sure I sounded tart. More like my normal self. I held my hand in front of him like he'd never seen the thin gold band.

"Oh, you'd like a gemstone? What kind?"

I didn't know anything about gemstones. "Now you're talking silly," I said. I was tired of sitting in this park, and tired of talking. "What do we need to do next? You've told me you're looking for the chest, and there's some man involved, and you have to get this right or your family is doomed. We better get cracking."

"We might have to interrogate someone," Eli said. He didn't sound happy about it.

"Interrogate" didn't mean ask questions. It meant *torture*.

"That's not good," I said. Gunnies did what they had to do to get the job done, but I had never heard of a job where that meant torture.

"Ritter or Seeley?" he asked. He wanted to know which one I thought would break first.

I pondered it. Didn't like either choice. I said, "Rogelio. I think he knows something. He'll cave faster than the Iron Hand people, specially if you offer to cut his face."

Eli brightened. "Good idea." He didn't have the stomach for this any more than I did, but he had taken a dislike to Rogelio.

If that was the best idea I had—picking the person who'd break under pain the fastest—I really needed to think harder.

"Can't you spell him to tell the truth?" I asked. Eli hadn't stretched his magic muscles in a couple of days.

"I can try," Eli said. "There's a new . . ." He slapped his chest, feeling for the vest pocket that wasn't there. "I'll have to go back to the room," he said. "People were staring at the vest and not listening to me, so I left it there."

I stood. I had more questions, but they would wait. I was going to keep us moving while we were temporarily at peace with each other.

## CHAPTER TWELVE

There was a lot of activity at the hotel. Not normal activity. There were people standing outside and in the lobby, all talking, all excited. There was a doctor running up the stairs, holding one of those black leather bags.

"I can *only guess* which room he's running to," I said, giving Eli a sideways look.

"But . . . oh, the vest," he said, smacking himself on the forehead. "Dammit. What was I thinking?"

A middle-aged woman turned and looked at him, her face in harsh lines of rebuke. "Watch your mouth, young man," she snapped, and let him see her back real pointedly.

"What should we do?" Eli asked me, almost whispering.

I considered. "We should find out why someone went in our room while we weren't there, since we'd already had maid service," I said. "We can't pretend we don't know about this hubbub. They're in the wrong." I straightened up to my tallest, which wasn't very tall at all, and I went up the stairs *mad*. Eli was right behind me. Got to the top to see that sure enough, the doctor was going into our room. Mr. Mercer was standing outside trying to make up his mind if he was going to cry or beat someone up.

"You fiend!" he'd decided to scream, to work himself up into hitting Eli.

"What has happened?" Eli said, managing to sound concerned without sounding guilty.

"My daughter! My daughter! Your damn magic has hurt her! She may not live!" Now Mr. Mercer's face was red and he lurched toward Eli, his chest leading, his arms pulled back, reminding me of a Tom turkey. It wasn't good that I had that thought, because it made me want to smile.

"Mr. Mercer, why was your daughter in our room?" I asked, working to keep my voice absolutely level, but also to make sure it carried. "I know the maid's already been in this morning."

All the people listening began to remark on this in low voices. They didn't want to miss anything. Good.

Why *would* the daughter of the house enter a guest's room?

Mr. Mercer said, "I have no idea why she was in there! Maybe she was checking to make sure the maid had done her work properly! Maybe she was . . . I don't know."

He'd lost a little of his steam.

"Surely she wouldn't handle our possessions," I said, trying to sound amazed. "Surely she wouldn't go through Eli's things. That's the only way I can picture her getting hurt in our room."

Eli put his hands on my shoulders. His grip was gentle. I was doing okay. Mr. Mercer didn't speak—how could he argue with what I'd said? He was peering into our room, his shoulders and hands jerking with anxiety. I did feel sorry for him, to my surprise.

"May we see how she was hurt?" I asked.

"It's your fault!" he said again. But much more quietly.

"Is it not clear that Eli is a wizard?" I asked.

"Yes, of course," Mercer said, paying little attention.

"And wizards have magic stuff."

"Yes, of course."

"So your daughter touched something of Eli's? Knowing he was a wizard and that wizards have to have magical things with them?"

"I suppose she did!" Mercer all but shouted.

"I'm sorry she was hurt, but no one can be surprised that that happened," I said, aiming for reasonable but gentle. "Please let Eli go in, to see if he can help her."

The look Mercer gave us would have made me feel ashamed . . . if I'd been at fault. I met his eyes. After a little more hesitation, Mercer stood back from the door. "Help my girl. You owe it to her," he growled, looking from me to Eli.

"We don't owe her a thing," I said. "But because we hate to see anyone hurt, we'll do our best." Somehow I'd gotten included in this, so I went in with Eli. I hoped I'd made our point. I hoped there wouldn't be a lynch mob outside the hotel.

I also hoped like hell that Eli could help Miss Mercer, because otherwise nothing would keep us from big trouble.

In our room the doctor was bending over the bed. Miss Mercer was sprawled upon it, her face covered in a terrible rash. I bit my lip so I wouldn't laugh out loud. Eli squeezed my hand, in lieu of exclaiming in relief.

The doctor was a young man with a small beard and gold-rimmed glasses. He looked up at us over the top of those glasses, as if that would scare us. "Are you responsible for this?" he asked, his voice not as sharp as I'd expected.

"No," Eli said. "This young lady appears to have entered our room and opened the pockets of my vest. Everyone knows a grigori's vest contains magic powders and potions."

"Did you hear that, Nellie?" the doctor asked. "Your curiosity almost killed you."

Nellie Mercer whimpered. "I didn't know . . . ," she said.

"You did, though," the doctor said, not unkindly.

I was beginning to like the man.

"I'm Dr. Jerry Fielder," he said, looking from Eli to me. "Can you help her?"

"I'm Eli Savarov, and this is Lizbeth Rose . . . Savarov." Eli tacked on my new last name just in time. "Yes, I think I can help her." He picked up his vest from the floor. Nellie Mercer had clearly rifled it, since the pocket flaps were all askew and there were some powders and a pebble on the floor.

"At least she didn't use the pebble," I said.

"What would have happened?" Jerry Fielder asked.

I met his eyes. "You really don't want to know," I told him, and for once, someone believed me when I said that.

Eli began murmuring a spell, and the air over Nellie Mercer thickened. She got all blurry. Dr. Fielder watched with great interest. He didn't seem alarmed, for which I gave him high marks.

I loved to hear Eli work magic. I hadn't realized it until that moment. Eli was saying a spell backward, an "undo" spell. I have just enough wizard blood to make me a little sensitive to magic stuff. My father's blood also gives me a little resistance to spells. The words were like music, said the right way or the wrong way.

Eli came to the end and blew gently on the girl, his mouth pursed as though he was whistling. Her skin began to look less angry right away. The redness of the rash faded, her features grew more relaxed.

The pain was lessening. After a moment Nellie lifted her hand to look at it. The skin was almost free of blemish. "Oh, thank God," she said, and her father rushed into the room.

Mr. Mercer gathered Nellie up, sobbed a little, and then he let her have it for coming into a guest's room and interfering with things she should never have touched. "You could have died!" he said, shaking her a little.

"But old Mrs. Ballard—" she began, and her father pinched her, and she stopped speaking.

I pretended I did not notice. "She surely could have died," I told Dr. Fielder. "Depending on which pocket she fooled with."

The doctor shook his head, looking admiring. "I wish I could heal like that," he said. "No pills or ointments or injections."

"You'd have to study as long as you did in medical college."

"But it would save expense to the patient. And time."

"Yeah, true. But Eli pays for it." Eli was sitting on the chair. He was fine, but a little tired. "As it is, your patients pay you," I observed.

"Your husband is lucky he could fix her," the doctor said. "Might not go well for him, otherwise, no matter if it was Nellie's responsibility or not."

Since the doctor was right, there wasn't much I could say to that.

Within the next five minutes, Nellie Mercer was able to walk out of our room. I expected Mr. Mercer to threaten us more, but he very politely thanked Eli and helped his daughter down the stairs. Dr. Fielder shook Eli's hand and sort of ducked his head to me and invited us to dinner at his house. His wife would be glad to meet us, he said. Eli and I looked at each other, he lifted one shoulder slightly, I nodded slightly, and we agreed to accept the invitation.

When we were alone, Eli pulled a piece of paper out of one

pocket on his vest. "This is for you," he said. "And if she'd only opened that pocket, she would have been fine."

I took the paper between my fingers, real carefully. "What is it?"

"This is a healing spell. It's against our laws for you to have it. But I think you have enough grigori blood to make it work, at least some, and God knows we get hurt often enough."

"I can't read this." The letters were English but the language was not.

"I wrote it phonetically."

I guess Eli could tell by my blank look that that made no sense to me.

"I wrote it like it sounds," he said. "Not the way it's really spelled."

*Phonetically,* I repeated silently. I read the words out loud. It was just a sentence.

"You say that and you pull out the grigori in you, it will help you heal." Eli said this with great conviction. Probably meant he wasn't sure at all, but he was hoping it would work.

I nodded, and tucked the paper into my repaired boot. I hoped I'd be wearing my boots the next time we got into a tight spot, not these shoes.

The afternoon was almost done, and we had only an hour to wait until we were due at Dr. Fielder's house. I made up a bundle of our clothes, at Eli's insistence, and we called the front desk to ask if a maid could come fetch the clothes for laundering. I didn't recognize the voice that picked up at the desk, but a young woman in a green-and-white maid's uniform arrived quick as a wink to pick up the clothes. She looked at us with an odd expression—half excited, half terrified. She agreed that our clothes would be cleaned and returned to us by nine the next morning.

After that, there was enough time for me to take another bath. The blouse and skirt were still fine, so I would put them on again with clean underthings. I looked at my jeans and my sleeveless shirt, which I had washed in the tub. I sighed. Eli had been right about what Dixie women wore. I hadn't seen a single one in pants. I'd seen no white women without dresses and a petticoat, plus hose and garters, even the poor ones. I guessed I had to put the hose back on. So I shaved my legs again.

Eli ran his hand up and down them to make sure I gotten them smooth. Then he ran his hand a little higher, where no woman I knew had ever shaved. "I like that, too," he said, and leaned over to kiss me.

"No, sir," I said tartly. Because otherwise I'd let him proceed. "You could have a bath or shower too, and we could both feel nice for the doctor's dinner."

"We could both feel nice a lot sooner than that."

"Eli. Not enough time!"

"Oh, all right. But later, when we come back . . ."

"Yes, later when we come back," I said, looking away. It felt funny, talking about what we did together. Did other couples do that? Were we a couple? But there was a huge gap between us, and before I could get broody about it, I shut down that train of thought.

Eli decided to shower when we returned, so I brushed and braided his hair again, to make sure it was neat. I'd pocketed the map of Sally I'd spotted in the shoe repair shop, and I'd studied it while Eli was getting dressed.

"Tucker Street," I said. "We go out the front door of the hotel, take a left, go south two blocks, take a right, take the next left, and we'll be there."

"Yes, ma'am," Eli said, and kissed my cheek, quick and sweet. We set out to our first engagement as a married couple.

If people stared at us when we were coming down the stairs, if an older man shrank away so we wouldn't touch him when we passed, well . . . I was used to that, and I was sure Eli was too. I suppose it was one thing to know grigoris cast magic spells, and another thing to see one work. We ignored them all. By the time we reached the sidewalk and turned right, Eli had taken my hand.

No one had ever held my hand before. Somehow people in Texoma always needed their hands free. I found it a little hot, a little sweaty, and since we were yoked we had to match our pace. But it made me feel good. The sun was setting, the air was a little cooler since it was breezy, and I thought the world was a tolerable place. Eli was holding my left hand, leaving my right hand free to draw my knife, which was a good thing.

Also, I'd put a Colt in my purse. I'm a gunnie. I just needed to have it.

The Fielders had a small house with a real pretty yard. Even in the heat, it looked green and tidy, and the flowers were blooming like hell. There was a brick walkway up to the steps leading to the front porch, which was across the width of the house. The house was painted white, like almost all the other houses in Sally. The shutters were dark green. I could not imagine having a house like this. "It's so pretty," I whispered.

I could not read Eli's sideways look. He'd lived in the San Diego palace, so to him it was probably the same as the hovels we'd seen in Ciudad Juárez. "I like it too," he said. I relaxed. Eli rang the doorbell once.

Dr. Fielder—Jerry—opened the door. "Please come in," he said, standing aside with a sweep of his hand. "Millie! Our guests are here!" he called, turning a little toward the back of the house.

Millie Fielder hurried into the living room. She was wearing a blouse and skirt similar to mine, but in a golden brown print. It really suited her dark hair and eyes. Over her skirt she wore an apron, which had seen some use. She became aware of it the same moment she shook my hand, and she looked mock-horrified. "I never remember the apron!" she said. "Excuse me." She untied it and bundled it under her arm. "Pretend you can't see it," she told Eli.

"See what?" he said.

"That's a relief." She smiled, and you had to like her when you saw her smile. Millie wasn't exactly a pretty woman, but that smile was a wonder. "Please have a seat, and I'll bring you all a drink. Wine or bourbon?"

"Bourbon for me," I said. "Eli?"

"For me also," he said, taking a seat. He gave me a complicated look. I realized I was supposed to offer to help Millie in the kitchen. "Can I give you a hand?" I said quickly. "I'd love to see your kitchen."

Millie looked a little surprised, but she invited me to come with her with another wonderful smile.

The floors were polished wood scattered with throw rugs. We went from the living room into the dining room, then to the right of a fireplace and through a swinging door into the kitchen. I stared around me at the gleaming countertops and the oven with a cook-top built in on top of it. The sink was white like the stove and the refrigerator. The floor was linoleum, a dark green. There was a big wooden preparation table running down the middle with a white painted chair pushed up under it.

"This is so pretty," I said. "And it smells so good." A pot or two bubbled on the stovetop and a chicken was in the oven. There was a small tower of dirty dishes by the sink, and a much larger tower of washed and dried ones on the other side. A platter and some vegetable bowls were set out ready to use.

Millie had her back to me while she poured our drinks, but she whipped around as if she thought I'd been mocking her. She relaxed when she saw my face. "You mean it! But I figured . . . when Jerry told me your husband was a grigori, I thought you must be real rich."

"Not me," I said. "Not us. We haven't been married long," I said, after another pause. "In case you wondered. What about you two?"

"Oh, for four years," Millie said. She tried to sound like it was nothing, but she turned her back to me again and began pouring into the glasses. Her back was stiff. What did this mean?

"You must have been real young."

"'Bout your age, I figure. You aren't twenty yet, are you?"

"No, a few months until then."

"When I say we've been married four years, most people say, 'And no babies yet?'" Millie said, her back still to me.

"Not my business," I said, surprised.

She stopped pouring and halfway turned. "Really? Because everyone else on God's green earth believes it's their business."

I shrugged. "Not me."

"Thank you," Millie said.

"Quite a few women don't even want any," I said, when I should have kept my mouth shut.

Astounded, she gazed at me blankly. "Like who?"

"Prostitutes," I said. "And people with an illness. And people who just aren't crazy about babies."

"You're the most interesting person I've ever met," Millie said, after a second of silence.

"That means I said something wrong." I couldn't figure out what it might have been.

"Not at all," Millie said. "Can you get the kitchen door? I can handle the tray."

Very soon we were sitting in the living room, Eli and I side by side on the couch, and the Fielders in matching armchairs, a table between them. Its surface was mostly taken with a pile of books, leaving just enough room for their glasses. It was almost dark outside, and the bugs were battering the screen doors. The wooden doors had been left open for the breeze, which almost amounted to nothing now.

I took a cautious sip of my bourbon, and it was good. I was working, and I would not finish this glass, but I could savor a sip or two. Jerry and Eli were chattering away, while Millie vanished to do something in the kitchen every few minutes.

I was quiet for the most part. I felt like I was visiting another world. Jerry was asking Eli a lot of questions about healing magic, and when that conversation had run its course, Millie asked me how Eli and I had met.

I glanced at Eli, who was looking like he wanted to hear the answer. Okay. "He and his partner Paulina hired me to guard them on a trip to Mexico," I said. "I'm from Texoma."

The Fielders looked a bit stunned. "And you guarded them?" Jerry asked slowly, as if he was feeling his way through a jungle or something.

"I did."

"How?"

"Oh, I'm a gunnie." They looked blank. "A shooter," I explained. "That's my job."

They didn't seem to know what to make of that. "You shoot people," Jerry said very cautiously.

"I do. If they attack whoever or whatever I'm hired to guard. Not for fun." I wanted to make that clear.

"Lizbeth is famous," Eli said, and damn if he didn't sound proud. I smiled right at him.

"Are you armed now?" Millie asked.

And then the gun was in my hand. "Yep," I said. And it was back in my handbag.

"We aren't going to go after your husband," Millie said teasingly.

"We got the walk back to the hotel," I said, matter-of-fact.

And there was another one of those weird pauses. Eli kissed my cheek, just when I was feeling pretty bad.

Millie stood, still looking at me like a half-dead bird her cat had dragged in. "Supper must be ready to go on the table," she said. She kind of braced herself. "You want to give me a hand, Lizbeth?"

"Sure." I hopped up and followed her back into the kitchen.

Millie got a roasting pan with a chicken out of the oven, and I held the platter while she eased it on. The juice went into a gravy boat. The mashed potatoes went into a bowl. The snap beans into another. And the rolls came out of the oven and went into a basket. The butter dish came out of the icebox. "This is it," Millie said. "I made a chess pie for after."

"It looks great and it smells wonderful," I said honestly. I hesitated, and then I said, "You know how people always ask you why you don't have babies? People who don't know the business, they always want to know how many people I've shot." Not that I'd ever met many people who didn't understand my line of work. But it had happened.

"What do you tell them?" Millie was fascinated.

"I tell them as many as it took to do my job," I said, and we began carrying the food through the swinging door to place on the dining table.

# CHAPTER THIRTEEN

Since Eli and I had only had ice cream for our lunch, we were very enthusiastic about Millie's cooking. And it was fun to talk to people we didn't have to lie to . . . or at least, we didn't have to lie to them much. Millie told me about her ladies' group at the church, and her gardening, and her elderly mother who lived two houses down. Jerry talked about going to medical school in Boston, and how living in Brittania and talking to its people had changed him.

Eli talked about wizard school (though the Holy Russians called it some fancier name than that). I hadn't been in school of any sort since I was sixteen, and old to still be learning. I stayed quiet, but that didn't mean I wasn't interested in what they were saying. I just couldn't imagine myself doing any of those things.

Millie said she'd been to two years of teacher college before she'd left to marry Jerry. "And you?" she said to me.

"My mother taught our school," I said. "I left when I was sixteen and started work. That's what kids in Texoma do."

"And you went right into shooting?"

"Yes. I was taken on by a gun crew pretty quick, because I was good and had the grit to do the job."

"What sorts of jobs did you take? Typically?" Jerry said.

He was trying hard to make it sound like I was a normal person, which I'd always felt until I'd come to Dixie.

"Typically," I said, savoring the word. "Well. We guarded farm people fleeing from Mexico to New America, most often. The Mexican government had taken their farms, and they wanted out. We guarded shipments that had to go from Texoma down to Mexico, and ones that had to come back up. We took up the bounty on some bandits, once or twice."

"Took up the bounty?" Jerry asked.

"Tracked 'em down and shot 'em."

He gave a decisive nod, to cover his startled reaction. "Someone has to do that," he said. "Lots of action, then."

My turn to nod.

"And you still work for this crew?"

"They are all dead, but me."

Nothing to say after that.

"Who wants some pie?" Millie asked with a bright smile, maybe not as real as her previous ones. "It's chess, my grandmother's recipe." She vanished to the back of the house, but after a moment—during which I thought I heard a dull noise—she pushed open the kitchen door enough to poke her head out. "Jerry, grab some plates and come help," she said. "Excuse us just a minute, y'all."

Jerry leaped up to stack some plates. He looked worried, to me.

When we were alone, I turned to Eli. "Sorry I made 'em so uneasy."

"It was the questions. If they'd asked me what I did with my magic most often, it would have been just as awkward."

I don't know what I'd hoped for in socializing with the Fielders, but maybe it wasn't this. I should have known.

Someone rang the front doorbell. My gun was in my hand before the chime had finished. I altered the way I sat on the couch so I could cover the door.

Jerry sped through the dining room, hurrying, looking unhappy. Millie appeared, her hip propped against the swinging door to the kitchen, a dish towel in her hands. She was frowning. Easy to see callers after dark were not the usual.

Millie said, "Lizbeth, could you give me a hand?"

I knew she wasn't asking for help with the dishes. I tapped Eli on the shoulder to tell him I was taking the gun. Millie held the kitchen door so I could scoot through, purse under my arm. Then she went to the sink to run cold water, soaking a clean dish towel she'd snatched from a drawer.

Millie was not the only person in the Fielder kitchen. A girl, Negro and wearing a maid's uniform, this time gray, sat hunched in the wooden chair, her hands over her face. I couldn't tell if she was crying or not, but she was doing plenty of trembling.

"I hit her," she said. Then she said it again. "I hit her." The girl didn't seem to know how she felt about that. She sounded kind of numb.

"Oh, yeah? Who'd you hit?"

She uncovered her eyes and looked up at me, startled. She didn't know I'd come into the room. "I hit Mrs. Moultry," she said. "She pinched me again, and I slapped her."

"I'll bet she was some kind of surprised."

"Lizbeth, can you go listen at the door and tell us what's happening out there?" Millie had come around the table with the wrung-out towel, and the girl accepted it and put it to her face.

I tried to remember how much noise the kitchen door made—not much, I thought. I pushed it open very gently and listened to the men at the front door.

"My mother isn't in her right mind anymore, Jerry. She's getting worse. We saw her pinch Willa May," a big man was rumbling. "Oh, I'm sure it hurt some. But Mama doesn't know what she's doing, and we hired Willa May to take care of her. Willa May hauled off and slapped Mama in the face, and then she ran out the back door."

"I know you and Carolyn Ann are upset," Jerry said in a soothing doctor voice. "Your mama wasn't hurt, though?"

"Naw. She said some pretty awful things. You know Mama! But then she forgot about it."

"So you don't need me and my doctor bag at your house, I take it." Jerry sounded friendly, like he was the man's uncle.

"Naw, naw. We just want to know where Willa May is."

I couldn't get a feeling from this man on what he wanted to know for. He didn't sound forgiving. But he didn't sound like he wanted to string Willa May up from a tree, either.

"All right, Norman. I still don't understand why you're here." The doctor echoed my thoughts.

"Occurred to me that Willa May might run straight down here. You treat those blacks, too. They like you. She might think she needs to hide somewhere."

I heard that trace of darkness in Norman's voice. He surely did not think Jerry doctoring on black people was something to admire. Norman sure wanted to know where Willa May was, but it wasn't because he was worried about her welfare.

"It's just been us and our company this evening," Jerry said in a neutral voice. "The ladies were about to cut the pie, and me and Eli here are about to have a drink. You want to have a glass with us, Norman? Or some pie? Or both?"

"I'd sure like to do both those things some other time, 'specially since you and me need to have us a talk about my mother. But I better go home and see how Carolyn Ann is dealing with Mama. We got to have someone with her all the time, and Carolyn Ann ain't up to it more than a couple of hours a day. It makes her nerves all frazzled. We need Willa May to get back to work."

"Then we'll have that drink some other time," Jerry said. "See you later, Norman."

"Have a good night. Give Millie my regards."

The front door closed behind Norman.

"Your husband's coming," I said, turning to Millie.

"Good," Millie said from the bottom of her heart.

I stepped away from the swinging door so I wouldn't get hit in the face as Jerry and Eli entered. The kitchen seemed real crowded all of a sudden.

"Now, Willa May. Tell me what happened," Jerry said. He was good at firm-but-nice.

"Miss Evvie pinched me for the hundredth time," Willa May said. "It hurt. I just couldn't take it anymore. I didn't think at all. I slapped her."

"Willa May, what do you imagine will happen now?"

Willa May had quit crying, if she ever had been. She did not seem curious about Eli and me. "I think I better not go back to Mr. Norman's," she said. "I think he'll do something bad to me if I do, even if I cry and repent and say I'll try again. I'm the third person he's hired to stay with his mama. The others found good reasons to quit. I think Mr. Norman hired me because I was the only one who showed up to apply. I think he and Miss Carolyn Ann figured I had to stay because I wouldn't find work anywhere if I left another job. So I think I'm done in Sally, 'specially since Carolyn Ann was a Ballard before she married. She musta told me that five times a day."

"Do you have a plan?" Millie said.

"I thought about it," Willa May said. "A few times. Since Miss Evvie started pinching me. And she bit me once, hard enough to bleed." Willa May was clearly angry when she thought about this. I was willing to bet this was a face Norman and Carolyn Ann Moultry had never seen.

"So what can we do to help?" Jerry said.

"You two are nice people," Willa May said. "I don't want to drag you into my trouble. Before Mr. Norman starts looking for me, I'm going to go home, grab my clothes, and head off to my cousin's house in Arkansas. My brother will take me to the state line, at least. Maybe farther. Then I'll decide what to do next."

The girl sounded calm and sure.

"Here's what we'll do," Jerry said. "You get in the back seat of my car, crouch down low, and I'll run you home. At least no one will see you on the street."

Willa May stared at him for a long moment. "No, sir. I appreciate you thinking of it, but I can get home without anyone seeing me. Or at least, anyone noticing me. Everyone knows your car: white people, black people. Someone will say you were out driving. It might get back to Mr. Norman. He'll have it in for you. He's already suspicious."

"I thought as much," Jerry said. He was trying not to be worried, but he was.

"Let me loan you a dress," Millie said. "That uniform stands out."

This offer really hit Willa May like a brick. Her mouth fell open.

"All right," she said, very slowly, as if she expected Millie to snatch back her offer.

"Come on," Millie said, and off they went to look in Millie's closet.

Jerry turned to us. He waited for us to say something.

"I knew they didn't ask us over because we're fun," I said to Eli.

He laughed, and Jerry looked mortified.

"You know why I'm here in Sally?" Eli asked our host.

I was interested in hearing the answer, since I didn't know myself.

"I've heard you're here to help change things," Jerry said.

"That's a good way to put it. Did you put up some of the money?"

"I don't really have enough spare money to make much of a difference," Jerry said. "We gave what cash we could."

Millie and Willa May came back in the kitchen. Willa May was wearing a dark blue skirt and a brown-and-blue patterned blouse. Better than the light gray uniform, if you wanted to blend in with the shadows.

Jerry did not look happy, though I didn't know why. But he didn't object, and with an awkward hug, Willa May thanked Millie and slipped out the back door.

Millie said, "What?" the minute the door closed behind her.

"Lots of people have seen you wearing that blouse," Jerry said. "If she gets stopped, people are going to know who helped her."

"I haven't worn it in three months," Millie said. "I'll say I gave it to her when I cleaned out my closet last spring."

Jerry didn't look like he thought that would erase all doubt, but he shook his head and pushed away the worry. Millie went into the kitchen, and I hoped we were about to have some chess pie.

"So now you know way more about us than we know about you," Jerry said to Eli and me. "You know if you talk about this to anybody here, we'll get run out of town. Maybe not right away, but people will stop coming to me with their ills, and Millie and I will have to move. Our families are here."

"I don't know why you'd even imagine we'd tell anyone," Eli said.

"It's not like we're so popular," I said, and I had to laugh a little. "Especially after the Nellie incident."

"Fool girl," Jerry said, and he almost smiled. The air in the room lightened up a little.

"Let's just carry on as we were," I suggested. "Best thing is to look normal. Be normal."

We all had pie. Millie and I washed the dishes while Eli and Jerry finished their drinks. After that, Eli and I took our leave.

He and Jerry didn't finish their talk about change in Sally.

## CHAPTER FOURTEEN

Walking in the dark with Eli was nice. Since I was supposed to be his wife, I could hold on to his arm. But I never forgot I was guarding him, too, and since the Willa May episode got me worried, I kept my gun in my hand. I hid it in the folds of the skirt. It would be better for someone to say, "Oh my God, that woman's carrying a gun!" than for me to be caught unawares.

And it was lucky I did that, because two men came out of the hedge lining the yard of a big house. They positioned themselves right in front of us. Eli's hands were ready and I moved a little apart from him, ready to bring up the gun and shoot. Wasn't pointing it at them yet, but they weren't armed. Not with guns. One had a length of wood.

"I'm Nellie Mercer's intended," the taller man said. The streetlights were on, and I could tell he was thin and broad-shouldered and a damn idiot. His buddy was shorter, broader, but no smarter.

"Listen, Intended," I said. "No one can see us. Eli and I can kill you quick as quick, and no one will know. Why are you doing this?"

"Nellie got hurt," Intended snarled.

"You two are a good match, 'cause you're both dumb," I said. He stepped back to get a good swing, and Eli hit him with some magic.

While he went down, I put the gun to his friend's head. "You want this fight?" I said.

"You'd really shoot me," Friend said.

"In a heartbeat," I said, and smiled. Because that would be his last heartbeat.

It was the smile that did it, I figure, because Friend broke and ran. He left Intended lying there on the sidewalk.

Eli and I circled the man sprawled on the sidewalk and went on our way. We were at the hotel in less than ten minutes, and then in our room with the door locked.

And then we were together.

Eli went to sleep right away afterward, but I was awake long enough to reflect. There was so much I wasn't clear about.

There was some kind of rebellion brewing in the Negro community, and Eli had come to ignite it . . . with a person Eli'd been supposed to bring with him, and that had some relationship with the Lucky Team's lost cargo. So why hadn't Eli brought the cargo? Who was the person, and where was he hidden?

The Negro community had been waiting for the arrival of that person. They didn't think their plan would succeed otherwise. Also, there were white people in Sally who were on the side of this rebellion. The Fielders were among 'em. Millie and Jerry were doing what they thought was right, though they stood to lose everything by doing so. And they seemed like good people.

I was getting used to not knowing what was going to happen when I was around Eli. That wasn't a good thing. I wondered if we could ever start out completely honest with each other. And then I fell asleep, because he was beside me snoring just a little. For now, that was good enough. But just for now.

I slept all night for the first time since I'd left Segundo Mexia, and that helped. A lot.

We went down to breakfast the next morning, each in our own silence. I had no idea what Eli had planned for the day. I hoped some of James Edward's amigos would report they'd seen the chest.

When we walked into the dining room, I could see we wouldn't get to talk to him anytime soon. The two Iron Hand people were waiting for us. When Seeley and Ritter saw us, they waved and smiled. Since they were sitting at a table for four, clearly they wanted our company. I said something unbecoming to my pretty rose blouse, and Eli's hand tightened on my arm, but over we went.

"You look adorable today," Harriet said, rising as if to kiss me on the cheek. I'd as soon be kissed by a rattlesnake, and I pulled back real definitely. Adorable, my ass.

"Thanks so much," I said, with the broadest smile I could muster. I was pleased when she came close as dammit to flinching. "You look nice too."

Which was a big fat lie. For once, Harriet Ritter looked tired and worried, and even Travis Seeley was not as smooth as usual. He'd missed a patch of whiskers on his chin.

A waiter, not James Edward, hurried over to see what we wanted to drink. Their coffee was so good, I was delighted to get a cup. I could hardly wait till it was drinking temperature.

When the waiter had gone to get our drinks, Harriet leaned forward to say, "There's no trace of the chest. We have to find it, and if that means we have to team up with you two, so be it."

"What will happen if you don't trace it?" I asked. I was hoping it would be something bad.

"We might get fired," Travis Seeley said. He was doing his best to look like that was something he didn't care about. I didn't buy that for a second.

"Why should we care?" Eli said, taking the words out of my mouth.

"Your gunnie was guarding it, and she has to find it too," Harriet said. "And I suspect you are looking for the same thing. Else why would you be here?"

"I am here to be with my wife," Eli said. "I'll help her do anything she wants to do."

"I hear you have a sister," Harriet said to me.

The hair on my neck stood up, and all the fun seeped out of me right quick. I determined at that moment that I would enjoy shooting this woman. "I don't know where you would hear anything like that," I said. "I grew up without brother or sister, my mom's only child."

"Who was your father?" Travis Seeley was smoking a cigarette, and he tapped the ash in the glass tray in the middle of the table.

I felt Eli tense beside me, but if he got upset too, it would confirm everything the Iron Hand people thought they'd dug up. "I am a bastard," I said. "I don't know my father." Both true things, in different ways.

"Hard to believe our informants were amiss," Harriet said. "But I suppose if you help us look for the chest, I could forget all about what we heard."

I turned to look at Eli. He gave a tiny nod. Somewhere along the line, maybe these two would die.

"Don't know why you feel you got to threaten me," I said, turning back to Harriet. "And I don't know why you feel it's got to be Eli and me who help you. Why do you think we'd want to or need to? We're here on our own say-so."

Just then the waiter poured my coffee and brought Eli's orange juice. He took our breakfast order.

But our two uninvited companions stayed on point. "Eli, you're clearly a wizard, and a powerful one. Lizbeth, you have a reputation as one of the best shooters in Texoma. And here you are together. That doesn't happen by accident."

"Actually, it did happen by accident," Eli said after he took a sip of orange juice. "I had no idea I would meet Lizbeth here, and I was happy as a man can be to see her at the train wreck."

"Not too many men would be happy to find their wives at a train wreck," Harriet said. Her polish was wearing thin, and she was almost snarling.

"We're a real unusual couple," I said, bending forward as she had earlier. "One thing we got in common, Eli and me: we like to eat breakfast by ourselves."

Harriet glared at me. After a moment, Travis said, "So be it." They both rose and marched out of the dining room.

"I bet they stuck us with their bill," I said to Eli. "What do you want to bet?"

"Not a nickel, Lizbeth. Not even a penny." He smiled at me and I smiled back. We finished our breakfast in a much better mood. We'd found something to unite against.

I ran up to our room to brush my teeth after we'd eaten. I love a cup of coffee, but having the taste of it on my teeth the rest of the day . . . not a good feeling.

The maid had already made the bed and put out fresh towels. I had felt guilty the first time I'd been waited on like this, but now I just felt glad. Housework had never been a calling for me, just a chore I had to perform to be decently clean.

In all the hotels I'd stayed in, the maid had never written me a letter after cleaning the room. I found a sealed envelope in my little suitcase. I'd only opened it to put my washed and dried stockings inside; I was glad I'd done that. Though I was mighty curious, I stuffed the envelope into my purse and hurried downstairs.

Eli was waiting by the front doors, and something in me kind of twanged when I saw him. I froze on the bottom step, suddenly aware that I was way too happy to see him, way too used to him being there, waiting for me. I could see disaster in my future, a totally different kind of disaster from the ever-present chance that someone would shoot me.

He turned to look just at that moment, and his calm face went all puzzled and surprised. He was over to the stairs in a few strides. "What's wrong, Lizbeth?" he asked quietly, taking my hand.

I had to jerk myself out of this bad moment, and I did, with a wrench that was almost physical. "Someone walked over my grave," I said.

Eli looked startled. "What do you mean?"

"Oh, it's an old wives' tale. When you feel a sudden . . . shakiness inside, or a shiver, you say that someone must have walked over your grave."

"Gruesome," Eli said. "Are they off of it now? Your grave?"

"Yeah, I'm okay." We went out the door side by side, me carefully not touching him. After we'd walked for a moment, I said, "We should find a bench or something. There was a letter in the room. I haven't read it yet."

Since we'd been headed nowhere in particular, and we had no plan for the day—at least that I knew of—we walked to the little park and settled on the same bench we'd used before.

"I hope this is interesting, because I feel we're getting nowhere," I said as I pulled the envelope from my handbag. I put my thumb under the flap to open it.

"Wait!" Eli took it from me and pressed his hand against the paper, his eyes closed. "Okay, no magic inside," he said, and gave it back to me.

"Magic?" I didn't know it could be put in an envelope.

"Could have been a spell inside, or it could have been spelled to react when you opened it," he said.

I shook my head. "That is . . ." I couldn't even think of the words. I felt real straightforward and simple. I opened the envelope to pull out a single sheet of paper. Hotel stationery. The message was not in cursive, but in the plain printing we'd learned when we'd first started writing. It was short. *Meet tonight after dark behind Mount Olive Church on Lee Street.*

"If it's a trap, it's certainly not a fancy one," I said.

"The handwriting could be because the writer can't do any better, or it could be a disguise."

"We know nothing." I was pretty disgusted with that state of affairs.

"We have to go," Eli said. "We go fully armed, though. Vest and guns."

I nodded. "I expect this is from John Edward, and it was the safest way he could communicate with us. But that's just a guess. Could be from anyone. Maybe the Society of the Lamb."

"Would that be connected with the pin the Fielders' neighbor had on his shirt pocket?"

"I couldn't see him. Describe it."

"A bleeding lamb superimposed over a cross." Eli made a face. "Of course, the lamb is white."

"Maddy told me about a girl who lived out by her, just thirteen, who was pulled out of her house and whipped by men who claimed she was a witch. They belonged to that Society of the Lamb."

Eli looked really grim. "This kind of ignorance is what we have to fight all the time," he said. "It's ridiculous. Our founder was devout, most of us are devout, and we would never . . ."

I knew why he'd trailed off. *Yes, you would. You do it all the time,* I thought. He'd been about to say, *We'd never use magic for evil.* But what had I seen during our trip to Mexico? Wizards using magic for evil. Because I defined evil as "trying to kill me and Eli," and there had been plenty of that. They'd almost succeeded.

"What do you think Iron Hand Security has to do with this?" I said. "I guess you know what's in the crate, and maybe your grigori organization was who sent it here. How did Iron Hand get involved?"

"While you were out on your own yesterday I sent a telegram, but of course I had to put it in the most general terms."

"Heard back yet?"

"No. I told the telegraph office I'd call back in today."

That sounded very familiar.

It wasn't the time of day for the tree to be providing shade, and I was tired of tilting my head to keep the glare out of my eyes. I tried to think of something I could do to move us forward. "Rogelio," I said. "Let's go get him. You said we'd have to interrogate someone, and now is a good time. Where could we take him?"

"We can put him in the car and drive out of town," Eli said. "It's hard to find a place around here that can't be seen for miles around."

"And this is a community of farmers, who are liable to be out and about all day. I guess we could find a patch of woods." I thought of the tall trees cutting off our view, and I didn't like the idea at all.

"I'll go scout out a place," Eli said. "You try to find out where he's staying."

"Okay." I got up, glad to have something to do.

"Be careful." Eli put his hand on my shoulder. "He may be more dangerous than he looks."

"The day I can't take down Rogelio is the day pigs fly," I said.

# CHAPTER FIFTEEN

I was sorry I'd said that two hours later. I'd found Rogelio sitting in another restaurant, having a long drink with lots of ice. He was alone. I'd waited outside, hard put to look natural while I remained out of his sight. He'd come out finally. By that time, I hated him because he had been under a fan having a cool drink while I was sweating.

I set out following him. In a little town like Sally, that wasn't easy to do. I was real glad when I spotted Eli cruising around in his battered car. Our eyes met, and I jerked my head at Rogelio, who was a block ahead of me. Eli was able to do a U-turn and pull up to the curb beside my former crewmate, who looked over when Eli leaned over to the passenger side and rolled the window down.

"Rogelio," Eli called. I sped up to box Rogelio in from the rear by then, and he still hadn't noticed me. Rogelio went over to the window and bent down. I closed on him from behind and stuck a knife to his ribs.

"Get in the car," I said.

"No." Rogelio began to push back against me, and I jabbed him.

"You bitch!" he said, and started to wheel around to hit me, but Eli got him with a spell first, contained in some powder he'd pinched from a pocket of his grigori vest. Rogelio went blank and silent.

"I love that," I said. I opened the passenger door and told Rogelio to get in. He did, without a word. I got in the back seat.

"Smooth as silk," I said, smiling. I kept the knife in my hand. "How long will the spell last?"

"It's unpredictable," Eli warned me. "So don't relax."

"As if I would." I was sitting forward on the seat, my knife almost at Rogelio's neck. It would only take a second to settle him.

We'd abducted Rogelio just before noon, and the streets were empty. People were home eating lunch, or inside a store shopping. Anything to be out of the sun. Of the few people about, no one had seemed to notice a thing. If they had, they were confused enough about what they'd seen to keep quiet.

We drove north out of Sally and into the countryside, which was gently rolling and cleared for agriculture for the most part. Cows and chickens, the occasional crop of cotton or . . . something else. I'm not real versed in farming.

Rogelio seemed to be more aware after ten minutes, and soon after that he was definitely stirring and muttering.

"Hold still!" I said, pricking his neck. "Don't talk till we're ready for you to talk." Our unwilling passenger quieted down for a minute or two, but then he was twitching again, and saying, "No, no, no." Which was not useful.

"We about there?" I was wondering how long it would be before I had to fight Rogelio, which would not be hard since I was behind him and armed. But we hadn't had a chance to search him. That made me anxious.

"Yes, here we are." Eli turned right onto a rutted driveway, very short, which ended in a ramshackle place that had once been—it was hard to say. Maybe a storage shed? Maybe a real small home?

Whatever it had been, now it was leaning to the side like it had had too much to drink. There were big trees around it, and the grasses and weeds had had their way with the yard. Pretty much ideal as far as concealment for the car, and there wasn't another building anywhere in sight.

Rogelio put up a fight when I told him to get out of the car, but Eli was able to give me a hand. "I don't want to hurt him too bad before you ask him questions," I said by way of explanation. It felt good to be back at work I understood, but very strange to be doing it wearing a dress. I was all too aware I was getting seeds and leaves and bits of stuff all over the skirt while I was maneuvering Rogelio to the back of the building.

To my relief, Eli had bought some rope. We secured our prisoner and sat him down at the base of a little tree. The high weeds closed in around him, and Rogelio looked like a small man.

I found a stump to sit on while Eli did his "questioning." I knew it was part of this particular job, but I had no stomach for it.

Rogelio turned out to be a tougher nut to crack than I'd figured. I made myself stand witness. If Eli had seen me shoot many, many people, I could watch him practice pain magic on Rogelio. I tried to figure out what was different about the experience. Magic seemed more personal than a bullet, I guess.

Rogelio groaned and moaned and screamed. In the end he wept and talked. As I'd predicted, it was a threat to Rogelio's handsome face that broke him.

Eli told him he was going to make all Rogelio's teeth fall out, and his hair, too. "And every hair will hurt as it detaches from your scalp," my "husband" promised. "Every tooth will ache and bleed."

Since Rogelio was already aching and bleeding from a few points on his body, he could appreciate what was in store.

The next time Eli said "Who hired you?" Rogelio began talking.

"The lamb people," he said. "I don't know how they got my name, but after Jake took the job of guarding the crate, I got a visitor at my house."

I didn't know where Rogelio's house was, but I assumed it was easier to get to than Segundo Mexia.

"What did your visitor tell you to do?" Eli sat back on his haunches, sweat trickling down his face and plastering a stray strand of hair to his cheek. It was hot, even under the trees, and the bugs and birds were making a ruckus. The country is not quiet, especially farm country.

"He told me that during the journey, someone would try to take the crate, and I should do everything I could to help it happen." Rogelio was crying, tears and sweat blending on his cheeks in a salty wash.

I nodded at Eli to let him know this was true. I had suspected Rogelio had pretended to be hit worse than he was during the train wreck attack. And he hadn't gotten in a shot in the earlier attempt, with the two men who'd charged into the car.

"What was the man's name?" Eli said.

"He didn't give me one. He wore one of those pins."

"What did he look like?"

Rogelio's nose was so runny by now that he had to snort for a moment before he could speak. "He was all dressed up. Good clothes and shoes. He looked rich. Maybe fifty years old."

"He was on the train, wasn't he?" It was the first time I'd spoken since we'd left the car.

Eli looked startled, like he'd forgotten I was there.

"Yes, he sat close to the doors." It was hard to understand Rogelio, because blood and snot were bubbling out of his nose.

"I didn't see him after the wreck. What did he do?" I bent closer.

"He left the cabin just before." Rogelio gasped desperately because all the fluids were choking him.

Our enemy had been so close. I could have killed him, if only Rogelio had spoken up. Rogelio himself could have shot the man when he'd come to Rogelio's house, and been true to his crew. I lost all sympathy for Rogelio in that moment. He'd sold us out. He'd let us be shot, would have let us die, for money. I didn't understand it.

My eyes met Eli's for a moment. We were of one mind on the subject of Rogelio. Then Eli looked back at his prey. He asked, "How were you supposed to contact him here?"

"He said he would find me in Sally. That's why I've been out in the streets and cafés so much."

"You idiot," Eli said. "Mr. Well Dressed thought you would die too. He never planned to meet you after the wreck. He was sure the gunnies he sent in would kill you."

Rogelio looked kind of confused and a little shocked, and then Eli snatched his life out of him.

I said some things in my head that people didn't say out loud very much, and I felt a rush of relief that this episode was over.

Then, since Rogelio had fallen silent forever, I heard a car coming.

There was a good chance it would pass by; our car couldn't be seen from the road, at least at a quick glance. But I had a bad feeling, maybe because I was half-grigori, maybe just from being cautious.

"We got to get him out of sight," I said, and when I used that tone Eli didn't ask any questions. "Open the trunk." Together we dragged the body over to the car and tossed it inside the trunk, snapping the lid shut.

I looked around at the trampled ground, the marks of Rogelio's boots, the drops of blood.

"Lie down right there," Eli said, pointing to the most marked area. Since he was using that voice too, I did so, though I had a twinge of distaste because that meant the damn skirt would suffer even more. Eli was beside me on the ground the next instant. He kissed me like he wanted to compress about ten kisses into one. Not what I had expected at all.

I heard a car door slam, distantly, and then a man cleared his throat. "Excuse me," he said apologetically. He also sounded a little amused.

I blinked to clear my vision. Standing a few feet away was a man I'd never seen before—but I'd heard his voice. This was Jerry Fielder's neighbor, surely, the one so upset about Willa May hitting his mama. The older man with him was the sheriff; I remembered him from the site of the train wreck.

Eli rose from the ground and gave me a hand up. "Gentlemen, good day," he said. He didn't explain or apologize in return. No law against having sex with your wife in a secluded spot, right?

I kept my eyes cast down as if I was embarrassed, but I was scanning the ground for any sign we'd just killed someone. We'd done a good job of muddling things up. Maybe we were okay.

"We just spotted your car parked back here, and wondered what business anyone would have behind this old place," the sheriff said. At least he was being straightforward.

Eli looked doubtful. "Have we done something against the law?"

"No, of course not," the neighbor said. "I met you at the Fielders', remember?"

"Norman Moultry," Eli said, breaking out in a smile. "This is my wife, Lizbeth."

"Mrs. Savarov," Norman said, nodding in my direction.

"How is your mother?" Eli sounded genuinely concerned.

Norman said, "She's well, thank you. Doesn't remember a thing about the incident. And Willa May never showed back up at our house. We got to find us someone else to watch Mama."

"I hope you find someone more to your liking."

Though I made myself look agreeable, I didn't like the way the sheriff was looking at us. I could see he was doubtful about our story. Maybe he didn't know why he was suspicious, maybe he thought this was a real odd place to be overcome with passion.

"Are you all just out riding today?" I aimed to sound a little amazed, because truly, unless you needed to torture someone in a quiet place, why would you ride out this way in the heat in the middle of the day?

The sheriff said, "No, ma'am, we're on our way to Bergen to court. Mr. Moultry here is a lawyer, and I have to testify, so we're sharing a car."

That was a lie. Eli squeezed my arm a little to let me know he thought so too. They'd been tracking us somehow. Maybe someone at the hotel had seen us driving out of town, but after we'd gotten Rogelio into the car. They hadn't asked about him, and I was fairly sure they didn't know he'd been with us. I could only be glad they hadn't gotten here twenty minutes earlier.

I would have had to kill them, too. Three bodies to dispose of was a lot.

"Well, honey, shall we go back to town?" Eli was smiling down at me fondly.

"Sure, let's get some ice cream." I smiled up at him. I was calculating who I'd have to kill first. The sheriff had a gun. I'd go for him with my knife. Eli could handle Norman Moultry, who looked like he wasn't used to quick action of any kind.

"We'll be getting on to Bergen, then. Sorry to interrupt you folks." Norman turned to go back to the car, a tiny dirty smile on his face. I held my breath until the sheriff turned to go with him.

After we heard their car drive away, Eli's shoulders relaxed. "I thought we were going to have to kill them both," he said.

"Me too."

"Which one were you going to take?" He was asking out of what appeared to be simple curiosity, but I didn't think it was.

"Sheriff was armed. I'd have taken him."

"But maybe he could draw fast."

"Not as fast as I could cut his throat. And he wouldn't expect a woman to attack, no matter if he knows what I am or not."

Eli looked down at me admiringly. "You are very cunning," he said.

"Does cunning mean I'm smart about fighting?"

"In this instance, yes."

"Okay then."

I shook out my skirt, trying to rid it of as much leaf and grass debris as I could. I couldn't see any stains, so I turned my back to Eli and said, "How do I look?"

"You look fine," he said.

"I mean my skirt! I can hardly wait until I can wear my jeans again," I said.

"I would never have known that."

"Okay, I may have mentioned it a few times."

"Ten or twelve," he muttered under his breath, as he dusted himself off. "Or twenty."

"I got your hint." If my voice was sour, it was not out of ingratitude for the clothes, which had helped me blend into this society. But maybe he thought so? "But thanks so much for getting them for me," I added with some haste.

Eli bent over laughing.

I shook my head, smiling a little myself. "All right, you've had your fun. Let's think about where to dump Rogelio," I said.

"If the sheriff and Moultry hadn't seen us here, this would be a good place," he said. "I'm tempted to use it anyway."

"No, that's a bad idea. Let's drive a bit and see if we can find a place that's better."

I made sure there weren't any blood smears on the outside of the car before we took off on the road east, the direction the sheriff had taken, which I assumed would go past Bergen.

We came to a sign telling us Bergen was three miles ahead, but we took a road north before we reached the town. We were in the middle of nowhere, and it was hot, hot, hot. My hair was blowing every whichaway since the windows had to be open, and I felt dust all over me. But I was with Eli, and the country was green, and we had learned something from Rogelio. Pluses.

After a while I spotted a large culvert in a ditch, over which a gravel road had been built to get tractors into the field. We listened and looked, and couldn't hear or see anyone approaching. To get caught in the midst of moving Rogelio's body would be a very bad thing.

Eli got out and opened the trunk, and we waited a bit again. When nothing kept happening, Eli nodded. I leaped out of the car, grabbed Rogelio's feet, and yanked. We went down the side of the ditch faster than we'd wanted to, and nearly all ended up in a heap at the bottom, but we kept to our feet with a struggle. At least, since it hadn't rained in a while, the ditch was dry.

It is harder to feed a body into a culvert than you would think, and it took more time than we wanted, even with Eli making the body lighter with magic. Our luck held: no passersby. And no snakes, which I'd thought of the minute my unprotected legs were surrounded by high weeds.

When the messy job was done, I scrambled up the slope of the ditch and back into the car. Eli stood by the driver's door catching his breath before climbing in. We returned to Sally on a road so hot and still and dusty that my mind went numb.

I had to at least wash my face and hands before I did anything else, and Eli agreed.

The car needed gas, so we stopped at a garage and I went into the women's room with no expectations. It was very clean and had a lock on the door, and I was glad of a chance to wash as much of me as I could and dry those bits with the white hand towel hanging on a rack. There had been towels made of paper in the train toilet, which had been a surprise. Who said travel wasn't broadening?

I felt refreshed but my skirt and blouse looked awful. No matter how I shook the skirt and brushed at the top, there were bits of leaves and grass seeds and stains. If I'd been wearing my usual clothes, that wouldn't have bothered me. Well, only a little.

Eli had washed too. His face was the right color and the hair at his temples was wet with water.

When I looked at the clock inside the gas station, I saw that five hours had passed since we ate breakfast. I wasn't hungry, but Eli's earlier mention of ice cream suddenly dashed across my mind, and I said, "You promised me more ice cream." Maybe I could have chocolate again.

"So I did. I saw a different place earlier, in a drugstore."

We parked on one of the two streets that comprised the main shopping area of Sally. The drugstore was dark inside, and the ceiling fans were whirring. There was a fan on a stand, too, and it was blowing down the line of stools in front of the counter. A girl was leaning on the cool marble, bored and vacant, but when she saw Eli, she perked right up.

"Good afternoon!" she said, with a big smile aimed at Eli. I got a little corner of it. "What can I get you? You two?"

"What kind of ice cream do you have?"

She had chocolate, vanilla, strawberry, and blueberry.

"I can't decide," I said.

"You can get two scoops," she told me, her eyes never leaving Eli. "Two different kinds."

"Chocolate and blueberry," I said.

"Vanilla and strawberry," Eli said.

So we got to taste all four, and it was the happiest fifteen minutes I'd had that day.

The girl's name tag read EDITH. Edith's gaze never left Eli. I was not the only one who found him . . . what did I find Eli? Attractive. He attracted me. I liked his grit and his skills and his little accent. I liked him clothed and awkward. I liked him naked and limber. I knew he would leave again when this was over. He'd go back to his world, and I'd return to mine . . . if we lived. And maybe I'd never see him again. If I got lonely enough, maybe I'd marry Dan Brick, since he seemed to be carrying a torch for me I hadn't ever noticed.

"What are you thinking of?" Eli asked quietly. "You seem so serious all of a sudden."

"I was thinking about Dan Brick," I said. "I was thinking that if he was my boyfriend, maybe I should have known that."

Eli grinned at me. "Especially now that we are married."

But it wasn't the right moment for that joke, which was getting worn out in a hurry. I turned my face down to the remainder of my ice cream and finished it off. No matter how down I got, ice cream was good, and I should enjoy what I could since it wouldn't last forever.

Like that wasn't a timely reminder.

## CHAPTER SIXTEEN

We had a long time until the rendezvous, so we split up. I went to the hospital to visit Maddy, and in answer to her anxious questions about Rogelio, I lied. Somehow, telling her he was rotting in a culvert in rural Dixie didn't seem calculated to make her recover any faster.

"I haven't seen him," I told her. I don't lie a lot, no reason to, and it grated on me. "How's the leg?"

Maddy seemed happy with the progress she was making, but bored as hell with only getting up to be taken in a wheelchair to the bathroom. "And these women are awful," she said, trying to whisper, which was not natural for Maddy. "They treat me like I got a social disease."

I handed her some things I'd bought at the drugstore: two magazines with pictures of Hollywood actors and Russian royalty and their doings, and a bag of candy. She said she was glad to get 'em. "Not much of a reader," Maddy confessed, which didn't surprise me. "But anything's better than staring at the walls, watching the nurses, and listening to that woman over there." Maddy inclined her head to her right. "She bitches nonstop."

I glanced over to see a gray-haired woman with her arm in a sling and bruises all over her face. Her mouth was drawn tight with either ill humor or pain or both.

"Does anyone come to see her?"

"No, and no wonder." Maddy's voice had started to rise.

I shook my head, and she looked contrite. "Well, it's true," she muttered.

No point in a range war, with the two beds side by side. "Give her your magazines when you're through with 'em."

"That'll keep her quiet for a while. Listen, that Harriet Ritter came by this morning."

"What did she want?"

"She told me Iron Hand is picking up my hospital bill," Maddy said. "So I asked the nurse today, and she checked, and sure enough, it's taken care of."

We looked at each other with matching expressions of huge relief.

"I'm really glad," I said from my heart.

"Me too. And she wanted to know where Rogelio was. She said she'd stopped by his lodging, but he'd left early this morning after breakfast."

"I guess she's out looking. Maybe wants to pay his doctor bill, too."

"So, that's good!" Maddy was glad for their good fortune.

"It is." They'd save money on Rogelio.

I couldn't think of any other chitchat to share with Maddy, and now that she was rid of the worst of her anxiety, she was much more cheerful about the world in general. I left her as she opened the first magazine.

Eli had been to the telegraph office and was back in our room when I unlocked the door. He had had a shower, and that seemed like such a good idea after the hard morning spent in the heat with

Rogelio. I pulled off my sweaty, stained clothes and tossed them in a corner. Maybe the maid could take the blouse and skirt to the laundry. Eli smiled at me before I vanished into the bathroom. I marveled every time at the luxury of having it, a private bathroom in a hotel.

I wondered if he might join me, but as I toweled myself dry I peeked into the bedroom to see he was fast asleep. Torturing Rogelio had probably drained him. A nap seemed like a very good idea. I stretched out beside him.

When I woke, it was two hours later by the little clock on the bedside table. Eli was still asleep, and I carefully rolled onto my side to look at him. While he slept, his mouth fell open just a little. I admired his white, even teeth. He needed to shave again; there were tiny bristles showing on his cheeks and chin.

This was a good moment. I added it to my little room of good moments.

It was time to eat, and since (again) we'd only had ice cream for lunch, I was very hungry. I gathered together my soiled clothes, intending to stop at the desk on our way out and ask that they be laundered. I was sullen, I admit, at having to put on the clean blouse and skirt and the damn hose.

Eli was stirring by the time I brushed my hair. He got dressed in about half the time. He added his dirty clothes to my bundle, and we set it in the middle of the bed. "Are you as hungry as I am?" he said, and I nodded.

Nellie Mercer was on duty at the desk, which made me want to walk right by, but Eli was made of sterner stuff. The woman actually jumped when he spoke to her. "Miss Mercer, we left some clothes that need laundering on our bed. Can you send one of the maids to pick them up? And if we could have them back by late tomorrow, that would be most welcome." Eli didn't smile.

"I don't know why Daddy lets you stay here," Nellie hissed. "After what you done to me, and to Harvey. He was just trying to . . ."

Harvey must be Intended.

"Make a fool out of himself," I said in a real low voice. "Miss Mercer, you need to learn something. If you're smart, you leave gri-goris alone." Of course, she wasn't smart, or she'd never have touched Eli's vest. Had she been told to spy? Or was she simply curious about something unknown and forbidden? Either way, she'd paid for it in humiliation.

Nellie Mercer gave me a look that would have made my hair fall out, if she'd had any magical ability at all.

As we walked out of the hotel, I said, "I hope our clothes don't come back with holes all in them."

Eli and I went out to the closest café, the one where we'd seen the Iron Hand people with Rogelio. We were led to a booth, and he slid in beside me, not across as I'd expected. We were both facing the door that way.

The menu offered a choice between two meats and a long list of vegetables. I got speckled butter beans and squash and chicken-fried steak, and Eli ordered corn and snap beans and fried chicken. Our orders came with a basket of corn bread and a lot of butter, which the waitress brought before the food. It was great. Hard to eat corn bread neatly, but I tried.

Eli's eyes closed in happiness as he chewed. "Can you make this?"

"I can."

"This good?"

"Yes."

He got ready to say something else, but then he didn't.

I didn't coax Eli to speak, but I did wonder what he was thinking.

Then Harriet Ritter and Travis Seeley came in and headed right for our booth, though the restaurant was only scattered with diners. Were they going to interrupt every meal we had?

The answer was yes. Without asking, the two Iron Hand employees scooted opposite us. "You seen Rogelio anywhere?" Harriet asked.

"No, not in a while." The red-haired waitress slid my plate over to me and put Eli's in front of him, moving real quick and light. I looked up at her to say thanks. She gave me a stiff nod back, but when Eli thanked her also, the waitress hurried away as fast as she could scoot.

"Did you need Rogelio for something?" I asked, cutting up my chicken-fried steak. I hardly needed a knife, it was so tender. Yum. Though a lot of things in Dixie disgusted me, the food was just this side of divine.

"He hinted he had some things to tell us," Travis said. He sure had a level voice. You couldn't tell how he was feeling. I kind of liked that.

"Like what?" Eli said, after he'd had his first bite of fried chicken with gravy.

"Like why the chest got stolen and who might have it."

I could have told them he didn't know, or only suspected—but that information was for us, because we'd done the work to get it.

"We have a meeting tonight with an unknown subject," Eli told them.

If I was surprised, and I was—a little warning would have been welcome—Harriet and Travis were just about dumb with shock. "Why are you telling us this?" Harriet said. "Do you want us to do something about it?"

"Might be good to have someone hiding out in the woods to see that this isn't an ambush," Eli said. "Whoever left the note in our room, they're expecting Lizbeth and me. But not reinforcements."

"Why would we do this?" Travis asked. "We hide out in the dark woods, bit by mosquitoes, chiggers under our skin, for what?"

"To save our lives?" I said.

Harriet snorted.

*As though I need your help*, I thought. I wished Eli had not said a word to them.

"A stranger couldn't walk into the hotel and up to your room and enter. If it wasn't one of the blacks, it was someone who bribed one of the blacks," Travis said.

I couldn't argue with him.

"You don't know who asked you to this meeting, how many will be there, and whether they want to help you or kill you." Harriet was just as good at summaries as Travis was at picking apart situations.

"That's right," Eli said, just as calm and level as they were.

"No, thanks, we have other plans," Travis said in a final kind of way. "Tonight is catfish night at the Livingston."

I took a deep breath. None of this sat well with me. But there was something I had to mention. "Thanks for paying Maddy's bill," I said. "That's a load off my mind."

"You were going to pay it?" Travis said, staring at me.

"Sure. She is my crew."

Harriet shook her head as if my ways were strange. "Taken care of," she said, dismissing me and my gratitude.

"All right then," I said. "We'll keep whatever we learn tonight to ourselves. You just stay safe in your little hotel. We'll be fine and dandy."

There was a long silence, during which I finished my butter beans. They'd been cooked with a ham hock, as butter beans ought to be. Couple of dashes of salt. "You should have ordered these," I said to Eli. "Yum."

His chicken was only bones now. "What makes these snap beans so good?" he said. "Try one." I reached over with my fork and stabbed a bean, tasted it.

"Bacon grease," I said. "Just the right amount."

"Mmmm," he said, his lips closed over his chewing. He agreed, apparently.

Harriet and Travis were trading looks. Finally Harriet said, "All right. If you tell us when and where, we'll watch for you."

"After dark behind the Mount Olive Church on Lee Street," I said.

We'd made our deal with the devils.

Harriet and Travis left when it became clear we had no more to say. We had a fine time finishing our food. I was used to a lot more exercise and a lot less eating, and I felt porky.

Eli suggested a nap and maybe a few other ways to exercise, and I was not against that, since we had nothing else to do. But on our way to the hotel we ran into a snag.

A short man stepped into our path, seemingly out of nowhere. He'd been waiting in an alley, of course. And he was also a grigori: long dark hair, tattoos, vest.

My knife was in my hand before I could think of it.

The dark-haired grigori saved his life by bowing to Eli instantly.

I'd been just a breath from stabbing the man. But I kept my eyes fixed on him, bow or no bow. The last person I thought I'd see in Sally was another grigori. Especially this one . . . the grigori from the first day on the train.

"Prince Savarov," the grigori said. He straightened.

"Felix," Eli said, giving the new guy a nod. He seemed kind of on-the-borderline cordial, like he didn't hate Felix but he didn't call him a buddy, either. "I didn't expect to see you here."

"Who is your lovely companion?" Felix looked me up and down, his eyes fastening on the knife in my right hand. It was clear he was really saying, *Who is this ugly whore?*

Right away I disliked Felix, who was short and slim and maybe interesting in a brooding, hairy way.

"This is Lizbeth, also known as Gunnie Rose," Eli said. "Lizbeth got me and the descendant of our leader out of Mexico alive."

"Oh, this is the one." Felix made it clear he was not impressed— and also that he didn't believe in my skill.

I hoped to demonstrate it to him, one-on-one.

"But Paulina and Klementina did not make it out of Mexico, did they?" Felix said, as if he was pointing out something Eli might have forgotten.

"No," Eli said, with almost no inflection in his voice. "We had a great many enemies."

"What a tragedy, to lose two such talented women."

Paulina would have eaten Felix for breakfast. You didn't sneer around Paulina. Sneering was reserved for her.

I couldn't help but notice there was no declaration by Eli that

I was his wife, as there had been with everyone else we had met in Sally. Not that it made any difference to me. After all, it was pretend.

Then I took a grip on myself. I wasn't here to play games I didn't understand. I was here to guard Eli and help him look for the chest that had been in my charge for a couple of days, the chest that was missing.

"Can she speak?" Felix asked.

He was trying to goad me into saying or doing something rash, something that would embarrass Eli.

"I'm real happy to meet you, Felix," I said in the flattest voice I could muster. "You didn't talk to me directly, so I didn't think a response was called for. I remember you from the train."

"It talks," Felix said in a bored voice. But I had seen the flash in his eyes when I spoke back to him.

"Lizbeth is my valued ally, and you must treat her like an equal, Felix," Eli said. "This is your only warning. What were you doing on the train?"

"Getting here. How did you come?"

"Part by train, part by car. How did you . . . what happened to you at the derailment?"

"My car was one of those that remained upright," Felix said, kind of smug.

Of course it was.

"Lots of people died . . . in my car," I said.

"Interesting." Then he dismissed the topic of transportation. "I have been sent to monitor your progress."

"By whom?"

Felix's eyes slewed toward me and then back to Eli.

*Not in front of the woman,* he was telling Eli.

"Lizbeth is my guard," Eli said. "And I have very few secrets from her."

"I'm sure that's true," Felix told him.

Again said with contempt, and the unspoken statement that Felix knew I was Eli's bedmate, and that Felix thought such a pairing was unworthy of a grigori like Eli.

The next instant I slid right up to Felix, my knife to his dick. "Anything else you want to say?" I whispered.

"Open street," Eli reminded me, though his voice was mild.

"Sorry, Eli," I said, and stepped back, the knife disappearing into my pocket.

Felix actually looked a little shook up. Good. "You dare to attack me?"

"No *daring* to it," I said. "You're lucky I didn't geld you."

Eli grinned. "How many grigoris did you kill in Mexico, Lizbeth?" His eyes didn't move from Felix.

I'd never added up. "Maybe . . . twelve?"

Felix made a face I couldn't understand. Disbelief? Disgust? Amazement? Or just surprise that I could shoot as fast as grigoris could sling spells?

"Are you two going to talk now, or are we just going to stand out in the heat swapping insults?" I thought enough had been said about me, pro and con.

"Yes, let's go to another restaurant," Eli said. "This time of day they won't be crowded, and we can get some pie. Or ice cream."

More food. I was going to be as tubby as Big Balls, the butcher's pig in Segundo Mexia.

Felix shrugged, and we walked two blocks to another place.

I was going to visit every restaurant in Sally, at this rate. They all seemed to be of the home-cooked variety, so they all seemed to offer the same things. I was pleased to see pecan pie on the menu at Aunt Lillybeth's. I'd never had that. Travel was going to broaden me if I didn't walk more.

The ice water was better than the pecan pie. Aunt Lillybeth had had a heavy hand on the crust this morning.

"Why are you here?" Eli said, when the waitress had delivered our orders and left to clean the counter.

Felix leaned back, like a man about to have his favorite drink. "Your patron sent me to check on you," he said.

"My patron?" Eli looked blank. "You mean Gilbert?"

"Yes, Gilbert." Felix, who did look a lot like a cat, practically had feathers sticking out of his mouth.

"Gilbert is my immediate superior in the Air Guild," Eli explained to me. I nodded. Paulina had told me the wizards had assorted special talents: earth, air, fire, water, death, and healing. But hadn't Eli mentioned someone else in Mexico? His mentor?

"What happened to Dmitri?" I said.

"Dmitri was executed," Felix said, his face empty of expression.

See, I hadn't known that. Eli and I needed to have a much longer talk. Maybe we needed to spend more time talking in chairs, and less time in the bed.

"Excellent," Eli said. "I need some help, Felix. This place is treacherous." He might as well have hit Felix over the head with a shovel.

"What has happened?" Felix seemed to have the malice knocked out of him.

"Someone prepared for the train wreck and caused it," Eli said. "It was no accident. We don't know whether it was caused so the chest could be stolen, or if someone simply took quick advantage of the chaos."

"If the train didn't derail so the thieves could take the crate, what reason could there have been?" Felix said, his forehead wrinkling.

"It could have been a guerilla strike." Eli looked thoughtful.

"Guerillas? There are guerillas here in Dixie?"

It was lucky I was looking down. I thought he meant "gorillas" for a minute, and I was having a picture in my head that was crazy wonderful. Then my brain translated.

"I'm not sure of the size and scope of the movement," Eli said. "The people involved know they will be killed if they're found out."

I thought about Galilee's parents in the back room of the shoe shop. I thought of the man who worked behind the counter there, and James Edward. You didn't get afraid like that overnight. It was in the air your whole life.

"You all talk," I said, and stood. "I got to go run an errand."

Both the men stood, which was real polite but not needed. Eli gave me a questioning look, but I just nodded to him, told Felix good-bye, and got out of there. I went to the Western Union office, found that the reply to Eli's telegram had been delivered to the hotel, and walked to the Pleasant Stay. Nellie Mercer was still on the desk. She tried to give me a face with no expression, but she couldn't carry it off.

"I understand a telegram for my husband has arrived," I said.

Nellie reached back to our little mailbox and plucked a thin sheet from it, which she gave to me by laying it on the desk and sliding it over the wood with one finger. It might as well have been a dead mouse.

I gave Nellie a real direct look. And had the pleasure of seeing her look as scared as she should.

A white-haired lady with a back as straight as a poker had approached the desk from the stairs, unheard by Nellie. After I'd turned away with my telegram, I heard her say, "I certainly hope you treat the elderly with more courtesy than the young, Miss Mercer."

I smiled to myself.

I sat on one of the dining chairs on the porch to open the envelope.

The yellow sheet read: *No connection Iron H here. Felix en route. Anxious. Tell no one. G*

Felix had sure made good time. I didn't know if it was Felix who was anxious, or "G." I guessed that was Gilbert, Eli's new "patron."

*Tell no one*, my ass. I had to know what I was looking for. This was ridiculous. I loved Eli's sense of honor, but I also loved common sense.

And as I sat there mulling this over—Iron Hand, Felix, the crate, the Society of the Lamb, the terrible wreck and its death toll (which a newspaper headline told had grown by fifteen)—I could not make any sense of it. While I pondered it all, a man came by with a dog on a leash, a sight so odd that I stared at him. Pet dogs are pretty rare in Texoma; dogs roam the plains in packs, and to encounter a pack is to encounter painful injuries or death.

I caught the man's eye as he spit out some tobacco juice. "Little missy, you ain't never seen a bloodhound?" he said.

"No, sir, I have not."

"Then let me introduce you to Clete, the best sniffer in Dixie," the man said, with a lot of pride. He walked over to the porch with Clete, who sniffed at my shoe with a lot of enthusiasm. Clete looked up at me with doleful eyes.

"He hopes you'll give him a pat on the head," Clete's owner said.

Real carefully I reached down to give the dog a little pat, and when that went over well, I scratched him behind the ears. To this he responded with a kind of happy moan, so I did it again. The dog sat and looked up at me.

"What do bloodhounds do?" I looked from the dog's big brown eyes up to the narrow blue eyes of the man. I'd never known a dog who did anything but attack or bark.

"He's a tracker, ma'am. He can track anything you give him the scent of. A missing person, a deer, and so on."

I hadn't had any idea dogs could do that.

"Thank you for letting me meet him," I said, not having much idea how to end this encounter.

"You're real welcome. Clete likes to make new friends."

I looked at the baggy jowls and the drool and I figured it might be a little hard for Clete to do that. Smart he might be, but he was not lovely or appealing, at least to this Texoman. The dog and the man resumed their walk, and I congratulated myself on avoiding the drool.

When I looked up from checking my shoes, Eli was there. He was alone, I was glad to see.

"My telegram came," he said, spotting the yellow paper.

I came down the hotel steps to meet him. "Sure did. Telling you Felix was coming, and telling you to share everything with your gunnie."

Eli looked away with a smile. "I'm sure it said that."

"It did. Doesn't make any sense to keep things from the one who's protecting you."

"Say anything about Iron Hand?" He was still thinking.

"That G doesn't know anything about Iron Hand."

"That doesn't make any sense."

"Lot of that going around."

"Like Felix's arrival," Eli said. He was frowning as hard as I'd ever seen him frown. "The guild either trusts me or it doesn't. Why send help when I hadn't given any sign of distress? When I hadn't been wounded, and the enemy hadn't even appeared to confront me?"

I nodded, but he was thinking too hard to notice. We were ambling along now, because he seemed to like to move while he worried at things.

I was looking around us, because that was my job. I saw a pickup truck creeping up the street after us. There were two men in the cab. Though he was wearing a hat pulled down and a kerchief over his lower face, I was sure the one in the passenger seat was Friend. There was another man in the truck bed. Intended—What was his name? Harvey?—Nellie Mercer's fiancé.

"Eli, they're coming for us," I said, and his head jerked around. "We don't want to talk to the sheriff."

Eli didn't waste time asking me if I was sure, and he didn't ask any questions. He blew out the two tires on our side with a gesture, and the truck suddenly sagged to the left. There was a lot of yelling, and Harvey leaned out as far as he could with a pistol in his hand. Eli blew a cloud on them, and while they couldn't see we took off walking as fast as we could. We took the first right, an alley, to get out of sight. When we emerged onto the street where the shoe repair shop was, I got my bearings, and steered us toward the back way to the hotel. Though it was now enemy territory, it was all we had. I figured neither Mercer, nor Nellie, nor her Intended and his buddies, would attack us in the Mercer place of business, which was also their home. Probably.

We scooted up the stairs to our room at a more unremarkable pace.

Closed the door. Locked it. Stood and stared at each other.

"I'm going to tell you everything," Eli said. "If I get killed, I want you to know why."

I didn't remark that I was just as likely to get killed as him. I just pulled off the damn shoes and scooted up against the headboard, while Eli collapsed into the armchair.

"You're not religious, so you may not know this," he said. "But our church, the church of Holy Russia, is Orthodox."

I nodded, to show I was listening.

"We don't believe everything the Catholics believe, and we worship differently from the Protestant churches, too."

I already knew that, thanks to my mother. I waited for him to go on.

"But we are a Christian church, and we have our own saints. One of our early saints is African."

I didn't care one way or another where his saints came from. I made a beckoning gesture to tell him to keep going.

"Saint Moses the Black—some people call him Saint Moses the Ethiopian—was a big man, a violent man, a runaway slave. He was a fugitive when he got to Wadi al-Natrun."

I had no idea where or what that was. Not going to ask, either, not now.

"Though Moses was a robber and a killer, he converted to Christianity when given shelter at a monastery. There are all kinds of stories about him resisting temptation to return to his violent ways, though he wasn't always successful. When he was old, his monastery was attacked by bandits, and he chose to be martyred."

"So in the chest . . . ?"

"His bones. The remains of Saint Moses the Black."

# CHAPTER SEVENTEEN

So the Lucky Crew's first and only job had been protecting a dead man.

"How long ago did he die?"

"Fifteen hundred years ago."

"And there are still remains?"

"Yes. If the British can find tombs of ancient Egyptian kings, and see their preserved bodies, the bones of a saint can certainly survive." Eli sounded very certain.

I didn't know about any Egyptian tombs, and I didn't care. I was concerned with the here and now. "So the thinking of the Holy Russian Empire was that . . . ?"

"Our priests have been in contact with the Negro people here for a couple of years, very secretly, spreading the story. Moses the Black has become the most beloved saint of poor people here in Dixie."

That sounded like a secret religion to me, and kind of creepy. But I kept my mouth shut.

"It's no surprise that the Catholic church—the priests who know about this—has become incensed."

"So why are you doing this, exactly?" I didn't disapprove, not at all, but it didn't seem like the kind of thing a government would do if it wanted to stay stable.

"Tsar Alexei loved his first wife. You may remember she was a Ballard, from Dixie—in fact, from here in Sally. Her name was Amanda."

A lot clicked together in my head when Eli said that. I remembered the newspaper coverage of the wedding, even in Texoma. An American tsarina.

"Amanda grew up on the largest Ballard-owned plantation, just outside of town. On her deathbed, the first tsarina asked Alexei if he could try to make things better for the downtrodden people here. She often told the story of the woman who was her nurse when she was little. The woman was whipped for some minor error, and died of infection from that. It was the tsarina's last wish, that the black people here be helped. She told Alexei he was the only person she'd ever met who was powerful enough to change things."

"It sounds like you were there." It also sounded like, though she was dying, the former Miss Ballard had appealed to Alexei's pride and vanity.

"I was there," Eli said. He looked sad. "It was a terrible day. The tsar loved her, truly."

"He's got another wife now, and an heir." I was just saying.

"Tsars have to have heirs. Otherwise, we have people like his uncle and my father plotting to overthrow him."

"So does his current wife know about any of this?" Not that it made a difference, I guess.

"Tsar Alexei set all this in motion soon after Amanda died. The tsar sent one of our priests to Africa. After much searching, he returned to San Diego with Moses's bones. My superiors thought our priests, or even our grigoris, would be too easy to spot if they accompanied the crate to Dixie. So gunnies were hired all along the way, and it was switched from one crew to another, to muddle the trail. I thought that the decision was made to hire Iron Hand to further make sure the bones arrived where they were supposed to go. But maybe not. Their presence is a mystery to me."

"So the Lucky Crew had the crate on its final leg." I had pictured a lot of things that might be in that chest, but not human remains.

"Yes. Until the train wreck, which I believe—now— was caused by these Lamb people. They took advantage of the train wreck to kill your crew leader and steal the chest, having tried to get it away from other crews several times before. I don't know how they found out. There are sympathizers with their way of thinking in places I would never imagine."

I could believe that easily. There were so many people who tried to find a reason for all the bad things that had happened in America, bad things that had destroyed the United States as a country. Blaming it on black people was the easiest solution to a big question.

"They killed a lot of people to get the chest," I said, thinking of the row of bodies on the hillside. The two funeral homes. How Jake had looked.

"Maybe more than they'd counted on."

"And what will they do with the chest?"

"I'm afraid they will destroy the bones unless we find them very quickly."

"It's been days already." If I'd been a Society member, I'd have powdered the bones beneath my boot and burned the powder.

I didn't want to start this venture unless there was a real chance of success. No point in risking death for nothing.

"Then we have to move fast," Eli said. He was nothing but determined.

"I would move fast if I knew where to move." I had not a single idea.

But we had a miracle. There was a knock at the room door, and I pulled my gun. I stood to one side while Eli, spell in hand, answered.

James Edward stood there, his arms full of folded linen, and he looked from side to side and stepped in without being asked. "Shut the door, sir," he said. He set down his stack of sheets.

Eli did, and I lowered my gun.

"Listen to me," James Edward said. "Juanita Poe saw the chest where she works, at the Ballards' house, out on the road to Bergen. Young Mr. Ballard brought it in two days ago after the train wreck and hid it in his attic. Juanita waited till they was gone and went up there. Way she described it, that's what you're looking for."

"Did you leave the note here about the meeting?" I said.

"I did, but I wanted to tell you . . . the man who gave it to me is someone I don't trust. Elijah likes money more than he's loyal to other black people. He's been keeping an eye on me to make sure I delivered it. He'd know if I hadn't. He has a friend who works here."

"So you don't know who will be at this meeting."

"I've asked around, to see if any of my friends know anything about it. It's not with any of them, that's for damn sure."

That was bad news.

"Sally is a complicated place," I said. Everyone I'd met had seemed like other people, some nice, some not so nice, but regular. But there was this whole secret underlying it all, this thing we were all supposed to assume.

"Yes, ma'am," James Edward said, and I didn't tell him to call me Lizbeth. He would not be able to.

James Edward left within a minute, because his absence would be noticed. He'd picked his time carefully. He asked Eli to look out in the hall to make sure no one was observing before he picked up his armful of folded sheets and carried them on to the big linen closet at the end of the hall. After that he went down the back stairs, which I figured ended in the kitchen area.

"Well, shit," I said.

"That sums it up." Eli threw himself on the bed. He lay his head back against his laced fingers. "We should have asked where the Ballard house is."

"Phone book," I said, looking in the shallow drawer of the bedside table. It was only a few pages long. Though Ballard was a common name for businesses and public buildings, I found only two private individuals with that name: one senior and one junior, same phone number. Looked to me, from the map, that if we hadn't turned onto Bergen Road we would have gone past the place.

There was no way we could drop in on these people. We were strangers, and Eli was clearly what he was. I couldn't think of a single story that sounded believable. Even if we could talk our way into the house, there wasn't any reason on earth we could give to ask if we could see what was in their attic.

"I'll tell you about the Ballard family," Eli said.

I loved it when he volunteered information. "I've seen the name on a lot of buildings here," I said, to grease the conversational wheel. "I've read about them in the papers, I'm sure. But it's been a long time."

"The Ballard family owns huge amounts of farmland in this area, and several businesses, too," Eli said. "They also have a sugarcane plantation in Cuba. They control part of an import firm in New Orleans. But they're based here. Tsar Nicholas was impressed with their wealth when he met the previous head of the family at a reception in Cuba."

"So he was open to the marriage of Amanda Ballard to Alexei. Pretty ambitious marriage on the part of the Ballards," I said. "Considering Alexei is real royalty."

"Yes, it was." Eli looked grim. "If Tsar Nicholas had been well, and not so anxious to find some financial backing for his new kingship, he would not have agreed when Samuel Ballard proposed it."

"I don't see why he would consider it at all. Considering royalty marries other royalty—at least that's what I've always heard." Not that I had thought much about it one way or another.

"You have to remember, this was some years ago. We were new to the continent and trying to make connections to all parts of it."

Connections that had lots of money. But I didn't need to point that out. The Russian court had hurried onto rescue boats with what they could carry, but jewels and silver wouldn't last forever, not after the long dreary period of sailing from country to country in search of asylum. When Nicholas was invited to stay at San Simeon, and afterward asked to set up a new government when the American system failed, there'd been a lot of hasty marriages. All the grand duchesses had more or less been auctioned off, the Texoma papers had said. Alexei had been the biggest prize, saved until last. "All right," I said. "What happened?"

My lip curled. This was awful.

"Alexei agreed to marry Amanda Ballard. He had always been sickly, as you know, and everyone was anxious for him to try to beget a son as soon as possible."

No pressure there. "I understand," I said.

"It was a really good thing when he and Amanda fell in love. They had more in common than anyone suspected."

"What?"

"They both had dark childhoods. Alexei had been held prisoner by the Bolsheviks and was living in the shadow of execution every day. He saw his whole family abused and mistreated, and he suffered great pain because of his illness. They kept him separated from Rasputin unless he was on the verge of dying."

Alexei, who had the bleeding disease, had been kept alive by Rasputin, a deeply religious grigori, founder of the order.

"And Amanda had her story about her poor nanny," I said.

Eli looked at me in rebuke. "Yes," he said, and I felt cheap. "Amanda told him the story of her upbringing, of the cruelty she witnessed almost every day of her life."

"Okay." I wasn't going to say that Amanda didn't seem to have lodged any protests until she was free and clear, and she hadn't asked her husband to effect any change until she was on her way out of the world. When she didn't have to bear any consequences.

"She grew up at the family mansion? The one here? The one where the chest is in the attic?"

Eli said, very heavily, "Yes. With her violent brother Holden, who once threw a boy down the stairs for scuffing his boots."

Okay, Amanda had had some bad times. "So I'm guessing the Ballard house is really big? Full of servants who are deathly afraid of the Ballard family?"

"Yes," he said again. "Amanda said so. Of course, some of them wish their employers ill. But a few others, the ones in favor, they will back whatever move the family makes."

I thought about the Fielders, who had helped a black woman in trouble . . . trouble that she'd gotten into through losing her temper.

"By the way," I said. "How come you called the tsarina by her first name? That doesn't seem very Russian court to me."

Eli flushed. "It's too familiar. But we sat together many nights when the tsar was doing badly. He fell on the stairs once. He was very, very ill. We talked as we waited."

There was a knock at the door, and we both sat up. The world was suddenly coming to our door.

I had my gun in my hand and I was standing to one side of the door when I said, "Who is it?"

"Felix," said a very quiet voice.

Eli nodded and I answered the door. Our visitor really was Felix, whose long hair was now wound up in a bun at the back of his head. Because he didn't stand out enough before. He gave a quick glance at the gun in my hand, and then focused on Eli.

"Something has happened out at the Ballard place," Felix said. "I don't know what."

I might as well not have been there, but that was all right. This was big news, and I was listening.

"I've been walking around the town, trying to be friendly," Felix said. Every single Sallyite who would respond to Felix had told him there was another magician fellow at the Pleasant Stay. Felix found that almost unbelievable. It was obvious he had never lived in a small town.

While I pretended to be part of the wall, thinking how wonderful it would be if Felix attacked Eli so I'd have a reason to do him some harm, Felix told Eli that the staff at his hotel had been gathering in clusters to exchange excited whispers, then shooting off in all directions as quickly as they'd gathered.

Naturally, Felix had wanted to know what they were saying.

"I cast a far-hearing spell," the grigori explained. "I heard one man tell another that someone had been killed out at the Ballard plantation. The Ballards did not call the hospital or the police or the funeral home."

"We don't do any of those things at home," I said, just to remind myself I was in the room.

"What do you do instead?" Eli asked.

"We go to the cemetery and dig a hole and put 'em in it. If they were believers, the minister comes."

"No coffin?" Felix was horrified.

"Not everyone can afford one," I said. "Wood is not plentiful where we are. Not like here."

Felix dismissed me and turned back to Eli. "One of us needs to investigate."

"We have the mysterious meeting tonight," Eli reminded him. "So it will have to be you."

Felix looked pleased. "Then I will do it. I will have to find out where the Ballard house is, but that shouldn't be hard."

I opened my mouth to tell Felix he had better be able to turn invisible, because going to the Ballard house was a very dangerous venture. But then I shut my mouth again. Felix would not listen to me.

Eli met my eyes. He said, "Felix, you'd do well to wait until I can go with you. The Ballard family are rulers here, in their way, and they can dispose of us without consequence."

"I think I'm a match for a backcountry tyrant," Felix said, smiling. There was no doubt he believed that.

I touched my forehead with the thumb of my right hand. I didn't know I was going to do it, I just did it. Gunnies did that sometimes when they were saying good-bye to a person who was about to die. Eli asked a silent question, but I shook my head.

Maybe Felix would get away with it.

He left a moment later, practically shining with the excitement of a chance to distinguish himself.

"What did that mean?" Eli asked, imitating my thumb-to-the-forehead gesture.

"Meant I think he's going to die."

Eli stared at me. "You didn't say anything."

"He's not going to listen to me, is he?"

I could see Eli trying to come up with a reason to tell me I was wrong, but he couldn't. He was fair enough to see it would be wasted breath.

So Felix had gone off to die, and we had to hope that Travis and Harriet would abide by their lukewarm agreement to back us up tonight. Otherwise, we might end up just like Felix, without the excuse of being ignorant.

"Do you think there's really a chance that this meeting is with the Negroes who are willing to help us? That they're just scared of talking to us in public?" Eli had resumed his pose on the bed, fingers laced behind his head.

"There is a chance," I said grudgingly. "I see we got to act on it. But I think it's a trap, myself."

Eli shook his head. "This is a bad place to be in."

"We've been in plenty of bad places. We made it through them." Though by a very small margin. At great cost.

I had a good idea. "Can you do that invisibility spell? The one Klementina blessed me with so I could get away?" There was no way the Mexican police would have let me go, not after I'd shot a lot of people in public in broad daylight.

"I haven't ever performed it, but I know the theory of it," Eli said slowly. Then he grinned. If no one could see us, we had a much greater chance of coming out of tonight's meeting in one piece. "Wait, what if this is a legitimate meeting? What if John Edward's people are there, and they can't see us? Can you see them agreeing to help us after we talk to them out of the darkness?"

"Can you see this being a real meeting? And are you sure you can turn us back to being seen? I don't want to be invisible the rest of my life."

Eli nodded after a moment of considering, his hair brushing against the pillow around him.

I decided it would be a good idea to kiss him. Then, *pop!*—we were doing what we did so well. He was inside me, and we were one being. It seemed to get more exciting every time, as we grew to know each other better and learned we could play with things we'd never done.

I'd had a pretty dim view of sex before Eli. Not much experience, and the little I'd had had not been thrilling. I had not asked Eli for details about his times with other women, and I never would, but I believed Eli hadn't had this much fun before either. When it was over, gloriously over, I wrapped my arms around the sweating man above me and hugged him close, locking my mouth shut on all the words I felt bubbling up.

No point speaking them.

Every time we left this hotel, I had the strong feeling that we might die here in Dixie, killed by one faction or another. At least we'd had this.

And that was that.

# CHAPTER EIGHTEEN

As soon as the sun began to go down, I put on my jeans and a short-sleeved dark blue shirt and my boots and my guns. As I glanced in the mirror, something inside me relaxed. For the first time since the train wreck, I felt like myself.

Eli was wearing his battered brown pants and his wizard vest over a long-sleeved ugly brown-and-green-checked shirt. We decided to wear the darkest clothes we had, just in case the invisibility spell didn't work.

Eli had bought some compound from the pharmacy that was supposed to keep mosquitoes away. I just about prayed it would work. Mosquitoes here were big enough to carry away a baby rabbit.

Eli brushed my hair, smiled as he watched it spring back into ringlets. He pinned it back from my face with two barrettes. Mine was way shorter than his—but then he hadn't cut his hair since he'd become an invested grigori.

We could hear the buzz of the hotel become concentrated in the dining room.

When it was gloaming, Eli cast his spell. He seemed as eager to use his magic as I was to use my guns.

Eli muttered, his hand on my shoulder and his eyes closed, and then he vanished. "Can you see me?" he whispered from just above my head.

"I can't," I whispered back. It had just been me all by myself when Klementina had worked magic on me before. I'd never been lonelier in my life than when I'd been invisible. On the other hand, I'd been safe.

"Can you see me?" I asked. Sounded like a kid's game.

"I can't," Eli said, pleased. "I don't know how long this will last. How long do you think it was, in Mexico?"

"About three hours. Maybe longer. Let's go." I opened our door, and since no one was coming—we didn't want anyone to see our door open and close with no human being visible—we moved quick.

We went down the back stairs John Edward had used, since the landing of the front stairs was blocked by two couples talking in a leisurely way.

We startled a waiter and a cook, who glanced around them when they felt someone pass. Though we were taking care, maybe they heard our footsteps, too. I don't know how they explained it to themselves, and I didn't care. As long as they made no outcry or tried to grab us.

After we'd gone by them, we were glad to find that the back door of the kitchen was propped open. One less odd thing that might be observed.

I was relieved to be free of the building.

The locusts were making an ungodly amount of noise, but the people noise had abated. Sally foot traffic was down to almost nothing. There weren't many cars on the streets. We had a long walk ahead of us.

Eli and I had agreed to keep talking to a minimum. After all, voices coming out of nowhere were both scary and suspicious. As we made our way to the street where the old church stood, I reminded myself to visit Maddy the next day, so she wouldn't think I'd forgotten about her. I wondered what the Iron Hand people were doing. I hoped Travis and Harriet had decided to back us up, though it was a real faint hope. Mostly I felt excited. We were finally about to see some action, maybe make some progress.

We'd driven by the site earlier in the day. It was in a straggly part of town, where the houses had thinned out, and there was the occasional little store. The church itself hadn't seen use in years. It was a small wooden structure with a caved-in roof, like a giant had sat on it. The white paint had mostly peeled off, and the hand-lettered sign above the door was hanging by one nail.

We hadn't been able to explore behind it. There had been too many people around. Now we discovered that the yard to the rear of the lot was an overgrown tangle, very like it had been at the abandoned house where we'd questioned Rogelio.

There was just enough light to keep us from falling over the remains of a cemetery, buried in the waist-high weeds and vines. Most of the headstones had been knocked over or defaced in some way. The vines and weeds camouflaged them, so we had to pick our way through with care lest we break our necks. The surrounding trees had rained down leaves and sweetgum balls and pine needles for many seasons. It was treacherous footing.

Luckily the trees were still green and bushy, because we aimed to climb them.

Eli turned out to be good at scrambling up a tree, which kind of surprised me. I listened to his quick progress and I could just see the leaves moving. "I'm reaching down," he whispered. I flailed around and finally connected with his hand. One boost up was all I needed. Soon we were perched against the trunk of an old live oak, Eli on one side, me on the other. I could feel his shoulder if I leaned to my right.

It wasn't especially comfortable, but all I felt was good. I was so glad to be doing something I understood.

The familiar weight of the guns in my belt, the welcome comfort of my jeans . . . though a skirt would have been cooler, I was delighted to be back in my own gear. I would have said that to Eli, but it wasn't any time for idle chatter. It was time to listen.

We heard 'em coming a couple of minutes before they arrived under us. It was full dark by then.

I couldn't see 'em any more than they could see me. One of 'em was a pipe smoker.

After five minutes or so, three more men made their way to stand underneath us. One of them lit a cigarette. By the light of the match I could tell, sure enough, they were all white men. They looked well fed. Naturally they weren't wearing their nice clothes. One of them was the man who owned the shoe repair shop. Kempton. The smoker was Norman Moultry. I smiled, all to myself.

After a long silence, one of the men spoke. "They coming, you reckon?"

"Don't know." That was Kempton. "They got the message, Elijah said. He saw 'em reading it."

Eyes were everywhere here.

"That magician, he's from the HRE." That was Mr. Mercer from the hotel. Well, crap. John Edward had been right to be so careful.

"All magicians are." Did not know the speaker, but that was not the truth anyway. Magicians could come from anywhere, but they could be trained only by the grigoris of the Holy Russian Empire. That's why so many had come over from England, where magic was not permitted.

"Yeah? How you explain that Calhoun boy, then?" Didn't know this speaker.

"He's just crazy, is all." That was Kempton. He sounded worried, like he had connections to the Calhouns and didn't want anything to happen to them.

"Jimmy may be crazy," said Mercer. "But he can also make some things happen. I'm surprised his daddy hasn't taken him out and drowned him. You better warn 'em, Kempton, or the Society will pay them a visit some night."

Eli exhaled real heavy. I don't know how Mercer heard him, but the hotel owner glanced at Kempton to see if the sound had come from him.

"They ain't coming," an unknown man said, after a little silence. "If they been looking around town for something and they ain't found it, they're gonna be here on time."

"'Less they're back in their room fucking like nutrias," Mercer said, as though the fact that we had sex was disgusting.

"Well, she's a pretty little thing," Kempton said. "When she came in to get her boot fixed, she was all dressed up and cool as a cucumber."

That's me.

One of the men I didn't recognize said, "Don't know what she sees in a spooky guy like Savarov. He might turn her into a dog or something, she don't mind him."

I felt a little shiver in the tree, and I knew Eli was laughing silently.

After some more fidgeting and grunting, maybe ten minutes' worth, the men dispersed. "Here, I'll put that rope back," Kempton said to the unknown man.

I felt a cold ball in the pit of my stomach. Would they have tied us up? Or would they have hung us? They would have *tried*. Did they not know we could protect ourselves?

"Wish we had got to use it," the man said. "I coulda knocked out that Russian with this sap, he wouldn't have had time to work any hocus-pocus. Maybe had a little fun with her."

"Clyde, we don't even talk about raping white women," said Kempton. "They got souls, they got feelings. 'Specially married white women."

"She wouldn't miss a slice off a cut loaf," said the man. He was earning my Most Hated Man award with every word. "But virgins, no, sir, we shouldn't touch 'em."

"I agree," said Mercer. "By the way, how's your little girl? She's been real sick, I know."

And there they were, human beings again, discussing the recovery of little Junie (who must be a virgin) like they were real men instead of monsters.

Being helpless in their hands would be hell. Junie didn't have a chance with a father like that. He would infect the child with his own hatred. He would think he was doing a good thing. Maybe he'd give Junie her own little lamb pin to wear.

I wondered if I could find occasion to kill them all. The world would be a better place.

We waited ten minutes after the last man walked away from the rendezvous, just to be cautious. It was good we were quiet on our descent from the tree, because we hadn't allowed long enough.

When we emerged from the weed-choked wilderness of the little cemetery, we found Moultry standing by his car while he smoked a cigarette and waited for his companion to finish peeing in the bushes.

Even though there were no streetlights close, we froze. I didn't think the men could see us even if Eli's spell wore off, but every instinct I had told me to stay still.

"Come on, Dill, this is taking forever," Moultry said. I matched his voice to his face. This was the man who had thought Eli might turn me into a dog.

"I got something wrong with my bladder," the other man said over his shoulder. It was one of the men from the first funeral home. "I got to go to Doc Fielder."

It was at least three minutes until they got in the car to drive off, so that doctor visit had better be soon, I figured.

We were in full view. The three minutes felt like an hour. I drew a deep breath the second they were far enough down the street.

"Those men are poison," I said. "I could shoot 'em all."

"You don't get to judge."

I couldn't see Eli, but from his voice he felt the same as me but thought it was wrong, that feeling.

"Eli, we judge every day. We decide that person is bad and this one is good." It was a struggle for me to talk about what I felt. I wasn't used to it.

"There is a difference. We have to fight people who are trying to kill us, to block our path to the goal we have promised to reach."

That was pretty much my job description, and I nodded. Of course, he didn't know that. "Yes," I said, but I was a little slow saying it, because we were in deeper waters here than I was used to.

"But that's different from picking people out of a crowd and deciding that person isn't worthy of life," Eli said.

"What makes it different?" When Eli didn't answer right away, I went on. "What's the difference between me deciding someone has to die because they're shooting at me, and me deciding someone has to die because they don't believe people different from them are human?"

"Aren't there any people you don't think are as good as you?"

"That isn't a real high standard, most people would say."

"What do you think?"

I had never questioned my right to make my own decisions about people. "I think I'm as good as anyone if you're talking about rich and poor," I said. "I see the differences, but I don't think they make me worse or better. If you're talking about morals, I try to do what I think is right. I don't know how else to act. And I think it's right that rapists and people who try to hold down other people should die." I'd messed that all up, but I hoped Eli understood what I meant.

An invisible arm found my invisible shoulders. We were silent the rest of the walk back.

# CHAPTER NINETEEN

Getting into the hotel was not as tricky as getting out because there were fewer people around now. The kitchen staff had left, but there were still some workers, and the guests were sitting around the public parts of the downstairs. The Mercers had an apartment at the back of the hotel. Its door was right where the stairs came down. There was a little plaque that said PRIVATE on the door. Just as we passed it, the door opened and hit Eli in the shoulder—at least, that was my guess, because I heard the sound of a stumble and the chair sitting against the opposite wall scraped its legs against the floor as it was pushed sideways.

Nellie Mercer stood frozen in the doorway, her hand over her mouth. Her eyes were wide. If she'd been a horse, I'd have said she was about to bolt. In fact, she stepped back into the apartment and shut the door. I could hear Eli right himself and then he was back by my side. We could not speak, of course, but I was sure there were a few words he'd like to say. I wanted to laugh, but at the same time I felt a little sorry for the woman. A little.

We had to wait at the foot of the main stairs for a guest to come down, then a maid, and finally, when the stairs were clear, we could see someone on the gallery above. I sighed, and shifted from foot to foot. After seven or eight minutes, we had a clear path and we went up the stairs as quickly and quietly as possible. At the door of our room we waited, looking, and then Eli unlocked it and we scooted in. Closing the door and locking it behind us made me real happy.

Eli said, "Bathroom," and I heard him peeing a minute later. Now that we were alone, I would be glad when we could see each other again. I had to give Eli credit, this spell was lasting a long time.

I wanted a shower, after pouring sweat and pushing through all the weeds—no telling what was in my hair. I'd just gotten my clothes off when I realized I could see my hand, and then the rest of me became visible. Eli was also taking his clothes off, and he turned to look at me. "Oh, great!" he said, and then we proceeded from there.

About an hour later I took my shower with Eli.

We went down to breakfast the next morning early. Eli wore his vest. Our laundry had been returned, and I again wore my white blouse and blue skirt. Now I almost didn't notice them. I still missed my guns, though.

I heard a guest at the next table say, "Honey, you know that blond woman we were talking to at the Western Union office?"

"The woman you thought was so pretty?" his wife said, in a tone as dry as toast.

"Oh, honey . . . she was pretty, but you are my wife," he said, and she laughed a little.

I half-turned my head to get a look at them, and saw a young man, brown hair, blue eyes, well dressed. The wife was just the same. I looked hard at Eli, and he nodded slightly, to let me know he'd heard.

"What about the blond?" the wife asked.

"I went over to Melvin's hotel last night to ask him if he'd heard from Mama, and he told me she and her man friend had gone miss-ing. Stuff still in their rooms, but they hadn't come in or out for hours."

I wasn't keen on Travis Seeley and Harriet Ritter, but I had to admit this worried me. Also, they knew a lot about us, and that could become common knowledge if someone really persuasive had got them.

Dr. Fielder was waiting for us in the lobby when we came into the hall from the dining room. He was holding his hat in his hand, looking uncomfortable.

"It's good to see you again," Eli said, sounding calm and matter-of-fact.

The doctor did his best to look calm. "Sorry to interrupt your morning, but I wonder if you have a moment?"

"Of course we do," I said. "We were just about to take a little walk; it's such a pretty morning. Come with us."

I hadn't been lying—it was nice and cool that morning. It was even pleasant to be wearing a skirt, because the cool air just flowed up under it. We strolled down the sidewalk until we came to the park across from the courthouse, and there we picked a pair of benches. We sat opposite the good doctor.

"Something's going on out at the Ballard house," Jerry Fielder said.

We nodded. "We heard," Eli said. "But we don't know what."

"You remember the girl who came to my kitchen?" He looked around before he said that. "Willa May?"

We nodded again.

"You haven't seen the place yet, but there are a number of cabins behind the house. They used to be slave quarters. Now that—after the Civil War, the Ballards prettied them up and a lot of the people who work for them live in those cabins."

I was not going to nod again. I just waited.

"Willa May decided to hide in one of them with an aunt, Juanita Poe, until she could arrange a way to get to her cousin's."

Juanita Poe had been the one who'd said she'd seen a trunk carried into the Ballard attic.

"Willa May said the Ballards wouldn't notice one more black face among all the others, and I guess she was right. She went into the house today and called me from the Ballards' kitchen telephone, which was pretty brave—or stupid—of her. She said people were dying out at the Ballard place. White people."

My first thought was of Felix, who'd been planning to go there the last time we saw him. My second was of Harriet and Travis.

"Since they couldn't get us, maybe they settled for someone else," I said, trying to let Eli know what I meant without naming names.

Jerry Fielder said, "I wanted to make sure it wasn't you two, and now that I know that, I feel better. But I thought maybe this was information you'd need to know." He hesitated. I wondered if he were thinking of offering to go with us.

Instead he said, "I'll draw you a map, if you want to go to see for yourselves." He drew a piece of paper from his doctor bag and hastily sketched out a route to the Ballard house. Then he took off for his office.

"We've got to check on Travis and Harriet," I said. "Maybe they've come back."

Eli didn't question that. "Where are they staying?"

I fished the name out of my memory. "The Livingston," I told him.

We walked into the Livingston lobby a few minutes later. It

was cool and dark. Overhead fans turned in slow circles. The lady behind the desk was smiling already, even when she saw what Eli was. "May I help you?" she said. Her blond-white hair was braided and formed into a little crown on her head, which was fascinating. I shook myself and got to business with an introduction. Her name was Mrs. Girtley.

"Ma'am, we understand some friends of ours have not turned up where they are supposed to be," I said. Calm and reasonable. "Travis Seeley and Harriet Ritter. My husband and I are concerned about them, and we wonder if—with you present, of course—we might look at their room to see if we can find any clue as to where they might be?"

Mrs. Girtley's lips pressed together as she thought this over. "With me present," she said, nodding. "If Mr. Seeley and Miss Ritter hadn't been so regular in their habits, I wouldn't be too concerned. But their rooms were supposed to be vacated today. They told me yesterday they'd be leaving this morning. I just don't believe it's like them to vanish, especially not without their belongings."

"We'd be much obliged," Eli said, sounding as Dixie as he was ever going to sound.

We followed Mrs. Girtley down the ground-floor hall. First Mrs. Girtley unlocked Travis's room, which was orderly. His suitcase was shut, his clothes still hung in the wardrobe, his shaving gear and toothbrush were in the bathroom.

"I'm going to open his suitcase," Eli said to Mrs. Girtley.

"Oh, I'm sure it's locked," she said.

But I took a cue from Eli and began to ask Mrs. Girtley how long she had worked at the hotel and any other questions I could think of. Eli made some small hand gestures. When he pressed the release buttons the locks popped open.

"Oh, my goodness, he left it unlocked!" Mrs. Girtley said.

I knew for sure something bad had happened to Travis when I saw his guns lying on top of his clothes. From Eli's sudden stillness, he'd reached the same conclusion.

Same thing in Harriet Ritter's room. Her guns were in her suitcase too, and it was locked until Eli stepped close. And Harriet's jewelry was in her suitcase. It was nice jewelry. Not showy, but not fake. Real gold, as far as I could tell.

"I should call the sheriff," Mrs. Girtley said. She shook her head. "You'd think since they worked for Iron Hand they'd be able to take care of themselves, even Miss Ritter. But you don't leave sidearms and jewelry behind."

Any dragging our feet would make us look real suspicious. "You should do that," I said. "This is a real mystery."

And it was. But I kept on talking to Mrs. Girtley about how worried I was, to distract her while Eli got hair from Harriet's brush, just as he'd done in Travis's room. I had no idea what he meant to do with it, but he knew what he needed.

"I'll go call the sheriff," Mrs. Girtley said, with sudden decision. "You lock the door behind you, please." I took the key from her, and as soon as she was out of sight I took Harriet's guns. I checked them to make sure they were loaded—they were—and I tucked one into my purse, where it barely fit, and handed the other to Eli to tuck into the back of his pants, under his vest. I wanted to be armed *right now*. I couldn't walk back to our hotel without something better than a knife.

Eli didn't say anything about this, so I figured he was trusting me to do my work. He searched the suitcase very thoroughly (nothing) before relocking it in his magical way. We left the room after a final look around for papers or anything else that might give us a clue. Nothing.

Once we were outside, having handed Mrs. Girtley the key and repeated our conversation several times (some people don't think saying something once is nearly enough), Eli said, "Quiet spot."

I pointed to the paved path going around to the rear of the hotel. I'd looked out of Travis's window to see there was a patio, deserted this time of the day.

There was one little area in some shade. That's where we headed. Three wooden chairs huddled in this bit of shadow. We had to sit close together. Eli drew out the hairs. "Hold them," he said.

I turned my palms up, slightly cupped, and he dropped the blond hair into my right and the dark hair into my left. Then he began to whisper.

My palms began to tingle. As I looked at Eli's face, intent and serious, and felt his power, I felt proud to know him.

At the end of the spell, if that's what Eli called it, he stood and said, "Come."

I was up immediately, carefully stowing the strand of hair from Harriet into my right skirt pocket, stowing Travis's in my left. We began walking. My purse, heavy with one of the guns, slapped my side.

"Does it mean they're alive, if you can follow them this way?"

"No," Eli said.

Eli was acting like he was blind except for the path only he could see. I had to steer for him. I took his arm and used pressure to control him. My hands were full with keeping Eli from bumping into someone or stepping out in front of a car. He wasn't following a scent, like the bloodhound would have done. I don't know what he was following, but he was definitely fixed on going that way.

Eli chose that moment to cross a street. I had to hold him back from stepping off the curb into the path of a car. It was like shepherding a very large sheep.

I was real glad there weren't many people out.

"Eli," I said. "Listen to me."

He stopped walking. That was something.

"I'm going to get the car and come pick you up. Can you stand still here until I get back?"

Eli nodded without looking at me. He was holding on to the track. He couldn't waver in his focus. Temperature was going up fast, and he was sweating.

It took me fifteen minutes to run back to the Pleasant Stay, run up to our room to get my gun belt, get in the car, and return. I was scared the whole time that Eli wouldn't be there when I got back, but there he was. People were walking around him, giving him as wide a berth as they could, because he was simply still.

I had to jump out of the car and run around to open the door. Then Eli climbed in after I pulled Harriet's gun from the back of his pants. He pointed forward, and off we took. I was driving slow so I wouldn't miss a change of direction. If I turned the wrong way, I might jar him loose.

I had four guns now, but it didn't seem enough.

We left downtown behind and drove through the pleasant streets where the people lived who had plenty. After that ran out, which didn't take long, we were on gravel instead of pavement. These were folks who were less lucky. Their yards were messy and any cars were beaten and rusty. The children wore faded hand-me-downs. And they threw rocks, sometimes.

Then we were driving on packed dirt. We were among the

shacks and shanties of the very poor. As far as I could see, the people in this neighborhood were all black. I knew there must be some white people just as poor, but even at the most desperate level the two races didn't mix.

If we were in Texoma, this was where I would live. The houses were kind of cobbled together, most of wood with the shine of age and weathering, a few with walls or roofs of tin, some with a pen of chickens and a garden, one or two with a cow in the yard, and every now and then a mule. There was always a vegetable garden. Children of all sizes played outside. Some were lucky enough to have a tire swing or a baseball or a jump rope.

But all these pastimes stopped when we rode slowly by. The children didn't follow us asking questions like kids in Segundo Mexia would have. These children stood in silent clumps as we passed.

These kids knew that white people in their part of town couldn't mean anything good.

And still I drove with my silent Eli, very slowly, windows down to admit whatever breeze might happen by. The sweat trickled down my back and under my breasts. This skirt might have to be burned after today, and I wasn't even thinking about the petticoat and the panties and the bra.

We drove at our creeping pace till there were open fields stretching far as the eye could see. The flat land was only broken by a little gentle roll here and there, or a strip of trees edging a bayou. The farmhouses were spaced wide apart and set back from the road, surrounded by trees. Some were real big and fancy, some were shacks, some were degrees in between.

A man passed us. He was riding a horse. He gave us a sideways look of alarm and urged the horse on. Odd. This was the only person we'd seen on this road, and he was going in the same direction we were.

We'd only passed the occasional farm vehicles rumbling down the road, and in the distance I'd seen small wooden sheds at the corners of the fields. I couldn't figure out their purpose. I learned later that was where cotton was stored when it was being picked by hand. Then it would be loaded on a truck and taken to the cotton gin in Sally. Other than that, the vast landscape seemed empty except for the rider.

I began to feel even more uneasy than I'd been, and that was saying something.

We'd been jouncing around on a dirt road that had not been leveled in a long time. Eli had not given me any signals in a while. I hoped we were nearing the end of our drive.

I caught a flicker out in the field on my left, and I leaned forward to look. A cluster of black people were walking through the cotton. They were empty-handed, most of them, and they were all heading for town. In a hurry. Surely taking the road would have been easier; maybe longer, though.

Eli hadn't spoken this whole time except to say "left" or "right." But now he said, "Stop."

Where Eli said to stop, there was a graveled driveway to our left leading to a huge white house, two stories with an attic. The windows all had green shutters. A broad front porch extended the full width of the house, and there were pillars supporting the porch roof. As we approached, I could see a big terrace at the back of the house, a sort of patio. Then there was a line of trees and bushes, planted as a screen.

Beyond that, there were little white cabins, planted all around with flowers, to make poverty pretty. There was a huge vegetable garden and an equally large woodpile. There was a long, low building that might be a garage for farm machinery or cars, or both.

This had to be the Ballard plantation. I had never seen the like.

Here was the oddest thing: at first glance, nothing was stirring. There wasn't even a breeze making the leaves flutter on the pecan trees. Not an old man rocking on the porch, not a bird flying across the grass.

Eli was coming back to himself, but I could tell it wasn't easy. I began talking to give him some time. "No way we can sneak up," I said. "Even if we got out of the car and crawled on our bellies. Probably someone in the house watching right now."

"They're there," Eli said, from a far distance.

"Harriet and Travis are in that house?"

"We must go find them," Eli said. He seemed stiff, like the long spell had taken away his sap.

"So here we go," I said, though I didn't want to even go close to that place.

I felt like . . . I felt like we were going to a hangman, as I turned the car to glide down the driveway. There had been no rain for a while, and the driveway was baked into a crust. The car's tires turned up a cloud of dust.

As we parked in front of the house, I saw I had been wrong about the place being empty. There was a black man standing by the blooming bushes that decorated the front of the house. He was clipping them with hedge shears. He had to have seen and heard us, but he was pretending we were not there.

I got out of the car first and faced the man squarely. I had one of Harriet's guns in my right hand, the one I'd pulled from my pocket.

I'd kept the other in my purse, but if I had one on show, I might as well have the other. Wasn't doing me any good in the purse. I pulled it out. I was saving my guns and my rifle in the trunk.

Slowly, unwillingly, the gardener turned to face us, and I saw he was shaking.

I didn't draw the guns to the gardener's attention, but he saw them, all right, clear as I saw the hedge shears.

"Yes, ma'am? Can I help you?" he said, evenly enough. He was a tall, wide man with a broad face, very dark. I thought he was bald under his wide-brimmed hat. His clothes weren't rags, but they weren't too far off.

"Some people we know are here, and we want to talk to them," I said. "Harriet Ritter and Travis Seeley."

"I don't know anyone of that name," he said. "Either one."

He hadn't done anything to me and I didn't want to shoot him, but I would if I had to. It occurred to me it might shake up his memory if I told him that, and I did.

"Why would you shoot me? I ain't done nothing to you," he said reasonably. There was a quaver in his voice, though.

"You are not telling me the truth. I want to see the two people I mentioned," I said. "Just so you know, shooting one more person isn't going to burden me any." That might not be the whole truth, but I wanted him to believe it was.

There was a long moment where nothing happened, and I was sure I'd have to kill him. But just when I decided to raise the gun, the screen door squeaked open and a woman appeared, wearing a gray uniform that didn't do her glowing brown skin any favors. The woman was scrawny, stiff with fear, and she held open the door to let Harriet Ritter follow her out onto the porch.

Harriet's nice clothes were rumpled as if she'd slept in them. Her face was bruised. Though Harriet looked at me directly, I could not read her face.

"Lizbeth," she said, without any expression. "Why are you here?"

"The hotel asked us to find you. They want to know whether you're giving up your room or not." I had hidden the gun in the folds of my skirt. I held it out a little now, to show Harriet I was armed. "I can go back to pack up your stuff. You let me know what you want to do."

"That won't be necessary." Another woman stepped out of the darkness of the house. Her iron-gray hair was rolled up behind her head. Her face was wrinkled and her eyes pouchy, but she wore a pearl necklace and earrings. Her dress was a limp print, dark green with light yellow butterflies. She was anything but a butterfly. More of a locust, or a scorpion. She had an ancient pistol in her left hand. She said to the black woman, "Myra, go back in the house and see to Mr. Holden."

Myra left the porch, but she didn't go anywhere to take care of anyone. She stood right inside the screen door. The older woman didn't seem to notice.

"I'm Lizbeth Rose," I called. "Who are you, to speak for Harriet?"

"I am Mary Ellen Ballard," the older woman said, as if that name should strike fear into my heart.

There was a dark kind of buzzing just at the edge of my hearing. Something was happening in the house, and it wasn't something good. Just when I was wishing Eli stood at my back, I heard him get out of the car.

"Mrs. Ballard," Eli said from behind me. "It's so good to see you again. I haven't seen you since Amanda's funeral. I hope you got the condolence card my guild sent after the loss of the tsarina."

"Cards don't mean anything at all when your daughter is dead," Mary Ellen Ballard said, each word heavy. "You damn wizards! Couldn't even save her life! And now you want to take away *my* whole life, in addition to my daughter's. And my son's." She was somewhere beyond bitter, into the real biblical zone.

Mary Ellen Ballard was drunk. Or crazy. Maybe both.

Eli ignored the speech. "We need to take Harriet away from here," Eli said. "You must let her go."

"Why? Why must I do that?" Mrs. Ballard said, with all the assurance of someone with an army at her command. Even the man with the shears looked scared. It was all I could do not to flinch, and I was the one holding a gun.

"'Cause I'll kill you if you don't," I said.

"My people will take care of you," Mrs. Ballard told me scornfully. "No one will ever see you again."

Jeez, she was creepy. "Yeah? Where are all those people? 'Cause I don't see anyone but these two."

Mrs. Ballard looked confused. She actually glanced around her. She appeared to be startled at the silence and the absence of her servants. "Well, I have called my friends from town," she said haughtily, putting her confidence back on like a coat.

"Friends" was a lot longer word, the way she said it. *FREEuhndss.*

"We need to get out of here," I told Eli in a real low voice. I made sure Harriet was looking at me. She still seemed stunned, not her sharp-witted self at all. But I gave my head a little jerk. She looked sideways at Mrs. Ballard and edged away from the woman.

"Don't you move, you hussy!" Mary Ellen Ballard said, her face in a true snarl. Mrs. Ballard lunged for Harriet, who pulled herself back so the older woman's hand missed grabbing her. Harriet scuttled down the few steps from the porch.

"Don't stand there like a fool, catch ahold of her!" Mrs. Ballard cried out to her yard man. He saw my gun and made the good decision to stand still.

Mrs. Ballard whipped out her gun and fired. She was no gunnie. The bullet didn't come anywhere close to Harriet.

I raised my arm to shoot the bitch, but Eli had already hit her with his magic. I didn't know what spell he was using, but it was effective. Mary Ellen Ballard went down like a lightning-struck tree, smoking and crackling. She didn't move after she hit the porch. The old gun lay by her twitching fingers.

That was new. I'd seen Eli knock down people in interesting ways, but this was . . . different.

Me, Harriet, the yard man, Myra, and maybe even Eli, were all startled. "My goodness. Did you kill her?" I said, which I thought was pretty mild.

No one moved.

"Would you mind seeing if Mrs. Ballard is alive?" I asked Myra, who was closest. I wanted to keep my gun on her, in case she roused.

"No, ma'am, I ain't touching her," Myra said. It was clear she'd rather play with a snake.

I went up the steps and squatted by Mary Ellen Ballard, who lay on her stomach with her face turned to one side. There was still smoke coming from under her collar, so I touched her bare neck real gingerly. Nothing. Her back wasn't moving up and down with breath. Just to dot my i's and cross my t's, I took Mrs. Ballard's hand

and felt her wrist. I shook my head. "She got struck by lightning," I said, and looked up into the clear sky.

"The old lady is dead, Franklin," Myra said. Suddenly, shockingly, she laughed.

Franklin dropped the shears and looked up to the sky, his arms extended, his palms up. I know praying when I see it. Harriet sank down onto the top step and put her face in her hands. Eli sat down hard, sideways, in the driver's seat of the car, his feet planted on the dirt. I looked at the body, so I'd know when it stopped smoking. I'm not sure why I thought I had to watch for that. Maybe I felt the porch would catch fire under her.

Myra said, "If Miz Ballard's friends get here and you're still around, they will kill you, and no one will ever know. Me and Franklin, we're getting out of here now. The rest left already." She ran into the house and returned with a sack. It clanked a little. I figured Myra was collecting pay owed her in a useful form. She beckoned to Franklin, and he took the bag and without any more words, they got out of there. Instead of walking down the driveway to the road, they took the route across the fields chosen by the other people we'd seen on our drive.

Franklin left the shears where he'd dropped them. Guess he figured he didn't work for the Ballards anymore.

"Harriet," I said. She looked up at me. "Where is Travis?"

"He's out back. He's hanging from a tree."

I won't say I didn't flinch.

"That old bitch hung him," Harriet said in an empty voice. "Her and her son. They made some of the colored men help."

"Where is the son?"

"Holden Ballard is in his bed upstairs." Harriet's face began to look firmer, more like herself. "I managed to wound him pretty bad before they locked me up. I had a knife in my stocking. I hope he dies of it."

"What is this all about?" Eli said, as he came up the steps. He was walking like a man who'd been carrying a heavy weight up a steep mountain.

"She hired us to watch everyone on the train," Harriet said, nodding toward the body.

Well, at least now I knew where Iron Hand had come in.

"She had heard through some of her connections . . . Ballards have fingers in every pie . . . that Russians were shipping something to Sally that would make Dixie erupt like a volcano. Mrs. Ballard hasn't been right in the head since her daughter died. We knew that when we took the job, but our employer really wanted to be hand in hand with the Ballards."

"So you looked the passengers over and fixed on us," I said.

"Of course. Gun team, at least two well-known shooters and the old man with the ax. And your buddy Rogelio. He told us where you were staying every time. Where is he?"

"Dead," I said.

"I figured."

"So was it you who stole the chest from Jake and killed him?"

"No. That was your little buddy Sarah Byrne."

"But why?"

"She was broke and banged up from her last job. She didn't want to go stay with her sister. She thought the crate was valuable. And it was." Harriet laughed, kind of bitter. "She thought Jake was unconscious, and she went to slip it away from him, and he woke up, and she killed him in a panic."

"What did she do with the chest?"

"She told us she wrapped it in a tablecloth from the dining car and carried it to town with her. Some woman who came out to see the wreck gave her a lift."

"How do you know all this?"

"She looked from hotel to hotel until she found us. She figured Iron Hand was a big deal; she could get money from us and be on her way. She was figuring that all the trains out of town wouldn't run again for a while. We all got stuck here in Sally. In nowhere. A town the Ballards rule. And since Mrs. Ballard called her friends in town about fifteen minutes ago, we need to get the hell out of here," Harriet said.

"What about the man upstairs? Ballard?"

"He can rot for all I care." Harriet made a face. "They summoned us to the house last night, sent a car and a driver. We couldn't very well say no. One of the waitresses in town had called Mrs. Ballard, told her she'd seen us all eating together. You and Eli, me and Travis, and Rogelio. She had some questions about our loyalty."

"And once you got out here?"

"We didn't expect what we walked into." It was clear Harriet was disgusted with herself. "Right when we came in, the old bitch got a big guy, white guy named Phelps, and a couple of his cronies, to pin us down. He's—he was—her overseer. And our friend Sarah Byrne was holding a gun on us."

"Where is Phelps?"

"Dead. Travis killed him with a knife he'd hidden in his boot."

"So that's why they hung Travis?"

Harriet nodded. "And they were going to do the same to me, or worse, after I stuck Holden. I want to go cut Travis down."

"You said we got to get out of here now," I pointed out.

Harriet looked like she wanted to argue, but at last she nodded again. I handed her her guns, and she was really glad to see them. I was tightening my gun belt around me as Eli began to look more aware.

"Sarah?" Eli asked. I was glad to hear him join the conversation, look livelier.

"I think she's run. She's not in the house, that I could see or hear. I plan on finding her." Harriet didn't have any expression at all in her voice. For the first time, I found her a little scary.

I heard engines. "They're coming," I said. "Let's get in the car."

"I don't think that will work. They see us trying to leave, they're going to block the driveway." Eli looked grim.

"Son of a bitch," said Harriet. "We've got to run."

"I have to get the chest," Eli said.

"You can't." Harriet was all but yelling. "You've got to come back to get it. We don't have time!"

So we ran.

# CHAPTER TWENTY

I caught a glimpse of Travis's body hanging from a tree branch as we sped past the brick terrace, a flowerbed, a white birdbath, a line of bushes before the white cabins, empty now. There were signs of work that had been dropped in favor of flight; a basket of wet laundry, a bowl of peas. The black people we had seen on the way here had hastened away. They'd been warned by the man riding the horse. They'd fled to town. I hoped they'd gotten there safely.

I hoped we would, too.

*I should have set fire to the house,* I thought suddenly. *Would have slowed 'em down.* Too late. Maybe they'd search the house, find the Ballard son that Harriet had knifed, spend time getting help for him.

Maybe the sight of Travis dangling from the tree would give 'em pause. But not enough.

Then I heard a dog baying, and I recalled my conversation with the tobacco-chewing man outside the hotel. Clete, or another hound just like him, was on our trail. I didn't know much about dogs, but I didn't have anything to bribe Clete with if he caught up to us. That was assuming he was bribable.

Eli was not at full speed because of the death magic he'd used on old Mrs. Ballard. (In hindsight, I should have just shot her the minute she started talking. But I'd thought we might learn something.) Harriet was sore from being beaten. I was hampered by my damn shoes and skirt. I swore to myself I would never wear such things again. See where blending in had gotten me? Running through some woods with a dog behind me.

At least Harriet and I both had our guns.

So we ran. We came to one of those meandering trails of trees that cut through the middle of the first field behind the house. I found that the trees were on the banks of a bayou. The water was dark and still, except for a ripple here and there.

I saw a snake slithering away from the bank. They had water moccasins here. Copperheads. Shit.

We leaped the water at the narrowest point. We raced along the other side, Eli picking the direction. Did not know why he went that way, but I followed. I was working on keeping my breathing even. Harriet sounded like a bellows. Weeds and stickers whipped and tore at us as we bulled our way through.

I finally figured Eli was following the trees because the people arriving at the Ballard place couldn't see us that way. We were close enough to be visible running through the flat fields. But the line of trees angled north, and we needed to go west, to town. Harriet had to stop for a minute, and I turned back to her.

"I got a stitch in my side," she gasped. "Go on. I'll catch up."

I took up running again. Didn't want Eli to get out of sight. The growth of trees and tangle of underbrush was thick unless you stuck to the edge of the bank, and I was scared I'd tumble into the dark water at any moment. The bayou was widening, and I saw turtles sliding into the water at the noise of our approach, and a slither or two from other snakes. This was its own narrow strip of swamp. At this wider place the sky could shine down onto the tangled green growth and the muddy bank . . .

. . . where there were alligators. I was so shocked it took me a moment to say *alligators* to myself. Three of 'em.

Eli didn't slow down, he ran right among 'em. I plunged after him. We were moving so quick, and in the heat and sun the alligators were slow and drowsy. That was going to change any second, because two people flying through was guaranteed to rouse 'em. I found I could run a lot faster than I'd thought I could. So could Harriet, because she passed me.

Two of them were small, one as big as I'd ever heard of. But the three gators might as well have been a score. The big one bellowed.

"I have a plan!" Eli called back to me.

Oh, I was *completely* at ease now. It better be a good plan. Did Eli's magic work on animals? Reptiles?

Since Eli's legs were longest and he was in the lead, I figured he was in the least danger. I dodged the snap of huge jaws and leaped over the fourth gator (I hadn't even seen it!) as it was twisting to bite. I noted Harriet veering away from the bank into the strip of woods and I wanted to follow, but I took off like a deer after Eli.

The gator came after me for a little bit, and I found I could run even faster. In fact, I could leap over a fallen tree, and the gator could not. That tree saved me, I figured.

When I caught up with Eli, he was bent over gasping for breath. When I looked down, I could see why he'd stopped. It was a drop of five feet down to the dark water. I couldn't hear any movement behind us, though I listened as hard as I could over Eli's rasping breath.

"Harriet?" he managed to say.

"Somewhere behind us," I said, with just as much trouble. "Why the hell did you . . . ?"

"If they're following us, they'll run into the alligators too," Eli said. "Only now they're all excited. The gators, I mean."

I felt a little bad about Clete.

In a couple more minutes we had gotten our breath back. We started walking parallel to the bayou. "What now?" I said. "Since you're the man with the plan."

"I'm all out of plan," Eli confessed. "That was all I had, getting away and having a chance to think."

"I reckon now is the time for the thinking part of it."

"You're not hurt?" He bent to look into my eyes.

"Nothing to worry about." Bruises, scrapes. Little things. I'd feel like hell tomorrow, but right now I was fine.

"Go back for Harriet?"

I thought about it for a few seconds. "No. We got her out of the Ballard house, which was more than she deserved." We were talking in spurts, because we were walking fast.

"True." Eli stared up into the blue sky. "Here's what we can try. We work our way back to Sally and find refuge with either some of the black people who are for rebellion, or we can go to the Fielders."

"Or we can steal a car and get the hell out of here." That was my very own idea.

"But we haven't finished our job." Eli said that with this real elaborate patience, like I was dumb.

"I got the bones as close to Sally as I could get with the train blowing up!" I was mad now. "That was my job, and I did it! If someone who knew what was in that crate hadn't blabbed, none of this would have happened!"

"Ssh, ssh," Eli said. He was looking at the way we'd come. Alligator alley.

I heard a shriek, faint and far away. And yelling. And gunfire.

"All right then," I said. "We can't go east, because the nearest town is twenty miles away and we have nothing. I have my guns. My clothes are back at the hotel. I got no money. I'll bet you don't, either."

Eli patted his pockets. "Not much." At least he had on his grigori vest.

"The bones were last in the Ballard attic. I guess they're still there. We don't know if Holden Ballard will live or die from the knifing. If he dies, we might be okay. There might be enough hoorah for us to get out of Sally."

We were in big trouble, isolated in a place where everyone's hand was turned against us—everyone who was powerful, that is. And the people who weren't powerful, that was a little chancy, too. They were terrified of failure. I could understand that. But they'd wanted the bones, they'd got the bones, the Holy Russian Empire was willing to back them to some extent, and if we didn't leave, we had to come up with another plan.

I was in favor of getting out while we could. My mission was over.

But Eli's was not.

# CHAPTER TWENTY-ONE

Our return to town took three times as long as it should have. We were both tired and aching, we had to stay off the road and in what cover we could find, and we were thirsty. I knew better than to drink bayou water, because it was full of alligator shit. No, thank you.

I'd seen enough of that bayou to last me the rest of my life. Which might not be very long, given the situation we'd put ourselves in.

Finally, we reached Sally. We'd decided we'd go to our hotel, openly, because . . . we needed our stuff. And we had to find another car, if that was possible. It was lucky the first person we saw at the hotel was John Edward. He was shocked to see us coming to the back door.

"Didn't sound like you, the man hanging on a tree at the Ballard place. But I was worried," he said, low and quick. "You go up our stairs, the servant stairs. You got your key?"

Eli did have our key, which was one good thing.

John Edward scouted the stairs and unlocked the door to our room so we wouldn't have to stand there, exposed.

"They're after us?" Eli asked, after we were safely out of sight.

"Nobody knows what-all is going on," John Edward said. "People are saying Miz Ballard's dead, man got hung behind her house, trackers going through the country with dogs. Those two white folks missing from the other hotel. All the people who worked out there are in town hiding with kin."

"The man that got hung is the missing man," I said. "The woman ran back to town with us, partway, but we've lost sight of her." We had to talk to John Edward, but I wanted to get in the bathroom so bad I was almost crying. "And Mary Ellen Ballard is dead."

"Oh my Lord." John Edward's eyes were wide, and I could not be sure what he was thinking.

"John Edward, now is the time," Eli said. He was using his serious voice, the one that pushed you to act.

John Edward looked terrified. He took some deep, ragged breaths, and then he said, "Yes. I see that."

"Are you sure the relics of Moses the Black are still in the attic?"

"Before she ran away from Miz Ballard, Juanita went back to the attic. She says the trunk is still up there. It has to be the right one."

It had been galling to have to leave the object of our search when we'd actually been at the house, but we couldn't have carried that trunk on our scrambling, running, gator-ridden trip to Sally.

I told Eli and John Edward I was going to clean up and they could keep talking if they wanted to. I grabbed what I needed out of my bag and the closet. I was really glad to have clean clothes. A clean bathroom. A bed with clean sheets. Not that I'd get to sleep in it.

It was a huge relief to shut the bathroom door behind me. I sat on the toilet with my hand over my face for a long moment. Then I started the water running.

I knew my day wasn't done, as much as I wanted it to be.

Eli stuck his head in the door as I was climbing out of the tub. "We have company," he said. "You need something?"

"I got all my clothes." My real clothes.

When I came out in my jeans and boots, feeling like myself, Jerry Fielder was sitting in our room.

"... whole town is ready to blow up, like the train," he was saying. He stood when I appeared. "Lizbeth," he said.

"Dr. Fielder ... Jerry. I hope your wife is well."

"She's pretty upset just now. I wish I'd gotten her out of Sally before today."

I looked a question at Eli. He shook his head just a trifle. Jerry Fielder did not know what had just happened at the Ballard plantation. Eli wasn't going to tell him, and I didn't know why.

I heard a scream outside in the street. For the first time, I wished our window overlooked the front.

"I'm sorry now that we talked to your representative," Jerry Fielder said. "When he first came to town and had such careful conversations with a very few people, I should have known ..."

"You should have known that drastic change doesn't come about without turmoil and bloodshed." Eli looked ... serious.

"I didn't count on all hell breaking loose," Jerry said, and now he was turning angry and bitter.

"This cause is a noble one, backed by our church," Eli told him in a low, steady voice. "A noble cause doesn't mean all the people who will benefit are noble. Or that the process of achieving our goal will be painless."

"This town will go up in flames!" Jerry said between his teeth. He was wound so tight he might explode.

I wanted to leave the room, go to the window at the end of the hall overlooking the street, to see what was happening. But I did not dare to. I was locked in on Jerry. He didn't sound exactly levelheaded. He and Eli were focused on each other.

"First off, maybe all hell needs to break loose here," I said, to break the glare-down. "When people are held down like this, they're going to rise up. Bad stuff will happen. There isn't any sweet, reasonable way to do this."

"This violence didn't have to happen," Jerry said, almost snarling. "I thought the bones of a saint would make the change . . . peaceful. We only have a *rumor* about the bones of Moses the Black, and everything is going to hell."

Eli didn't know what to say.

"What do you want?" I asked. Get it over with.

"I want you to bring the damn bones to town to see if you can calm things down."

As soon as Jerry Fielder left, I went to look out. For the first time, I noticed how quiet the hotel was. I didn't think there was anyone left who would have heard Jerry, even when he'd raised his voice a bit.

The hush was eerie, especially since there was so much noise outside. Since we'd come in the back way, we hadn't registered what was happening on the main street. I saw whites running down the sidewalk throwing their luggage into their cars, driving away like they were possessed. The reason? The street was sprinkled with little clusters of men armed to the teeth. Some clusters were white, some were black. None were mixed.

As I watched, a brawl started. Neither of these groups was carrying guns—yet—but there were rocks and two-by-fours and iron palings and baseball bats.

I didn't need to watch them slug it out. And they'd be running home to get their guns soon.

I went back to the room and nodded at Eli. "Bad outside," I said. "Jerry was right. All hell is breaking loose."

"We have to go back out to the Ballard place. We have to get a car."

"I know where one is."

"How so?"

"There's a man out on the front sidewalk, dead, right by a car with its door open. I'll get his car keys."

Before Eli could object, I ran out of the room and down the stairs. I had my gun in my hand and I looked both ways before I ran out to the body. Keys were still in the dead man's pocket, which was a stroke of luck.

The car was well-kept and old, an early model of the Celebrity Tourer that Eli and his late partner, Paulina, had rented for our trip to Mexico. It was a luxury car, with a panel in the roof you could fold back. That had already been done.

We piled in with all our possessions. We were not coming back to the Pleasant Stay. "You drive, I'll shoot," I said.

Getting to the road we'd followed before was not easy. For a while we were followed by a crowd of armed black people, who were ready to kick some white butt. I didn't blame them. There was no way for us to explain we were on their side.

No sooner had we gone fast enough to lose them than we were surrounded by a white group coming around a corner just as we passed through an intersection. They were angry because they were sure we were fleeing. "Stay and fight!" screamed one man, waving a rifle in our direction.

"This is depressing," Eli said.

That was not the word I was thinking of, but it was that, also. "At least we got away."

A brick hit the hood and bounced to the ground.

"Spoke too soon," I muttered, and Eli sped up.

I'd been threatened and chased. Someone would pay for the tension that was making my muscles tighten and my nerves hum.

When I saw a man running straight for the car with a burning bottle in his hand, I popped up through the roof and shot him. Lucky I did. The bottle blew up in his hand when he hit the ground.

Eli yelled. My gun going off had been a complete surprise. He hadn't seen the man coming, he'd been concentrating so hard on driving.

And that was why he needed me.

Eli was more alert to our surroundings after that. "Group coming up on the left," he said, steering closer to the curb on the right. I was up and pointing both guns at them before he finished. It was a group of black men and some women, too.

"It was her," one of the women shouted, and I recognized the maid, Myra, from the Ballard place. "She's good."

And they all halted in their tracks, and let us go by.

"Did she mean 'good' as in 'good shot,' or 'good' as in against the forces of evil?" Eli said.

"Don't know, don't care. As long as they held back." All of a sudden I felt how tired I was. It had been a long, long day and it was not yet over. We were on our way back to the Ballard house. I dreaded it.

At least some things I'd feared came to nothing. When we turned into the driveway, the men who'd tracked us were gone. The lawn and driveway were marked with the tire tracks of several cars or trucks, and there were footprints everywhere. A dog had been all over, I could smell the scent of its markings. There was a sad air hanging about the huge house.

"My car is still here," Eli said, wonder in his voice. "They didn't disable it."

"No one was around to tell them whose it was," I pointed out. "We can take it back to town when it's safe to go."

I got out of the car quick, keeping my eyes on the house. But no one appeared. The windows were empty.

We approached the porch slowly. Eli's hands were up, and so were my guns. Mary Ellen Ballard's body was no longer there. The wooden front door was still open. I pulled the screen door handle, and it made a terrible screech as it opened.

Eli made a quick step inside and to the right. I followed him, going to the left, letting the screen door bang shut behind me. Anyone alive would know we were in the house by now.

The wide hall had a chandelier hanging down. There were shadows everywhere. There was a dark red carpet with a pattern, there were a few upholstered chairs, a small table or two. A long mirror. I'd never been in a house this big and fancy. All I felt was gloom.

Nothing stirred. After waiting a long moment, we wandered through rooms as big as my house. One was real fancy, so I guessed it was the company parlor. A bathroom, but with just a toilet and sink, no tub. There was a dining room, I could tell from the furniture. There was a smaller room I decided must be a sitting room for the family itself. There was a big kitchen, a pantry containing a refrigerator, and a locked closet.

"Should I break it open?" I whispered. Then I wondered why I hadn't just asked out loud.

"No, it's for the family silver," Eli said, and I noticed that his voice was pretty low too.

Out the kitchen door on the north side of the house, there was a plain back porch where wooden chairs served for the help when they were shelling peas and so on. There may have been more, but that's what I saw. The last room I entered was a study, or library, or office.

"I'm going outside," Eli said from the hall, as if he'd spotted something that needed his attention. "Find the chest." I only nodded, not even turning to look at him. I wanted to keep my eyes ahead. There was something bad in this house.

I heard his footsteps fading away, sometimes muffled on the carpets, sometimes loud on the polished floor. I took off my own boots. I hoped nothing could hear me coming now.

The doors were all open, and most of the windows, too. In the study, the only sound came from the blessed breeze. It made the curtains ripple and it flipped at the corners of the papers on the study desk. Lucky there was a paperweight to hold 'em down. At the other end of the same room, someone had lowered a wounded white man onto a couch, removed his boots, and carefully placed those boots where he could see them.

But this man would never pull on his boots again. His face was slack and empty. I bent over to look at him, saw he'd died from a knife thrust to the belly. Made by a big knife, maybe a machete. The wound wasn't new. This wasn't the overseer Travis had killed.

His eyes opened, giving me the shock of my life.

"Watch out," he said. "Watch out." And he was gone for real.

My heart was thudding so hard I had to hold on to the edge of the desk. He was the fifty-ish man who'd been on the train in our car, watching us.

I gave the study a quick search. Nothing I found made any difference to me. Eli might find the letters of interest, but I wasn't about to take the time to read.

I spared a glance for the dead man, who was still dead, before I looked at the clock. With a dart of alarm, I realized I had not seen or heard from Eli for maybe ten minutes.

Yet something in the silence of the house made me not want to call out.

I was torn between running out to look for him and doing as he'd bid me. I reminded myself that Eli was as capable of defending himself as I was.

I went up the stairs as silently as I could.

## CHAPTER TWENTY-TWO

When I reached the landing, which looked out on the back of the house, I saw Eli through the large window. He was balanced on a ladder, and he was sawing at the rope that dangled Travis Seeley from the thick tree branch. When the rope severed, Eli lowered the body to the lawn, his magic making it float down gently . . . more or less. When Travis's corpse lay on the ground, a cloud of flies flew up in agitation.

Eli scrambled down the ladder and threw up.

I eased up the remaining stairs. Behind the first closed door, there was another set of stairs going to the attic where Juanita Poe had seen the chest. That's where I wanted to go. But before I did that, I had to make sure this floor was clear.

A guest bedroom was first. It was bright and dustless and empty. The next bedroom was for the son of the house, and there I had more luck.

A man I assumed was Holden Ballard lay in the large bed. His blood had seeped through the bandage around his chest. He was in bad shape, which pleased me. Harriet had stabbed him on the upper left, aiming for his heart. She'd almost made it. He might die yet. Ballard looked terrible, his color bad, his gray-sprinkled hair all rumpled. His sunken eyes opened just a bit when he realized someone was there. "Where is my mother?" he said. "Where is Myra? Or Juanita? Who are you? Hand me some water."

"No."

His eyes got all the way open in a hurry. "Dammit, give me some water, woman!"

"No." This was the man who had gotten my friend Galilee pregnant by raping her. This man was why she'd had to leave her parents and begin a new life in a new country.

"How does it feel to be in pain yourself?" I said, with some curiosity.

"It hurts, dammit. What do you think?" He shifted around a little, trying to get comfortable. "Who were all those men downstairs? I called and called, and no one heard me." He was angry about that. "For that matter, who the hell are you?"

"I'm a friend of Galilee Clelland."

Holden Ballard's face was blank for a minute. Then he said, "Galilee. I remember her. Where did she go?"

"She made you a daddy."

He looked confused for a minute. Then he looked disgusted.

That pretty much sealed his case.

I heard footsteps behind me. Two people.

I whipped around and found I was pointing my gun at Hosea and Reva Clelland. They were not the people I thought I'd see, and I was glad of it. "You got here just in time," I said.

"You come here the same reason we did?" Hosea was a little wheezy from the stairs.

"Hosea, Reva, take this woman's gun," Holden Ballard said. He sounded almost as wheezy as Hosea, though he was a good thirty years younger. His wound was killing him, but not fast enough.

"Not too likely," Reva said. "We come to kill you."

"It had crossed my mind, too," I said, and smiled at the old couple.

"You hold down his hands, we'll put a pillow over his face," Hosea said.

"I'd just as soon shoot him," I said. "That way, you can say you came out to help him and found him dead, if you have to."

Holden struggled to sit up. He was making all kinds of noises, but we ignored him. His ideas didn't count.

"Or here, sir," I said, holding out the gun to Hosea. He hesitated, and in that moment Reva took the gun and turned to the bed. Though I think it was a lucky shot, Reva killed Holden Ballard with one bullet. He was a mess afterward, but she didn't even flinch.

"Oh, thank you, Lord," Reva said. "That I lived to see this day."

That's where Galilee had gotten her quickness and her grit.

The two old people stood there for a long moment, amazed they'd got vengeance for their daughter.

When Reva and Hosea could move, they made their slow way out onto the landing. Reva handed my gun back as she passed. "Can you two do me a favor?" I said. "My friend Eli is around here somewhere. Last I saw him, he was cutting down the hung man. Can you watch the front in case someone else comes? I'll need to know. I have to go up to the attic."

"Yes, we'll sit on the front porch," Hosea said, his arm around his wife. "Won't no one surprise you." He and Reva started down, step by step.

I figured Eli would have been startled by the shot and come a-running, but he didn't show. I didn't like that.

After a moment of waiting, I went up the attic stairs. They were broad. The servants could carry big things up or down. But the boards were plain, no carpet or rail, and the stairs were steeper.

There wasn't a handrail. I hugged the left wall, carried one of my guns in my right hand. I kept my eyes focused upward. I was wavering on the edge of something, scared I'd fall. I'd seen a woman walk a wire once, strung between the grocery store and the jail. It had made a big impression.

The attic door was open. Light came through the unshuttered windows. Dust motes floated around lazily in the glow.

I mashed myself against the wall, staring in. There was no movement in my range of vision, but there was a corner of the attic I couldn't see. As silently as I could, I stepped across the landing and scanned the other side. Nothing.

It occurred to me, way too late, that I should have questioned Holden Ballard about the chest, how he'd gotten it. Too late now. And he wouldn't have told the truth, anyway.

I took a small breath and stepped into the room. And stopped dead.

In Texoma, we used everything till it broke. When it broke, we used the parts. But I saw that in Dixie, people like the Ballards put all their broken or outdated stuff into the attic. They thrust the smaller stuff against the walls where the roof was the lowest. The bigger stuff was in the middle. The room was jam-packed.

I felt helpless for a minute. Then I recalled the size of the crate. The chest could not be much smaller than the crate. It had only slid around inside a very little. So I set to searching. All the stuff in the attic blocked the light.

Since I needed all the help I could get (*Where was Eli?*) I pulled the string dangling from the lightbulb in the middle of the room, the point where the ceiling was highest. Then there was light, but there were also deeper shadows. And for a minute, the bulb rocked back and forth, and it looked like everything was moving, just a little.

I had to make myself stand still. I wanted to get out of this damn house. I took a deep breath and set my jaw.

Chairs, both grand and plain. A chest of drawers . . . or two. Old trunks, very dusty and square. A long, cracked mirror with its own stand. A battered bookcase, two children's desks.

I realized I was gasping for air, and made myself still my breathing. What was wrong with me? I was looking at old furniture! Then I caught up with my sense and glanced down at the floor. Two sets of footprints, both man-size, approaching one particular spot and returning. Both sets of tracks led to and away from a big sheet of canvas draped over a group of things. I carefully placed my own feet by the prints and that was where I ended up, just as I'd suspected. I flipped back the canvas sheet, and there, pushed up against a discarded wardrobe, was the chest. It was the only thing that wasn't dusty.

There was a half-dried puddle of blood in front of it. I thought instantly of the dead man on the couch downstairs. Who could have killed him? Holden put the trunk up in the attic before Harriet had gotten to him with her knife, which had been yesterday. This blood was fairly fresh, and the man on the sofa hadn't been lingering long. That kind of wound, you don't last more than a couple of hours.

Holden had not killed the man on the sofa. I tried hard to figure it out. But my brain was a tangle.

I knelt to deal with the lock on the trunk. But the lid opened with my first pull. I was looking down at a mess of cloth. Maybe once it had been fine stuff, and I could tell it had been blue. Now it was rotted. There were wads of it on either side, and what looked to be a single fold in the middle. I lifted it as careful as I could.

And there was Moses the Black.

Over the bones lay what had once been a short sword. There was blood on it. I caught my breath in a gasp.

The bones were ancient, but I could tell they'd been those of a big man.

Jammed in beside the bones was some kind of paper. It might once have been a Bible. Or almost anything. I reached in and touched a leg bone with one fingertip. This man had been a real person before he'd been a saint. He'd been a killer, like me.

I felt very strange. I made myself stand up. I had to push off a vanity table with a broken drawer. I propped myself against it. Something else was in the attic with me, and it was not happy.

"I don't want to steal your remains. I want to take them to the people in town who need you to lead them." I was talking to a chest full of ancient bones, but it didn't feel strange.

Next thing I knew, the bones and sword were gone and a man was standing between me and the trunk. He was big and very dark. I didn't know when I'd sunk to my knees, but I had a terrible hard time not bowing my head.

"Who are you?" he said.

If thunder could talk, its voice would be like his. Though this man—this saint—had died in Africa, I guess one language is universal. The language of death.

"Moses," I said, struggling because my lips were numb. "I'm one of the guards who brought your chest to Dixie, as a . . ." I struggled with how to say it. "As an inspiration for the black people here. They're treated a lot like slaves."

I forced my chin up. I looked into his terrible face. Something inside me relaxed. He was a fighter. I was a fighter.

Moses had long black hair mixed with gray, and a full beard. I didn't know if he'd straightened it somehow, or if his hair was naturally less curly than I was used to seeing on black people. Though a robe or tunic covered his chest and his legs to the knees, on visible skin he had scars from here to glory. Sword and knife wounds, looked like.

"Your bones were stolen from my crew," I said. "I was the only one able to look for you."

"Talking a lot," Moses the Black said.

I looked up at him sharply. I thought something you should never think about a saint. "I figured you might want to know why you were so far from Africa," I said in a real pointed way.

"There is no home for me anymore," he said, in a way I decided was a bit more civil. And a little sad.

"Your home is everywhere," I said. "You're a saint."

It was like a bass drum laughed. *Boom, boom, boom,* low and slow. "I am? Whose misguided choice was that?"

"The Russian church," I said.

He looked at me blankly.

"That came after you died." It didn't seem polite to mention his death, but I figured he was used to it.

"I stayed," Moses the Black said, as if he'd just remembered. "I stayed when the marauders were coming. Live by the sword, die by the sword."

I shrugged. I didn't know what else to do. I didn't know what marauders were.

"Now you're here, I wish you'd help," I told him.

"Petulant child," Moses said.

I bit the inside of my lip. I wasn't a damn dictionary. "Desperate woman is more like it. There is chaos in town."

"Is this your town?"

"No. I live in Texoma. We're in Dixie, the town is Sally. We got here on a train."

"You guarded my remains?"

"Yes. But the train wrecked, and I got shot, and my boss got his throat cut, and Charlie died. Maddy still ain't—isn't—good to walk, and Rogelio was a traitor. My friend the grigori showed up—he's on your side—and now I don't know where he is."

"I understood almost none of that."

"Can you come talk to two of your people on the front porch, and then we can go into town to help 'em out? I'll give you a ride if you need." Maybe he could fly. "I'm gonna run and look for Eli."

"There are Ethiopians on the front porch?" Moses the Black rumbled. He now looked as solid as I did.

"Yes," I said. "Descendants of slaves."

The big man followed me down the stairs and out the front door. I could hear his footsteps. I could not hear him breathing. He was barefoot, but he carried the sword in his right hand. It wasn't real long or real skinny.

Pretty much the size of blade that had caused the wounds of the unknown man on the sofa.

I could not imagine the bones forming together and making the man, scraps of iron creating the sword—surely a monk had not been buried with a sword?—in time to kill the human man standing over it. That was outside my world.

Reva and Hosea were sitting in the rocking chairs only white people had ever used before. They seemed quite comfortable until they looked up to see my companion, and then they slid out of their chairs and onto their poor old knees. Maybe fear is a joint lubricant. Moses looked down at them and his stern face softened.

"My children," Moses rumbled. "Do you know me?"

"We know you are a holy man," Reva said, after a cautious pause. "I'm sorry, we don't know your name, sir."

"I am Moses the Black," he said.

"Oh!" she said. Reva seemed too overcome to say anything more. But her husband said, "This white lady came to help us, and now her friends are dead. She almost got killed. Please, sir, let her keep healthy and help get our community out of this mess we're in."

I appreciated Hosea's kind words while I pulled on my boots. But I was so anxious about Eli that I couldn't stay, even for a saint.

While the three talked, I eased down the steps and around the vast house. The sky was darkening. I saw the leaves of the trees and bushes stirring. The same breeze, which promised rain, also brought me the terrible reek of Travis Seeley's body.

I turned to look up at the house. No faces at any windows. The fields to either side of the house were flat, empty of anything taller than cotton. And I couldn't imagine Eli, for any reason, returning to the bayou, which was the only cover in sight.

Except the cabins.

I had to get near to the body after all.

The ground was hard and dry, and there were so many scuffs and prints under the tree that trying to pick out Eli's seemed useless. But I held my hand over my nose and mouth while I tried to make out what the prints were telling me. Finally, I picked out one toe mark I was pretty sure was Eli's. Then I followed it. There went Eli, away from the body, walking on the dirt path that led to the white-washed cabins. The cabins had been made to look pretty, with their paint and pretty flowers, but they didn't even have running water. There was a pump smack in the middle, a bucket lying on its side underneath.

Why would Eli go out here?

Maybe he'd heard something, or seen movement where there shouldn't have been any. I could search each cabin, one by one. Or I could try something else.

"Eli!" I called. "Eli! I found the chest. Moses the Black is here."

The door of the second cabin jerked open and out Eli came, not of his own choice. He was shoved. Sarah Byrne was hiding behind him, and she had a gun to his back.

Ah. This I understood.

"Listen, Lizbeth!" Sarah shouted. "I'm getting out of here! This Eli is going to drive me to town, and then I'll let him go. You won't see me again." She leaned out from behind Eli, just a sliver, to see how I was taking her proposal.

I shot her through the forehead.

"You got that right," I said.

# CHAPTER TWENTY-THREE

I could tell Eli was glad to be rescued because his shoulders kind of sagged.

"How the hell did she get the jump on you?" I said. I didn't know whether to slap him or hug him, so I didn't do either.

"After I got through being sick, I saw there was a pump out here, and I wanted to wash out my mouth," Eli said. "Next thing I knew, there she was."

"You missed a few things."

"Did you say Moses the Black was here?"

"He came out of the trunk."

Eli stared down into my face. "He . . . manifested?"

"If that's what you call becoming a real person with a real sword, yes."

"Where is he?"

"On the front porch, talking to Reva and Hosea."

"Galilee's parents?"

"Yep. They came out here to kill Holden."

"Holden Ballard."

"Catch up, Eli! Yes, Holden Ballard. Remember, Harriet said she got him with her knife?"

Eli nodded. He was still looking at me kind of doubtfully, like he wasn't sure if I was making all this up.

I never made stuff up.

"So Holden's dead now. And I went up to the attic, and the trunk was still there, and I opened it."

"And his bones?"

"Were still there. And a sword, about in the same shape as the bones. And what used to be a book or a scroll. Writing, anyway."

"He has the sword?"

"Yes."

"What about the book?"

"I don't know."

We walked around the house. I had wondered if Moses would disappear just to make me look a liar, but he was still there. The sword was in a scabbard at his side. I hadn't noticed that before, the scabbard. Hosea and Reva were still on their knees.

Eli stopped dead.

"I guess we'd better kneel," I muttered, and down we went. On the gravel driveway, this was not comfortable. With a lot of effort, I met Moses's eyes, which were deep as wells and just as dark. The wind picked up around us, and loose strands of Eli's hair whipped around his face. His braid was coming undone.

"Saint Moses, this is my friend Eli, a wizard of the Holy Russian Empire."

Moses didn't say anything.

"The Russians found you, remember? Brought you here?"

"Stand. This makes me feel ridiculous." His big hands reached down to Hosea and Reva, and in a jiffy they were up.

I scrambled to my feet, giving Eli a side look to make sure he was doing the same.

"You are a priest?" Moses rumbled at Eli.

Real thunder sounded, far away. The clouds were advancing from the east, and the sky was darkening.

"I am a grigori, a wizard, in service to the tsar. The Russian ruler."

I'd never heard Eli sound so formal, so awed. He was a true Orthodox believer. He'd never talked about that; I hadn't known.

What Moses the Black would have said in reply I will never know. Reva had latched on to the important thing.

"Moses," Reva said. "We have to get you to town. That's where you're needed." Her rusty voice was strong and sure. Hosea stood behind her, his hands on her bony shoulders.

Moses the Black laughed. "Let us go," he said.

He couldn't fly, it seemed. I was disappointed when he had to get in the car to be driven. I never thought I'd chauffeur a saint. I drove Moses in the car Eli and I had stolen. Reva and Hosea rode with Eli in his car. It seemed like a much shorter trip back to town.

Sally was in chaos.

Picking among clumps of brawling people, mostly men, we made it back to the courthouse. Fighting was especially intense there because of all the open space. There was a lot of gunfire, and lots of bodies. I'd never seen anything on this scale. This was a little war.

We all got out and waited for whatever the saint decided to do.

I figured Moses would weigh in with his sword, and I was looking forward to seeing that. He would step on the bodies piling up.

What happened instead was completely different.

Moses began singing. Didn't make no nevermind whether his voice itself was beautiful, made no nevermind what he was singing. I felt my scalp tingle all over. Was this a church-type miracle? Was this magic like Eli had? No one besides me seemed to be asking any questions.

Hosea and Reva went to stand by him, their arms spread at shoulder level, floating in the voice. Eli came to stand by me, and he put his arm around my shoulders.

Rolling out from the sound of the saint's voice, the fighting stopped. I could watch the progress of it, like a wave. All up and down the street, people came walking, staggering, bleeding, carrying all kinds of sharp things, and guns, and crowbars. And they came side by side, not trying to kill one another.

Not even looking at one another.

Not talking to one another.

And they kept coming.

This would have been the time I started shooting, if they'd been hostile. But they weren't. They were empty: not angry, or terrified, or vengeful.

But I was relieved *and* angry at the same time. I wasn't under the same spell everyone else was. Neither was Eli.

That was something I should have been thinking about.

I should have been wondering what was going to happen next.

But no matter what I'd guessed, I would have been wrong.

Instead of telling the black people who had been stolen from Africa that they were free and equal to the white people, instead of advising the former slaves to rise up and take over the property of their former owners, Moses told the whole crowd, "You must love one another."

The skies opened and the rain fell. And they all laid down their weapons.

# CHAPTER TWENTY-FOUR

T his is just spooky," I said. We were sitting on the hood of Eli's Carrier, parked by the car I'd stolen. It was pouring rain, and we were as wet as we could be. But there was so much to watch.

The people of Sally had begun to straighten up their town. They had shaken hands with one another, then cooperated with piling the bodies in the back of a two-ton truck and pushing abandoned cars off the streets.

Then they'd faded away. We were almost alone at the recent battleground.

"I wonder where Felix is," Eli said. He hadn't spoken in a long time.

"Do you think Felix did this?" Though I'd had a wonder or two when Eli and I hadn't become lovey like all the other people, I still hoped this was God doing stuff.

"Moses the Black hasn't moved in twenty minutes," Eli said. That wasn't an answer.

"Yep." I hadn't had much else to look at. We were sitting in the rain watching a saint turn into a statue.

I slid off the car hood and went over to Moses. I was watching him at every step. His eyes did not move to track me. His black skin was smooth and hard to the touch. The sword in his hand had turned into a scroll that read, *Turn away from violence and love your fellow man.* So he'd had the book after all, tucked under his robe.

I thought about this piece of advice. I didn't often *begin* the violence. And I loved *some* of my fellow men and women. That didn't seem too bad a start.

"What do you want to do now?" Eli asked from right behind me. He reached out a finger, as I'd done, and touched Moses's shoulder.

"You reckon everything is over?" I would have to check to make sure Maddie would be able to mend and go home. Charlie dead. Rogelio dead. Jake dead. Harriet, who knew? Travis, dead. Sarah, dead. The contents of the chest (standing before us and looking serious, maybe forever) recovered and delivered.

"I don't know." Eli put his arm around me again. "I'm thinking about it."

Leaving this town, leaving Dixie, would be great. But I would also be leaving Eli. I sighed real heavy.

"What's the matter?" he asked me.

At the edge of my vision, I caught a movement, and I was shoving Eli down as I heard the shot. I stood over him, my Colt in my hand, firing.

Then nothing. Nothing moved. I crouched over Eli in the rain, which had turned to a light mist. I ran my free hand over him without glancing down. "You okay?" I said. I was keeping watch.

But he didn't answer.

I glanced down to see blood soaking his shirt and vest.

I needed help. Fast. "I got a man down!" I yelled, hoping someone could hear me. "I need a doctor!"

"Do you need help?" a voice answered from maybe thirty feet away. Coming from the trees.

"Yes," I called back, but I felt this wasn't someone who wanted to help at all. "Eli's been hit," I added, hoping the voice would answer, so I could get a better fix on it.

Mr. Mercer from the hotel rounded a car maybe ten feet away, his arm already up with a gun in it. I fired before he could. And I fired more accurately.

His bullet missed me by a foot.

Mine did not miss him.

I went to him to be sure. His eyes were open and filled with hate.

"I guess you have magic blood too," I said. "You can resist Moses's message of love the same way Eli and I can. No wonder you hate us so much."

I turned and went back to Eli. I found I didn't care if Mercer was dead or not, as long as he was down. It was hard and took longer than I wanted, but I managed to get Eli into the back seat of the stolen car—the owner wasn't going to need it again—and drove to Ballard Memorial Hospital. I followed the signs to the emergency entrance. I honked the horn until the double doors opened. Two men in orderly white came out, but they weren't moving fast enough to suit me.

"Move faster than that, or die," I said, showing them a Colt.

"No call for that," said the larger one. "We'll hurry."

And they did, skillfully getting Eli out of the back of the car and onto a stretcher, with a little help from me.

"You need to move this car while we take him in," the smaller orderly said. "We're gonna take care of him now."

I did move the car into a parking space. Ran into the hospital. Noticed it had quit raining. Got stopped by a nurse behind a desk, who had paperwork.

There hadn't been any new patients for an hour, since Moses

had sung, the admissions nurse told me. "You're lucky—the doctors have just finished operating and stitching and bandaging. We've been busy all afternoon."

"If I was lucky, Eli wouldn't have been shot," I said, and she began filling out forms real quickly.

The two orderlies had carried Eli into an examination cubicle—I could just see the end of the table from where I stood—and a doctor (name tag read GIMBALL) and a nurse (ALLEN) were already on either side of Eli, whose eyes were closed. The nurse began cutting off Eli's shirt, while the doctor listened to his chest, asked Eli questions he didn't answer, and began to examine the bullet hole.

The canvas curtains were drawn around the booth beside Eli's. From the sounds, a woman was having a baby.

"Are you the wife?" Nurse Allen called. She was stocky and middle-aged. She looked tired. I signed the last piece of paper and ran over.

"I am," I said, and gasped like someone had stuck me with a needle. I landed back in my body from wherever I'd been.

"You all right?" Nurse Allen's heavy face was creased with concern.

"Yes, ma'am. Just work on him! Please!"

"We'll take care of your husband. Please take a chair outside."

I didn't want to leave Eli, but there was no room in the cubicle, even I could see that. I collapsed into a wooden chair against a wall opposite the canvas she pulled across. I could hear the doctor talking to the nurse, but I couldn't understand what he was saying.

From my pocket I pulled the healing spell Eli had been trying to teach me. I began chanting the words just under my breath. The spell flowed out, all the words making sense to me. I kept it up, over and over, while I heard Dr. Gimball give orders to Nurse Allen. After twenty times, I had to stop for a minute.

So this time, I heard what they said.

"Bullet's still in there. Where's Dr. Fielder when you need him? Have you seen him, Nurse Allen?" Dr. Gimball was grouchy and tired.

There was a heavy little pause.

"I'm sorry to spread bad news, Dr. Gimball. Dr. Fielder went home to check on his wife, and someone had thrown a brick through their window. It hit Millie. She's not conscious. Nurse Mayhew lives down the street, and she ran over when she heard him yell. He's not going to leave her until he knows she's going to recover."

"Poor fellow." Dr. Gimball seemed more curious than grieved.

"You taking the surgery?" Nurse Allen asked, after a respectful pause.

"I have to. I guess I have one more left in me."

This did not inspire confidence. I doubled down on my chanting. I had my hands together, just in case. When Nurse Allen stepped from behind the curtain, she said with approval, "That's the way to ask for help."

"You going to operate?"

"Dr. Gimball has to get the bullet out. We'll take him into the operating theater, prepare him for surgery, and then the anesthesiologist will make sure he stays asleep." She explained all this as if she had done it twenty times today. I figured maybe she had.

"How long do you think it will take?" I asked her, my voice sounding stiff and odd to my own ears. Inside, I said, *If he doesn't live, I'll kill you all*. If I told her that out loud, she might not be more skillful, but she would sure be more shaky.

"At least an hour, maybe two," Nurse Allen said. "There's a lounge down the hall, opposite the operating theater."

"Thank you," I said. "I got to go do some things, but I'll be back within an hour." I looked directly in her pale eyes. "Don't let him die."

Those eyes widened, and I saw that she understood me.

"He'll live," she said, struggling to sound calm.

I raised my eyebrows to let her know he'd better. And I left the hospital.

When I got back to the courthouse, Mercer's body was still there. He was for sure dead, now.

I went over to the statue. "You could have told us your song wouldn't work on us," I said. "Did you know that would happen?"

I didn't really expect Moses the Black to explain this to me, and he didn't. I wondered if he'd ever walk and talk again.

I was leaving the stolen-from-a-dead-man car, with its rear seat stained with blood. Nellie Mercer was standing beside it. She looked like she'd been dragged through a bush backward. She was scratched and disheveled. But she wasn't armed.

I waited to see what she would say.

"We were wrong." She tilted her head and looked at me. "You were right."

"I am sorry about your father," I said. I nodded to her, stepped around her, and left.

This day had been one surprise after another. I had expected Moses the Black to bring a sword. He had, but he had changed it into words that would alter the way people thought. I hoped that would last, but I wasn't putting money down one way or another.

It was beyond my responsibility, and I was glad of that.

I reloaded my guns, got my rifle out of the trunk and put it under the front seat where I could reach it. Then I drove back to the hospital.

## CHAPTER TWENTY-FIVE

Eli came out of surgery about thirty minutes after I'd returned to the waiting room. There had been a few other people slumped in the chairs that lined the wall, and they'd all looked exhausted . . . but not too tired to give me a long stare.

I was past trying to pretend I was a Dixie woman, and our mission was over here.

After a nurse came out smiling to talk to him, a man with two children left. I figured he'd been waiting to hear about the woman giving birth. Beaming, he took the kids' hands and off they went.

A white-haired man, slumped in the corner, had fallen asleep. No one but me was awake and waiting. It was black outside the window.

Harriet Ritter walked into the waiting room. She'd had a chance to clean up sometime recently. She had fresh clothes, her hair was done, her shoes were polished. Once again, she was wearing confidence like a dog wears hair.

"Why are you here?" I said.

"What do you mean? I've been looking for you. I spotted the car outside, so I walked around the hospital until I found you."

"Why?" I asked again.

"Has something happened to Eli?"

I nodded. "They're getting a bullet out."

The Iron Hand agent looked as unsettled as I'd ever seen her. "I'm sorry for my part in this," Harriet said. "When we took the job of watching your crew, we didn't know what you had. We did know how the Ballards were, though. And our job was only to watch, because Mrs. Ballard wanted to know who was going to receive the chest, so she could take care of them."

My brain wasn't sparking after the long day, but a question drifted up. "You said you and Travis fired on the men attacking our car, after the wreck. Were you lying?"

"No. We took care of two of them, at least. We didn't know if the Ballards had sent them, or someone else. No one told us not to interfere. So we did."

"But . . . you went out to that awful house when Mrs. Ballard summoned you. What did you expect would happen?"

"We expected we'd get a chance to explain to Mrs. Ballard. By then we had realized what a mistake Iron Hand had made taking a job from the Ballards."

I looked at her with some doubt. Harriet flushed.

"We got our payback for being stupid," she said.

True enough.

"Sorry about Travis," I said. I waited to see how she would take that.

Harriet looked like her face was made of iron. "I'm going to find that Sarah Byrne. I'm going to kill her slowly. After she cut Jake's throat and grabbed the chest, she was spied by a man who worked for the Ballards. He told Holden, and Holden drove into town, picked her up, brought her and the chest out to the plantation. He paid her off big-time, asked her to stick around to help out. She was there when we arrived. She was waiting to get behind us with her gun."

"You don't need to look for her."

After a moment of silence, Harriet shook her bright head. "So I won't have the satisfaction of killing her myself. At least the bitch is dead."

We sat quietly, waiting together. "What will you do now?" she asked.

"I got to find out how Eli is. After that, I may have to help him get home," I said. "Then I'll go back to Segundo Mexia."

"I may not have mentioned that I own a chunk of Iron Hand," Harriet said.

That was more startling news, but I was too tired to give it much energy. "No, I don't believe you said anything about that."

Harriet smiled. "You need a job, you come see me. Our headquarters are in Britannia, in North Carolina."

That explained the accent. "I appreciate your offer."

"I'll wait with you until the doctor comes," Harriet said. And she did.

We sat without speaking until Dr. Gimball came in. His white apron was bloody. Eli's blood. "Mrs. Savarov," he said. "Your husband is out of surgery."

"Okay," I said, to show I was listening.

"I got the bullet out. I stopped the bleeding."

I nodded.

"The bullet didn't hit anything vital. I sewed him up again. I think he'll be all right."

Harriet patted my shoulder and left. I exhaled, felt everything inside me relax. "What now?" I said.

"Lots of bed rest," Gimball said. "No stairs, no walking for a few days. You can give him a sponge bath, but avoid the area of the incision. He'll be taking antibiotics to avoid infection. I want to keep him in the hospital for two days, and then you can take him home. I'll want to drop by to see him again, two days after that."

I wondered where I was supposed to take Eli. Where I could spend the night, for that matter. No matter what apology Nellie had given me, I didn't want to go back to the Pleasant Stay; besides, it had stairs, which would be bad for Eli when he got out of the hospital. Of course, the Ballards' house was empty now. That was an awful thought. I bit my lip to suppress a crazy giggle.

"Do you know a place I can take Eli until he can travel?" I was not happy about asking, but I didn't have the energy to scour Sally, which I wanted to leave at the first opportunity.

Nurse Allen, who'd come out of the room where Eli was—at least, I figured so—said, "I don't know about anything other than tonight, but I have an extra bedroom at my house, and that's where I'm headed now."

"I sure appreciate the offer," I said.

"I'll be ready to go as soon as I hand off to the night nurse."

"Can you show me where Eli is, first?"

Nurse Allen took me to a two-bed room not far from the operating theater. He hadn't been wheeled past me, so there must be another way out of the operating theater.

Eli was in the bed closest to the door. The curtain was drawn between him and the other sufferer. I stood looking at him, biting my lower lip, trying not to cry. Eli had bandages all around his chest. He was white as a sheet. He smelled like medicine.

I stood by him for a long time, watching his chest go up and down. Then I pulled the wooden chair up to the bed and sat, my hand on his. Then I lay my head on the bed, and I slept.

"Mrs. Savarov?"

It was a gentle voice, a woman's. I was on my feet in a snap, my hand on my gun.

Nurse Allen stood her ground, giving me a very disapproving look.

"Yes?" I said, relaxing a little.

"Let's go."

"Who'll be on duty tonight?"

"Nurse Underwood."

A tall woman stepped out from behind Allen. She had her hair up in a bun behind her white nurse's cap. She looked strong.

"Mrs. Savarov," she began in a smooth voice, "we let you stay longer under the circumstances, but you have to go now. I promise you I'll call Nurse Allen's house if there's any change in Mr. Savarov's condition."

"I need to take all Eli's possessions with me."

Both women looked surprised.

"When he gets out of the hospital, I'll bring 'em back, clean."

Underwood went to a narrow closet by Eli's bed and pulled out a bag. "Everything he was wearing, it's in this bag," she said.

My arms full of Eli's clothes and boots, I turned back to the bed. I was self-conscious because the two nurses were standing there. After I looked down at Eli for a long moment, I bent over and whispered in his ear, "I'll be back tomorrow morning."

And I followed Nurse Allen out of the hospital.

"We need the car?" I asked.

"No. It's a block away."

So we walked. It was easy to see the nurse was worn out by the way her shoulders slumped. She turned in to a little house, and I could tell it was neat as a pin by the light of the street lamp. She unlocked the front door, and then we were in a tiny living room with shining polished furniture.

Nurse Allen said, "I'm not being real hospitable because I'm dead on my feet. You need anything in the kitchen, you're welcome to it. Here's the guest bedroom. Here's the bathroom. I'm in the room across the hall if you need me, but I pray you don't."

"Thanks again, and good night," I said, turning in to the room she'd pointed to as mine. It was small, but I didn't care. I waited to hear her go into the bathroom, and when I figured she was in bed, I took my own turn, leaving it as clean as I'd found it.

Before I climbed in the bed, I checked the window to make sure it was locked. The bed creaked and shook with age. I had my guns beside me. The night was cool enough that I didn't have to turn on the fan.

It felt incredibly good to lie down.

I tried to think over the day. Too much had happened to remember all of it in the weariness of the moment. I didn't feel well, and I realized I hadn't had anything to eat in many hours. But I couldn't imagine trying to find food, or even getting up from this bed, and that was the last thought I had before I said hello to sleep.

# CHAPTER TWENTY-SIX

I t was full light in the morning when I woke. I was real hungry. I got dressed, made the bed, went to the bathroom. Loaded myself down again with everything, including Eli's clothes, which were still dirty. I hadn't had the energy to wash them. The shirt couldn't be mended anyway.

The house was silent.

I wondered if Nurse Allen was already at the hospital, or if she had the day off and planned to catch up on her sleep. I left a five-dollar bill on her kitchen table to thank her, and I left as quietly as I could.

My plan was to eat breakfast and go see Eli at the hospital. I would have all day to figure out what we'd do next. I stowed Eli's stuff in the car as I passed, and it felt good to have my hands free.

There were only a few people in the nearest restaurant. Maybe people were scared to come out after the day before. The waitress looked kind of jumpy, but at least the place was open for business, so I ignored that. I drank as many cups of coffee as the waitress would pour. I also packed in the pancakes and eggs and bacon.

I got to the hospital just a bit before visitor's hours. I couldn't see anyone over the counter barricading the duty nurse from the public. But I looked over it to see a woman slumped over the desk, asleep.

I froze in place.

Hospitals are noisy places.

But I couldn't hear a sound.

I leaned against the wall and slipped off my boots. I went to Eli's room very quickly, very quietly, my socks padding over the boards.

There was someone bending over Eli when I eased the door open, a short man wearing a hospital gown. In another second the man had a gun in the back of his skull.

"You idiot!" said Felix, keeping his voice low but mean. "I'm here to get him out before they kill him."

"Last night he was doing fine. They made me leave. I came back this morning and everything's strange."

"I'm going to turn around really slow," Felix told me.

"Arms away from your sides." Just in case he ... where were his clothes? Why was he dressed in a gown like Eli's?

Felix actually did what I told him, to my surprise. He turned around as slowly as I could have wanted. But then he snarled, "Where did you spend the night? Did you find some other man?"

"Could you be any more of a ..." I couldn't think of a word bad enough. I took a small step back, all that the room allowed, and said, "I stayed in Nurse Allen's extra bedroom."

"What was she like when you left this morning?"

"Too quiet. I didn't see her or hear her."

"I hope she's alive," Felix said.

"Why wouldn't she be? Has Dr. Gimball been by?" I asked, still keeping my voice very low.

"Yes." Felix smiled broadly, but there wasn't any mirth in it at all.

"What did he say?"

"He tried to kill Eli."

"Where is he? The doctor?"

Felix said, "He's dead. I put him in my bed." Jerked his chin toward the curtain around the other bed next to the window.

"You killed Eli's doctor?"

"I told you, woman. He was going to kill Eli."

"Why didn't he just mess up the operation last night?"

"Too many eyes on him, I suppose. I think Nurse Allen is a good woman, or at least an upright one."

"What are you going to do if I holster my gun?" My arm was tired. Also, I was feeling silly, because I believed Felix was telling the truth. Though it didn't make sense.

"I'm going to tell you to help me get Eli out of this place before someone else shows up to kill him. I can't keep everyone asleep forever. And the other grigoris are coming nearer every moment."

That tipped me over onto Felix's side. I stared into Felix's little brown eyes, wanting—real hard—to call him a liar and hit him in the head. But I couldn't do it. "Get your clothes," I said.

Felix disappeared behind the curtain and reappeared within five minutes, fully dressed. Since I didn't want to have to kill any of the nurses, I was relieved. Eli's color was better than yesterday, but he still seemed to be unconscious.

"Why isn't he awake?" I asked Felix, since he was being so quick with the answers this morning.

"He will be soon," Felix said, real shortly.

"Where were you wounded?" I said, suddenly realizing I ought to know why Felix was in the hospital.

"I became unconscious," Felix said. "Too much magic use."

In other words, he had fainted.

"You full strength now?"

"No. Close enough."

"Should I get a stretcher for Eli?"

"We should put his arms over our shoulders and walk him out. They'll all be waking up soon. Except for Dr. Gimball." Felix actually smiled.

"The car is out front."

"Drive around to the back door."

I set off down the hall again. I gave the reception nurse a sideways glance. She hadn't moved, but her fingers twitched. I took a fast detour into the women's ward. Maddy looked a lot better. I put half my money into her hand. Then I ran.

I pulled up under the awning at the emergency entrance. Two orderlies were sitting on wooden chairs outside the big doors, sound asleep. One was white and one was black. Surely that was unusual; maybe Moses the Black had made a lasting difference, here in Sally, at least.

I jumped out of the car, leaving the doors open to be ready for anything. I hurried inside, to find Felix sort of dragging Eli. Felix was so short and Eli so tall that it would have been comical . . . if anything could have been. I ducked under Eli's free arm and took my share of the weight. We moved much faster. When we came to the door, I pushed with my left and we sidled sideways out under the awning. Eli stirred at the brightness.

We shifted Eli into the back seat. I was getting good at the maneuver. He was lying down, as much as we could arrange him. His knees had to be drawn up a bit. Felix got in the passenger's seat, and I scrambled behind the wheel, put the car in gear, and off we took.

In the rearview mirror, I saw one of the orderlies rub his face. I made my turn out of the parking lot very smooth and slow, because the last thing I wanted to look like was fugitives escaping.

"Do you have a goal?" I figured I better find out.

"Get out of this town as fast as we can without attracting any attention."

I could do that. For a few minutes we were silent as we drove through the streets of Sally. The town was not silent, like the hospital, but it was what I'd call subdued. Despite the cleanup of the big objects yesterday—cars and bodies—there was still plenty of evidence of the violence: broken windows, overturned trash cans. But the rain had washed away all the blood.

The statue of Moses the Black stood in front of the courthouse as if it had always been there. People of both races were standing before it, gazing upward at the terrible and beautiful face.

I drove real careful. After what seemed like way too long, I was on the highway west out of Sally. There was still debris scattered in the field where the train had crashed, but there was a crew at work laying new tracks.

"You put everyone at the hospital to sleep," I said. I'd been thinking.

"Sleep is like a form of death," Felix said, without opening his eyes. I'd been sure he wasn't asleep.

I finally understood. Felix was a death wizard. He could kill. And he could reanimate the dead.

"That gave you control over the bones of Moses the Black."

Felix nodded.

"You made him stab the man we found on the couch."

He nodded again. "If the trunk was opened by an enemy, that

was going to happen. I thought it might come to be seen as the first miracle. When the story was told."

I felt a rising tide of anger. "He might have stabbed me. You weren't there in the attic, were you?" I pictured Felix crouching beside some of the broken furniture under the canvas sheet.

He opened his eyes and slid his gaze over to me. "No. All that time? No."

"So how come Moses didn't kill me, too?"

Felix did sit up then. The full weight of his gaze was on me. I didn't like that at all. "Wasn't Eli with you?"

"No. I was alone." Eli had been outside being taken hostage by Sarah.

"You were alone. But the spell recognized you. That's very interesting."

Well, shit. Felix now knew I had grigori blood.

I couldn't think of anything to say. I wasn't going to beg him to keep silent. I wasn't going to kill him, not after he had saved Eli.

Seemed he wasn't going to kill me, either.

We had to stop for gas thirty minutes later. The kid who came out to pump the gas and check the oil was full of the amazing happenings in Sally—that blacks there were equal with whites, that some foreign god had made it happen.

"Sure gives you food for thought, when God tells you to alter your ways," I said.

The kid could not bring my change fast enough.

Off we went again. I had a lot of questions I wanted to ask Felix, but he was truly asleep now. I looked back at Eli pretty often, and it seemed to me he was lying more naturally. Eli had been sent to sleep by Felix's spell just like a regular person; I figured it was because he was weakened by his wound. I thought it was good he slept. He would be hurting when he woke. But I was worried.

It was lucky the road was clear when I heard Eli say, "Lizbeth? Where are you?"

I pulled over and parked and opened the door behind me. Eli was struggling to sit up. I helped him and climbed in beside him. He leaned against me and held my hands. We didn't speak for a little while. Then, because I knew the other wizard was awake, I said, "Felix is here. He got you out of the hospital. With me helping."

"Felix?" Eli's voice was weak.

"Yeah. Felix."

"I think he killed the doctor this morning."

"He did."

"Why?"

"He says the doctor was going to kill you." I kept my voice going right down the middle.

"I had no idea," Eli said, and his tone was the same.

"You see Felix in the front seat? He said we need to get out of Sally now that our job is done."

"Felix?" Eli said.

"I'm right here, Eli."

"Why are we leaving town? I was supposed to stay to see what happened after the arrival of Moses the Black."

"I had to get you out of there as soon as possible. That's what I am doing, with the help of your charming friend. You knew she could resist magic spells?"

If Felix was trying to be casual, he missed his target.

Eli had not told anyone. He had kept a secret I had not even dared to ask him to. With a lot of neck-twisting, I looked him in the eyes.

"Are you sure?" he said now, looking back. "Maybe she is just lucky. Gunnies often are."

"Or else they're dead gunnies," I said, making myself sound cheerful and stupid.

"I have to get out and relieve myself," Eli said, sounding like he was apologizing for something.

"Sure." I scooted out, reached in to help him.

It took some shifting around to get Eli out of the car. Felix didn't offer to help. Whether he knew I'd seen all of Eli (who was still in the hospital gown) and that wouldn't bother me, or whether he planned to steal the car while we were out of it, *something* was going on, and I didn't understand what it was.

"The car," Eli gasped as we moved a few feet away behind a tree. He was in pain.

"I got the keys," I said. "And I got my guns."

I lifted Eli's hospital gown for him. When I saw it was all he could do to lean up against the tree without aid, I held his dick. With a sigh of relief, he let go. When he was done, I took the opportunity to squat and do the same. Eli eased around the tree to keep an eye on the car.

Since Eli remained silent, I took it that Felix was behaving. Of course, maybe he was behaving because I had the car keys. Or an invisible someone might have snuck up and stabbed him while I was holding Eli's dick.

I couldn't help but think that would solve a lot of problems.

When I was put back together, I tucked myself under Eli's arm and we began working our way out of the woods and back to the road. Eli was already tired after that short side trip into the trees.

"Hey, I even said the healing spell on you about a million times while they were operating," I said, trying to sound cheerful. "Guess I am not such a good half-grigori after all."

"It's bad that Felix knows," Eli said.

"I don't know what I did to make him suspect, except not get killed by Moses the Black. Oh, I didn't fall under the singing spell. Do you want me to kill Felix?"

Eli kissed the top of my head as we moved slowly onto the road. He was shaking all over now. "You are wonderful to offer," he said. "But we'll keep on as we are, until he wants us to do something we know will lead to our imprisonment or death."

I had never thought of imprisonment. The idea made my stomach curdle. I hadn't been in jail before, much less a prison. Take that back—I'd been in jail once, overnight, due to a case of mistaken identity. More or less. Being locked in a cell, unarmed, with people I didn't know . . . I was a good fist-fighter, but I was small with a short reach. Size matters, in a fistfight.

"Have you always fought with magic? Or have you been in any kind of brawl where you had to use your hands?" I asked Eli, just as we got to the car door.

"I hit other boys when I was small," he whispered. "Before I found that I had magic ability. Are you asking if I can still do that?"

"Yes."

"Some days there is nothing I would like better than to hit someone square on the chin. But then I think of what we were taught, that magic users should think it below them to use their bodies to fight."

"Don't you *ever* think any form of fighting is below you," I said seriously. "You weigh in there with whatever you got."

"All right," he whispered.

Eli was about to fold up, so I opened the rear door—thinking a little help from Felix would have been welcome—and got him in. But I looked at Felix as I was about to close the door. "Eli," I said. "Felix is dead."

Eli was so done in it took him a minute to gather up the idea. "Shake him," he said. "I didn't do anything to him. You didn't do anything?"

"No. You're the boss, and you said not to." I opened Felix's door and looked in. "He's absolutely dead," I told Eli. Just for form's sake I put my fingers to Felix's neck. "*Shit*," I said with disgust. "I had twenty questions I wanted to ask him. When he felt better."

"He was ill?"

"He said he'd been unconscious last night because he used so much magic in resurrecting Moses the Black. And then turning him into a statue. Maybe this morning, killing Dr. Gimball and putting everyone at the hospital to sleep so we could get you out . . . maybe that was too much."

Eli slumped against the doorframe. "Lift my arm," he said.

"Put it where?"

"On Felix's neck."

"We were just talking about killing him! I don't want both of you dead from your own magic overuse."

"Do it."

Eli sounded pretty stern. I said a few things to myself, but I lifted his arm and blessed the length of it. I put Eli's big hand on Felix's neck, still warm.

"Keep your hand on top of mine."

I pressed his fingers hard. And I felt Eli's magic flicker into being, run through me like I was an electric cord, and magnify through my strength into something big and powerful. It passed into the blood vessels and muscles of Felix's scrawny neck. I felt the magic falter when it met up with death, but it kept pushing at that thing in Felix, pushing it out of his body, replacing it. I was getting weaker and weaker, but I couldn't let go of Eli's hand.

"Eli," I said with great effort. "I can't." I thought I was going to die giving Felix life. And that was not my way to go.

"Just a minute," he said. "One more minute."

My life was going to last one more minute.

But it didn't have to. Felix whispered, "I'm back."

Then I was on the ground.

I was never completely out. That meant I could hear a car coming fast from the direction of Sally. As Felix and Eli climbed slowly from the car to tend to me, I croaked, "Car! Car!"

They both turned their heads to the east at the same time, like deer on alert . . . or birds when a hawk flies above them.

A car pulled in behind us, and to my shock and dismay, who should climb out but Mr. Mercer. Still alive. "You took everything away from our town!" he yelled. "Everything!" He was wearing the clothes he'd had on yesterday, which had been soaked in the rain and then bled all over. And he was staggering. And he was a terrible color.

Would he never die?

Oh, for God's sake. We had gotten away from Sally and its weirdness and nastiness. But here came Sally after us.

Mercer still didn't know shit. As Felix and Eli raised their hands, with the slow movements of exhausted men, I eased my Colt from its holster with the sloppy movements of my weak hand. I gathered the little bit of energy I had left. As Mercer yelled at Eli and Felix, I whipped up the Colt and I fired.

Got him. In the foot.

## CHAPTER TWENTY-SEVEN

W e loaded him in his car and pushed the car out into a field," Eli was saying. He was looking down at me, and we were moving. "We made it look like a snake bit his foot. We fired his gun, like maybe he'd seen the snake close to his feet and shot at it, and hit his foot instead."

"Not bad," I said. My voice was weak and faint.

"Felix made his foot swell up. What was left of it."

I nodded. Just a little bit, since otherwise my skull might crack; that was how delicate I felt. I was not used to this at all. Also, my head was on Eli's lap. Not used to that either. We were in the back seat. I rolled my eyes to see Felix's dark ponytail. He was driving.

"We're back in Texoma," Felix said. "Just barely."

Show-off. I'd been just about to ask where we were. From the light, it was late afternoon. Days were getting shorter. That was good.

"We'll stop soon," Eli said, stroking my hair back.

"Okay," I said. Or I think I said it, before I went back to sleep.

Next thing I heard, Felix and Eli were arguing over my head. Not about my head, just over it. Two angry but quiet voices.

"We need to stick together." Felix.

"We need some quiet privacy." Eli.

On it went, each restating his own opinion. Finally I realized I'd have to intervene. "I'm not going to bathe in front of you, Felix," I said. "I get a room alone with Eli."

So then we were stumbling down a hall. Eli was laden down with our bags and his own weakness. I was walking, but I had one hand on the wall to keep me straight. He unlocked the door. Then we were in, and there was a toilet and a sink in the room. I used both, and brushed my teeth, and crawled into the bed in nothing. Oh, it felt so good. The sheets felt clean, the night was cooler, and when Eli slid in beside me, I felt like everything was right. I was asleep the next second.

After all that, I woke the next morning by five. It was dark, but dawn was approaching. Eli was still asleep. I crawled over him as careful as I could to use the toilet, and I noticed a note had been pushed under our door.

That was a bad way to start the day. No one ever slips you a note to tell you that all is well with the world, or that they love you more than anything, or that breakfast will be ready whenever you want it.

The room was too dark to read the writing, the toilet and sink weren't in a separate room, and I was anxious. I found a match in my bag, flicked it with my fingernail, and it sizzled into life. The message read, *Eli, I must go. Take the car and get out of here. They're on our track; they'll catch up today.*

"Well, *hell*," I said, loud enough that Eli made a mutter of protest.

"Shake a leg, Eli," I said. "Your buddy Felix says you and I got to get out of here. Except he forgot to mention me." In ten really unpleasant minutes, we were in the car and on our way. We'd left some money under our key on the front desk. For the first time,

I saw that our hotel was almost by itself in the woods right off the highway. There were a couple of cottages and a body shop business.

I volunteered to drive. I was more alert than Eli. "Look at the map, if Felix didn't take it," I said.

Eli found it folded in the glove compartment.

"I think we need to get off this highway," I said. "We got half a tank of gas, so if we find a good paved road to turn left on, we can dip south a bit and then meet the highway again farther west, if the roads are real bad."

Eli had to switch on the overhead light to study the map. It was hard on my eyes. I was glad when he switched it off. "We're coming to an intersection in seven miles," he said.

I kept looking in the rearview mirror to see if there were any lights behind us. Not yet.

"You got any idea how Felix left?" I said, since the darkness and monotony of the empty road were about to make me crazy. I was hungry and thirsty, I felt grubby, and worst of all I felt separated from Eli in a way I couldn't pin down. Maybe because I thought he and Felix knew each other better than he and I did, and that hurt, which was stupid. Felix and Eli had trained together and lived in the same circle for years, I figured. Felix probably knew Eli's sisters. Maybe he partnered with them at dances, if Russians had dances. Felix didn't think I was good enough for Eli. I could not talk to Eli about that. It would mean I thought Eli and I had a future together, which was something I tried not to imagine, because it wasn't going to happen.

I spotted some lights, way back.

I said, "Someone's behind us."

"Turn right as soon as you can."

I saw a decent road coming up, and I turned.

"First open area you see, park."

We went a ways before I spotted a good place. The side of the road was open, both north and south, for about ten feet. Looked like there had been a small fire there that had gotten out of hand for a few minutes. I pulled over to the right.

"Go into the trees. If they try to kill me, shoot them all."

Without a word, I grabbed my rifle from the back and took off running. Had the guns all ready, of course, and they were fully loaded. I always checked that first thing in the morning, if I hadn't remembered to do it last thing at night. The sky was lighter by the minute. The sun was just up.

I found a good tree and scrambled up it so I could get some oversight. When I looked down, there was a sleeping black bear about ten feet away in a natural depression in the ground lined with old fallen leaves and pine needles.

I tried not to picture what would have happened if the bear had woken as I started up the tree. You never could tell with bears. Sometimes they did their best to get away from your area. Sometimes they charged. I had not been careful to be quiet.

I made myself forget the bear and sight through the Winchester on Eli, who had gotten out of the car to lean on the trunk. He wasn't wearing his hat, and he hadn't had time to tie his hair back, but at least today he was wearing real clothes. He did not look my way. After a moment I could hear the car coming up fast.

And then it skidded to a halt.

Three people piled out of it, two women and a man. The women were both redheaded, and though it was hard to tell in the light, I thought they were twins. The man was black. They were all wearing grigori vests, which settled that.

Eli had said that I had to wait to kill them until they tried to kill him. There was a long, uneasy silence among the four grigoris.

"Where is the woman? The gunnie?" The black man had a heavy accent. I couldn't place it.

"I left her to make her way home," Eli said. "You needn't bother to look for her. You won't find her. Why are you here? I did what I was sent to do."

"We don't believe you should have come at all," said one of the women, her voice calm and confident.

"Why?" Eli sounded truly surprised. "This was the wish of our late tsarina, that people here should see a better way, that black people should be free. Kasper, you should understand that."

The black man said, "There's more to this than freedom, Eli. There are economic . . ."

"Oh, bullshit!"

I'd never heard Eli say that before.

Then he said, very clearly, "There is no point in waiting."

*That* was clear.

The red-haired woman on the left raised her hand to fire some kind of power at Eli. It was too dark to be sure I had a killing shot, but I could hit her. I shot her and she went down. Quick as a wink, I shot the other woman, a gut shot. By that time, Kasper was running back to their car, and he was harder to hit. But I winged him in the right shoulder, and when he was on his way down I shot him again. Took care of him.

And the bear woke up, of course. It charged Eli.

"Get in the car!" I screamed, and by some miracle he made it into the passenger seat and slammed the door behind him. I didn't want the car any more banged up than it already was, and I prepared to shoot the bear. I didn't want to. It went against my grain to kill an animal I couldn't eat.

And then a good thing happened. A deer, really a fawn, maybe startled by the gunfire, blundered into the clearing and ran for the other side.

The bear took off after it.

I didn't question luck, good or bad. I was down the tree and dashing for the car. Eli leaned over to push open my door, and he took my rifle from me and put it in the back seat. When I was sure the bear wasn't coming back, I took the grigori vests off the dead people and handed them to Eli. I had to shoot one of the women again; she wasn't quite gone. I had to move their car, too.

Finally, we took off. The whole thing had taken maybe ten minutes, but it felt like a lot longer.

I kept driving until we had to stop for gas.

No one else came after us. Or if they did, they didn't catch us.

We didn't see Felix—or anyone else we knew—and we joined back up with the highway about thirty miles later. It was easier and faster driving, but it was also the road anyone searching for us would take.

We ate quickly in a diner in Texoma. Chicken-fried steak and the last of the summer squash and biscuits. I felt real glad to be in my territory. We were low on money, and that worried me along with about ten other things.

I began driving for Segundo Mexia. Eli didn't say a word, yes or no. He slept a lot of the time. When he was awake, we didn't do a lot of talking. But I was thinking as I drove, and the first night we turned to each other in bed—he mostly had to let me take the reins because he was so fragile—I had some questions afterward.

"Did you know Felix was going to do all that with the bones?" I still felt kind of hurt when I thought of it. I had believed the bones were alive, that Moses the Black was with us, and I was not much of a believer in anything. I hated Felix for doing his sorcery well enough to make me wonder, and I also thought the better of him for trying to do such a bold thing. And he had done it so well. I would sure like to punch him in the nose, though. Now that I'd brought him back to life.

Eli ran his hand across my stomach, up and down it, rubbing it and patting it. He really liked my stomach. He said, "What would you do if you thought I was running after someone else?"

That was a shocker of a subject change.

I started to give a teasing answer. Like, *I'd shoot you first and her next*. But I thought again. Eli had sounded serious.

"I would walk the other way," I said. "I am too proud to try to hold on to a man who would treat me that way. I would tell you I wished you well, but for a while that would not be true. I would hate you. But in time, weeks or months, I guess . . . I would get over the worst of the pain. And I would hope someone new, someone better, would cross my path."

"You would not hope that I would come back?"

That surprised me. "I would not take you back." That was all there was to it.

"Why not?" He was dead serious.

Seemed so plain to me. "You did it once, you might do it again. I try to learn from my mistakes."

"That seems almost . . . manlike."

"Don't you *ever* think women are always the ones who ruin relationships. If you stray, you deserve the backfire. I'll tell you something. Dan Brick isn't any more than a friend to me. But I know he would never do me that way if I took him on."

Eli was silent after that, and I was glad. I had said my say, and I meant every word. I knew Eli must have some princess or a fancy rich woman to go back to. How could he not? And I knew when this little jaunt was over, he'd go back to the HRE. He'd probably get some title or medal for helping the black people of Dixie get some rights, since of course they'd want to join the church that had taken off their chains, namely the Russian Orthodox Church. And if all the blacks in Dixie joined the Russian Orthodox Church, and they began voting, they might think it was a good idea to be allied with the HRE. And if that alliance didn't work, it had only cost the tsar some money and some expendable gunnies and grigoris. I knew the grigoris I'd killed had another point of view, but I could not imagine what that was.

We reached Segundo Mexia after three more days of hard driving. We arrived after dark and helped each other up the hill to my cabin, leaving the car parked outside of John Seahorse's combination stable and garage. I'd left a note on it that said, *$75 and it's yours to turn into what you want, if you do it quick.* Lots of people in Segundo Mexia could use car parts, no matter where they'd come from. It would be like holding bait over a hungry fishpond.

I unlocked my cabin door and turned on the lights. Someone had been in it while I was gone. There were flowers in a jar on the table. Nothing else was changed.

"Your admirer has been here," Eli said, caution in his voice.

"Me and him's going to have a talk real soon," I said.

"I believe you," Eli said. "But right now, even if I didn't, I'd say I did, because I have to lie down on something that's not moving."

I figured out after a second that he meant the bed, not me. I'd been thinking, *I move plenty when the occasion calls for it.* "Okay, let's go to bed," I said.

We both used my bathroom (consistent running water courtesy of Eli) and washed our faces and necks, and I pulled on an old night-gown, and Eli pulled on nothing, and I got him to climb in first against the wall. We were in my place and it was my job to defend him. It felt so strange to be sleeping with him in my home.

It felt good.

Early next morning, I walked down to my mother's and Jack-son's house. I hadn't wanted to leave Eli, but I had to. Mother hadn't left for work, and Jackson was reading his morning paper. My mom hugged me and didn't cry, which was the best I could hope for, but Jackson gave my battered self a steady look.

"I'm back, but I don't know how much peace I'll have," I said. "I got Eli with me, and he needs some days to get better. Then I'll try to get him on the train for the Holy Russian Empire."

They both stared at me with real serious faces. Mother and Jack-son both wanted to know whether my relationship with Eli was one that would break me, or just a little thing. I could not tell them one way or another.

"So I don't need nobody—anybody—to tell strangers where I am or who's with me. I might not get the drop on 'em next time. Might not have any warning."

"You need me to bring you some food to cook?" Mother asked me.

"Yes, ma'am, since I can't go shopping. I know that everyone on the hill will know I'm home, but I think I can trust 'em to keep their mouths shut."

"I'll take care of 'em if they don't," Jackson said. "You in love with this man?"

"I am."

Mother's eyes widened. "You love a grigori."

"He isn't anything like Oleg Karkarov." My father. Whom I'd killed.

"Must not be," she said quietly. "You got good sense."

"But I know he's gonna leave," I said. "He's got to go back." I shrugged. "That's it."

They both stared at me, and then my mother nodded. Jackson touched my shoulder. Conversation about Eli was over.

"You heard about the train wreck?" I asked.

"Charlie's wife and Jake's man came by to tell us how much they appreciated your letting them know, and that you were fine when you sent the message."

"It was terrible," I said. I had never told my mother something like that. I nodded again, when I couldn't think of anything else to say. "Well, I better get back home."

"Here, take you some eggs and some cornbread."

I gladly accepted a bag from my mother. She'd stuck in some pears, too. "Thank you, Mom." I couldn't manage a big smile, but I hugged her as I gave her a little one. "I'll pay you back."

She knew I would, too. "Maybe just shoot me a deer when you're up to it," she said.

I told her I would.

Off I went home, to find that Eli had gotten into the shower and that Chrissie had left some cookies in a little basket at the door. I had passed her cabin on the way up. I retraced my steps and knocked. Her pretty blond head stuck out.

"Thank you," I said. "I got company. You don't know about him, and you don't know I'm back."

"I understand," she said. "Hey, look here." She showed me a little bundle wrapped in an old sheet.

"Ohhhh," I breathed. "What is it?"

"Got me a girl," Chrissie said proudly. "Her name is Emily Jane."

"Your husband must be proud."

"He acted fussed at first, like boys were the only ones could help out. But after he held her and looked at her, I caught him singing her a song, and swaying with her like he was dancing."

"Sometime I'll babysit if you need to go to the village by yourself," I offered. "In a week or two." I don't know how I decided Eli would be gone by then.

"I thank you," she said. "And you two enjoy the cookies. You got that tall man back?"

I grinned. "I do. How long has Dan been leaving me flowers?"

"Every other night, lately. He got real worried when you didn't come back when you'd told him you would."

It hadn't been Chrissie's job to keep Dan out of my house. Chrissie and Dan (and my mom) knew where I'd hidden a key, in case they needed something while I was gone. Chrissie enjoyed using the refrigerator. I'd asked Dan to check on the cabin once while I was gone, make sure everything was running okay. That had been a mistake made by me.

I admired the baby for a minute more and went uphill.

Eli was out of the shower and toweling off. There was a lot to admire. "My wound is much better," he said. "I think you made a good start, with that healing spell." Eli felt so much better that we didn't get around to doing much of anything for another hour. It was slow and easy, because we both felt battered.

"I went down to see my mom," I said. "And talk to Jackson." I told him what I'd asked them to spread around.

"People here will know that, and they won't try to earn money by informing?" Eli said.

"If I get put in jail or killed, Jackson will take care of 'em."

"They will hide me, a stranger?"

"They will hide you if I ask them to. I grew up here. And they appreciate that I'm real accurate with a gun."

"Two good reasons." Then he bent his mouth down to mine, and he said, "I think we could do this again."

"Right now?" I couldn't help but smile.

"Right now." He smiled too.

So we did.

In seven days, no one came for either of us. I had seldom had seven days in a row of doing very little, and I had never had seven days with Eli when we weren't on the road. I cleaned my guns and my rifle, with Eli watching closely. I went out hunting for a morning, and Eli stayed at home and made bright magic bubbles for Emily Jane, which she watched with a solemn look, he told me. Chrissie said he was a great babysitter, that he knew how to change a diaper and everything. She was able to get her washing done.

Dan Brick showed up after four days, looking hard. Like he had his mind made up about what he wanted to say. When I saw him coming up the hill, I took off the wedding ring and put it on the table. It would set him off, and I couldn't bear it. I met him outside the door.

"Don't speak, Dan. It's too soon," I said. "And Eli is still here."

Dan turned without a word and walked down the hill.

Eli had stood back from the window so Dan wouldn't have to stand the sight of him, which was real thoughtful. But when I closed the door and turned back to Eli, he said, "What will you do about him?"

My ring was gone.

It was like a bucket of cold water thrown in my face. I shut my eyes and breathed hard for a minute. We would not talk about this, because there was no point. We would not speak words that really didn't make a difference, because Eli had to leave. Besides, I didn't know how he really saw me. I wasn't like the women he knew.

It took me a big twist of pain to say, "I'll take care of it after you leave."

And we both fell silent for a long time.

The next two days weren't as nice. I waited for him to tell me, and maybe he was waiting for me to tell him something, beg him, announce that I would not let him go. But I knew he would leave. He had family in San Diego. He had those sisters to marry off, his mother to care for, his brother still in grigori school. He knew all this as well as I did.

Still, when Eli told me he would leave the next day, after I'd returned from a quick visit to my mother, I had to turn my face away from him. We were in bed. We had just been together. I had seen fireworks.

"When?" I said, when I was sure my voice would be normal.

"I went to the stable while you were gone. I can ride to the station. Someone's coming in on the train who can bring the horse back here."

"All right then," I said, trying to sound brisk. "I'll make you some food for a basket to eat on the train."

"Aren't you going to talk to me?"

"I am not." I could not think of what to say. Or maybe I was thinking of too many things. "I'm glad you stayed awhile. You should be strong now." I forced the words out.

"You're always strong," he said in a brooding kind of way, and then he pretended to go to sleep.

I lay awake too, and stared into the darkness.

I got up early. The sun was not yet up. I wanted this to be over with, because it was so painful. I gritted my teeth and made breakfast and packed Eli a bag with some fruit and bread in it. I had a canteen I could spare. I filled it with water and put it in the bag, too. He was eating at the table, not saying a word.

When Eli was through, he gathered up every item and slung his duffel bag over his shoulder, and the smaller bag, too. Then he looked at me, helpless. "They're going to be coming here, Lizbeth," he said. "You tell them I'm long gone. They'll search your house for me, maybe."

"Go on," I said, jerking my head at the door. Eli stepped forward aiming to hug me, but I said, "No." I was gathering myself all up to get through him walking out the door.

And he left.

I collapsed onto the bench by the table and strained hard to keep myself together. I worked and worked at it, and I did it.

The next day the grigoris showed up at my door.

It was two men, one English and one Russian. The Russian was almost as tall as Eli, and his name was Simon. The English one was Godfrey.

"May we come in?" Godfrey asked, real polite.

"No," I said. "You want to sit on the bench out here, you can, but you're not coming in."

"We could spell our way in," said Simon.

"You think your presence here hasn't been noticed?" I said.

They both looked irritated, and they swapped glances.

"We had heard that our brothers Felix and Eli might be here," Godfrey said, not nearly as politely. "One of them, anyway."

"Neither," I said. "Last time I saw Felix and Eli, they were driving away in a real dump of a car, going back to San Diego." At least, I figured that had been Felix's destination. I just tacked on Eli. Seemed safer.

"When are they coming back?"

"Never," I said, in as level a voice as I could manage. "Never."

Then I was in a tunnel in the dirt, and a mongoose was coming in after me. I was tiny and the mongoose was huge, and it was going to bite me in two. When I came to myself I had my gun at Godfrey's temple.

"You do that again, I'll shoot you through the brain," I said. "Who told you Eli and Felix were here?"

"A man named Dan got drunk in a bar last night. Simon and I were there," Godfrey said, smiling. "Dan is despairing of ever regaining your love. Please move your gun away from my head."

"What are you made of?" Simon asked, all suspicion.

"I'm made of pissed-off and real-tired-of-you," I said. "I answered your question. You get off my land and away from my town. I guess Dan didn't tell you he's never spent the night here. He's never had any love of mine in the first place."

The grigoris looked at each other, like, *A man with a grudge. We should have asked more questions.* They knew I was telling the truth. And Simon stepped to my open window and had him a quick look all around the cabin. He would not see any hint of Eli. I'd spent three hours this morning scrubbing everything in the bathroom and kitchen, dusting and polishing all the wood, washing the sheets (even now flapping on the clothesline in back), burning the garbage in the metal drum outside, mopping the floors.

That was a good thing, because Simon worked a spell.

"If anything of Eli's is in the house, it will come forth," Godfrey told me, still smiling.

But because I'd been a hard worker, mostly to keep my mind off my misery, nothing "came forth."

Simon and Godfrey looked at each other, gave a little shrug, told me good-bye, and walked down the hill. When they passed Chrissie's cabin, they didn't see her step out behind them with her husband's gun in her right hand, Emily Jane in her left.

We both stood in our places, not moving, until the grigoris had descended the hill and walked back into town.

Chrissie climbed the slope until she was close to me, Emily Jane fussed, and Chrissie bounced the baby gently. "Boys are at school with your mom, thank God," she said. "They woulda swarmed right over those two."

"They're lively," I said. I felt like I'd been beaten up. I was bewildered I'd lived through their visit. And now I had nothing ahead of me.

"Saw your man yesterday, digging a hole," Chrissie said. She waited until I looked directly at her. "Up yonder, by the oak."

The little oak tree stood upslope and east from my place.

"Yeah?" I didn't know what to think.

Chrissie nodded and carried Emily Jane home.

Since I had nothing better to do, I went to see. Sure enough, there was a bit of disturbed earth visible under the edge of a large rock. I shoved the rock over with my foot. Something had been buried there. I knelt and began to dig with my hands, which was not smart, but I couldn't wait to get a trowel. The top of a jar came into view soon enough.

In the jar were our wedding rings.

I held them to me for a long moment, flooded with feelings. Then I reburied them, to be safe.

When I stood, I could see into Segundo Mexia from my vantage point. The grigoris were at the stable, and I watched them get into a car.

All of a sudden, I knew what I had to do. I had to have a talk with Dan Brick in private. I'd have to do some planning on how it would come about.

But I had plenty of time.